FOUR
STEPBROTHERS
& I

D. E. BARTLEY

VINCI
BOOKS

By D.E. Bartley

O'Reilly Fight Club

To all those who feel they are unlovable.
You are loved. You are wanted and you matter to me xx

Vinci Books

vinci-books.com

Published by Vinci Books Ltd in 2025

1

A CIP catalogue record for this book is available from the British Library.
Paperback ISBN: 9781036709655

Trigger Warnings

This book briefly touches on substance addiction and its effects on a person's loved ones.
If you or someone you know suffers from substance addiction and you want advice please know there is help out there.

Choking Kink
Murder of a Loved One

Prologue

Sitting on the soft sand with my long legs in front of me, I close my eyes and breathe in the cool sea breeze that gently flows over me, relaxing my tired mind after a long day.

Today, I watched my mother marry Tommy O'Reilly, a guy she met only four months ago. I didn't want to attend, but Tommy offered to cover the costs for me to travel to Majorca with them and stay in his family villa with its own beach; I couldn't turn down the chance of some time in the sun. I might as well get something out of this marriage, as I doubt it will last.

Mum's relationships never seem to last more than a year, not since Dad left when I was eight. He went to work one day and never came back. He sent a few letters saying that he was struggling with Mum's drinking and spending, and then one day he just sent his wedding ring with a letter saying he wasn't coming back with a cheque for five thousand pounds with strict instructions for it to be put towards a trust fund for me. I never saw the money, Mum spent it on drink, and god knows what else, but I saved each letter and his ring and used to believe that one day he would come back and save me from Mum and her abuse. He never did.

For years, Mum went back and forth with drugs and alcohol, occasionally getting sober enough to live a relatively normal life; this is the longest she's been sober in years. Tommy seems to make her happier than I've seen her since Dad left, and I hope it works out. When she introduced me to Tommy, I'd been dubious, to say the least. It was apparent he has money and isn't afraid to splash it about. Not only does he come with money, but he also has four sons from his first marriage. Christian is the eldest at twenty-five, Jason's twenty-two, and the twins Sean and Maximus are two years older than me at twenty. I know I shouldn't find my new stepbrothers attractive, but I swear they look like four gods.

Tommy made his money by setting up boxing clubs after Christian became a well-known boxer, and his brothers quickly followed in his shoes. All four have an impressive history of competitive fighting, which shows in their physique. I all but drooled when I first saw them standing together when they arrived this morning. All four are well-built with dark brown hair and wear perfectly tailored designer clothes. They stood out by miles, and every woman in the complex where Mum and Tommy got married couldn't get enough of them.

My body has been on fire since I met them, and I've soaked up every touch, look, and compliment they've given me. If only they weren't just being nice. I learned never to let anyone in long ago; everybody eventually leaves.

"Mind if we join you?"

I open my eyes and look up to find Christian and Jason standing over me. Both are still in their suit trousers, Christian still wearing his suit jacket whilst Jason has lost his and rolled up his shirt sleeves, revealing some of his tattooed arms.

"It's your beach," I reply with a smile as they both sit on either side of me.

"Why are you hiding out here?" Christian asks. I shrug as I look back out to sea.

"It seemed like a good way to end the day."

"It was a lovely wedding," Jason says, leaning back. I nod, closing my eyes again and taking a deep breath.

"Yeah, it was. Mum seemed happy anyway."

"Tommy, too. Carol seems good for the old bastard," Jason chuckles as he stretches his legs out in front of him, crossing them at the ankle.

"He seems to look after her, which is what she needs," I add as I sit, hugging my knees to my chest, making sure my long dress covers my legs as the evening chill starts to sink in.

"Here, put this on, sweetheart." Christian places his suit jacket over my bare shoulders. "You look like you're getting cold," he adds with a smile that softens his whole face.

"Thanks," I reply, pushing my arms through the sleeves. The jacket's huge and smells of his aftershave and him. I take a deep breath of his masculine scent, hoping he doesn't notice.

"There you all are!"

We turn to see Maximus and Sean walking towards us, grinning, having ditched their suits at the earliest opportunity and settling for jeans that hug their thighs and ... other assets and tight-fitting polo shirts, the material stretching over their broad chests. They aren't quite identical, but there is no mistaking they're twins.

"We came to toast the happy couple again," Sean announces, holding two bottles of champagne they'd stolen from the venue before we returned to the villa, leaving Mum and Tommy to stay in the bridal suite.

"Any reason for a drink, Shorty," Maximus winks, sitting next to Christian and taking a drink out of the bottle before handing it to me. Christian snatches it from my hand and gives it back to his brother.

"She is underage, you idiot."

"Only just. I'm eighteen next month," I point out as I take the bottle off Maximus, who grins broadly.

"I'm sure she can handle a couple of glasses," Sean laughs, holding his bottle out for me. "Cheers, princess."

I tap mine against it before taking a sip.

"Jazzy could probably drink you under the table, you lightweight," Jason laughs, taking Sean's bottle and drinking from it himself. I sip mine again whilst looking at a smirking Sean.

"Will you be moving into Tommy's when your mum's house is sold?" Jason asks next to me as he hands the bottle to his brother. I quickly shake my head.

"No, I will advance in a year and aim to get my dance degree. So, in the meantime, I'll find a small flat to rent."

"That can't be cheap. How will you afford it?" Christin asks.

Money's no issue for these guys. They've continued to build the business their father started. They now make more money in a month than I could in years.

"I can teach at the dance school to help with money, and I have some savings from my grandparent's inheritance," I explain, smiling.

"I'm sure your mother would prefer it if you moved in with them," Christian comments with a frown.

I can't help laughing as I take another sip of my drink.

"She really wouldn't; we aren't that close."

"You seemed close today," he points out, reaching around to take the bottle from me and hand it to Maximus. I roll my eyes and reach around to take Sean's bottle before having another sip.

"Only because it suits her. What better way to have everyone paying attention to you than to act like the loving mum and bride," I sigh as I hand the bottle back. "I've lived *away* from her more than *with* her. I'm used to being alone, but it's easier that way," I add before forcing a smile on my face.

Jason puts an arm around my shoulders and pulls me against him. I'm not used to people showing affection. I freeze for a moment before resting my head on his shoulder.

"Well, you have us now, so you aren't alone anymore," he says, kissing the top of my head before releasing me with a smile.

I roll my eyes as I look out to sea, knowing that after this weekend, I'll probably never hear from them again.

Chapter One

Two and a half years later

Chucking my bag onto the bed, I rush to the wardrobe and start rummaging around for something to wear. After a long week of essay deadlines and exams, I need a night out to clear my head. Amber and Sophia, my best friends, will be here soon to start getting ready. It's already six, and we plan on being out by eight.

The three of us have the best nights together. It started when we were sixteen and used to attempt to sneak into pubs and clubs pretending to be older than we were. When that didn't work, we used to go to the local woods and drink whilst trying to keep warm.

Since we turned eighteen and can now get in every-where, we take full advantage and go out whenever we get the chance. When we can't afford to go out, we come back here to the house I rent from my stepfather and stay in drinking and partying, still managing to have the best time.

I'm just pulling out my favourite little black dress when I hear my phone ringing. I look at the screen and smile.

"Hey, Christian."

"Hey, sweetheart, you sound happy."

"I'm getting ready for a night out. I'm in serious need of letting my hair down," I reply as I start looking for the shoes that go with the dress.

"Who are you going out with?"

I pull the shoes out of the wardrobe and throw them next to my outfit.

"Amber and Sophia." I open the drawer out from under my bed and start going through all my handbags for the perfect one.

"Is Damien going?"

I roll my eyes as I activate hands-free and place my phone on the side. Christian and the guys don't even attempt to hide their dislike of my boyfriend, even though they only met him briefly once.

"No, it's a girl's night out. No men allowed."

"Just be careful, don't drink too much and make sure you get a taxi home."

"I will, Dad," I sigh, rolling my eyes again. "I'm not stupid; I know how to look after myself. I've done it my whole life," I add as I start pulling my long hazel hair out of the top bun it's been in all day. Luckily, it falls in long, loose waves down my back. Perfect, one less thing to worry about.

"I know that, sweetheart, but I worry, we all do. It's only because we care."

The guys have shown me time and time again that they care about my safety, sometimes though it can be smothering. My mother doesn't care what happens to me when I go out; it's hard to accept that the guys do.

"Jaz, you up there?" Sophia calls from downstairs.

"Yeah, come on up!" I call back before picking up my phone and turning off the hands-free. "I have to go, but I promise to behave and will text when I get up tomorrow."

"Okay, enjoy yourself."

"I will. See you later, Christian."

"Bye, sweetheart."

I hang up and turn to see Sophia and Amber looking at me with big grins on their faces, holding a bottle in each hand.

"Jaz, get the music on; we have these to drink while we get ready to hit the town!" Amber declares, grinning. I place my phone into the speaker and put on my favourite band, Nickelback. We quickly open a bottle of wine each and tap them together before taking a drink and giggling at each other.

I laugh as I watch my friends starting to dance around my room with their bottles in their hands; I quickly jump up and join them. Tonight, I'll drink as much as I can and dance until my feet hurt so much that I can't stand. Let's face it: there is no one to tell me no and stop me anyway.

I'm so drunk. Actually, I'm too drunk. I want to say it's thanks to the shots we've been doing, but that's a lie. I was drunk before we even left the house.

Tonight, I seem to have lost the ability to say no. I've gone so far past my limit that it's not even funny anymore. If any of the O'Reillys saw me now, I'd be in the shit. I know Damien wasn't happy when he saw how drunk I was. But the thought of disappointing him doesn't bother me anywhere near as much as disappointing my stepbrothers.

Sophia called her boyfriend earlier to meet us. The

problem is her boyfriend is friends with Damien, and he's now here in the club watching me like a creepy stalker as I dance with my friends. He keeps coming over and dancing with us, but he's getting very handsy. At first, it was fun grinding up against him, but the more I drink, the more I realise sleeping with him is the last thing on my mind tonight.

"Come on, Jaz, I need to sit down for a bit," Sophia calls over the music. I nod, letting her lead me to the table where Amber is talking to one of Damien's friends. The only empty spot on the table is next to Damien. I don't manage to hide the eye roll when I realise I have no choice but to sit there. As soon as I sit, Damien places his arm around my shoulders and leans closer.

"What's going on with you?" he yells into my ear. I turn and look at him, forcing a smile.

"Nothing, just having a good night." He leans forward and kisses me. I kiss him back because it's what I should be doing, not because I want to. I quickly break the kiss and force a smile, ignoring the annoyance I can see in his eyes.

"Shots!"

We all look up to see one of Damien's friends walking to our table with a tray of shot glasses. Oh fuck, this is the last thing I need; I've had enough to drink already. I try to decline, but no one's taking no for an answer, especially Damien and his friend.

"This is a bad idea," I sigh, looking at the green shot in my hand, but Damien just nudges me, chuckling.

"Come on, babe. The last one, I promise," Damien laughs with his friends who wink at him. I shrug and down the shot, quickly shivering as the liquid burns its way down my throat, and I cough whilst frowning from the horrible taste.

"That was foul!" I cough as Damien and his friend laugh at me. I feel Damien's arm tighten around my shoulder, and he pulls me against him.

"You don't have to do any more, I promise."

I have a feeling that one may have just been the nail in my drunk coffin.

"Fuck Jaz, you're wasted!"

I look up from where I'm sitting on the cold concrete ground outside the club. Damien's standing over me with his friend, and they are both looking angry.

"I told you I shouldn't have done that last shot," I slur at them as the world starts spinning. I look around and can't see Amber or Sophia anywhere. Have they left already? I try to open my handbag to get my phone, but I can't see properly.

"Fuck I'm drunk," I slur as I close one eye to try and focus on my bag.

"You okay, miss?"

I look up and see a bouncer looking down at me. He's not much older than me but looks every bit the part, and I have no doubt anyone who caused trouble in front of him would soon find themselves wishing they hadn't. I shake and moan when everything spins.

Crap.

"Are you with anyone?" he asks, squatting in front of me.

"She's with me," Damien announces behind him. The bouncer looks at him and then at me.

"Who is he to you, miss?" he asks. I'm about to reply, "A pain in my ass," when Damien interrupts.

"I'm her boyfriend," he declares, standing tall. The bouncer stands up and looks down as he towers over Damien, forcing him to take a step back.

"Well, you've done a piss poor job of looking after her, haven't you!" he points out, and I can't help laughing. I quickly place my hand over my mouth as Damien glares at me.

"Come on. Move it, now!" he snaps through gritted teeth as he reaches down and grabs my arm roughly, trying to pull me to my feet.

"Get off me!" I protest as a hand grabs his arm, and I look up expecting to see the bouncer, but instead, I find Maximus O'Reilly glaring at Damien.

"Get your fucking hands off her now!" Maximus growls as Damien quickly does as he's told.

"You know this girl, sir?" the bouncer asks as Maximus squats in front of me.

"I sure do," Maximus answers, looking at the bouncer before smiling at me. "What's going on, Shorty?" he asks softly as he tucks some hair behind my ear and cups my cheek.

"I'm fucking drunk," I slur as I close my eyes, leaning into his touch.

"I can see that," he chuckles as I open my eyes because the world starts spinning. "Pass me that bin," he orders to someone behind him. I look up as Sean passes his brother the bin from the side of the door.

"Hey, princess," Sean says with a smile.

"Hey, your…" I don't finish as I turn my head and throw up into the bin Maximus is holding. I hear Damien and his friend both cursing as Maximus grabs my hair from my face and holds it out of the way.

"Okay, Shorty, get it all up," he coaches softly as I throw up again.

"How much did she fucking drink?" I hear Sean growling and sneak a peek to see him standing in front of Damien and his mate, glaring at them. I don't hear their response as another wave of sickness washes over me, and I throw up again.

"Shit, Shorty! Have you eaten anything tonight?" Maximus asks as he hands me some paper towels the bouncer gives him. I shake my head as I wipe my mouth, instantly regretting it as it makes me feel sick again.

"I'm okay," I whisper as I push the bin away from me. Maximus frowns and takes a bottle of water from the bouncer. He opens it and forces me to take a sip.

"You're far from okay. We're taking you home," he says as he takes my bag and hands it to Sean before helping me to my feet. As soon as I'm up, I start swaying and have to grab him to stop myself from falling over.

"I'll take her home," Damien declares as Maximus and Sean both look at him with raised brows. I can see the worry on Damien's friend's face.

"You think we trust you to take care of her? Look at the state of her!" Maximus growls as I almost fall over on my heels. In one swift move, he sweeps my legs from underneath me and lifts me into his arms. I lean against this hard chest and instantly feel a lot safer than I did with Damien. His smooth black shirt feels warm against my cheek as I close my eyes, savouring his touch.

I must be drunk as I don't usually allow myself to enjoy any affection they show me; well, I try not to anyway.

"She's *my* girlfriend. You are *just* her stepbrothers," Damien yells as he becomes braver and takes a step towards us. I can see his friend looking at the twins with fear in his eyes. He knows the twins could take them both easily if it came to a fight.

"Go home, Damien, before they kill you," I sigh as I close my eyes, relaxing into Maximus's chest.

"She's not wrong. Go home now before I show you why she is more than *just* anything to us," I hear Sean warn as Maximus turns around and walks away with me in the opposite direction to Damien.

"Feel better soon, miss," I hear the bouncer call.

"Thanks for your help, man. What's your name?" Maximus asks.

"Layton, sir."

"Get a business card off my brother. If you fancy doing more than bouncing, give us a call," Maximus says as he starts walking again. I hear Sean talking to the bouncer.

"Where were you? I didn't see you in the club?" I ask as Maximus continues walking with me in his arms.

"VIP section, Shorty. If I'd known you were in such a state, I'd have found you sooner," he answers as he comes to a stop, and I open my eyes to see Sean opening the car door for him.

"I can't go in there! What if I'm sick again?" I protest as Maximus places me on the passenger seat of his expensive car.

"Then I get the thing cleaned or buy a new one. Do you really believe I would put a car over your safety?" he asks, frowning. I shrug as I look around.

"It's a nice car; you were so excited to get it."

Maximus squats down in front of me as I look into his chocolate-brown eyes.

"And you're still more important. The car is replaceable; you're not. You will *always* be my priority. Do you get that?"

I nod as I close my eyes, feeling a little sick and very tired.

"Relax, Shorty. We'll get you home safely," I hear him whisper before I feel a kiss being pressed to my head as he fastens the seatbelt around me.

"Thank you, guys," I sigh as sleep takes me.

Chapter Two

JASMINE

Before I even open my eyes, I regret waking up. My head hurts so bad, and my mouth's drier than a badger's ass. How much did I drink last night?

I go to roll over and fall out of bed, hitting the floor with a thud.

"Fuck!" I groan, wrapping my arms around my head and moan into the carpet.

"You're alive then."

I cautiously lift my head to find Sean casually leaning against the doorframe in jeans and a fitted t-shirt that's pulled tight by his crossed arms.

"Oh shit," I groan, placing my head back on the floor and under my arms. I hear Sean approaching before he lifts them away from my head.

"Do I want to know why you're here?" I ask, looking at him, nervously. Sean smirks at me as he takes my hands and pulls me up so I can sit back against the bed.

"Drink this and take these, and then we will talk." He places a glass of water in one hand and two tablets in another. I murmur a 'thank you' as I swallow both down before closing my eyes and leaning my head back. I think I'm dying. Actually, I may already be dead from embarrassment. If Sean's here, that means I did something really stupid and I'm too scared to hear what.

"Do you want to talk about last night?" Sean asks, sitting next to me. I shake my head and groan from the pain. I turn and look at him and hate the disappointment in his eyes.

"I honestly don't remember much," I admit quietly. Sean looks at me for a moment before putting his arm around my shoulders and pulling me against him.

"Princess, you were lucky we were there. You were so intoxicated you couldn't stand, let alone have protected yourself if you needed to."

My body tenses before relaxing against him. I don't think I'll ever get used to how much affection the guys show me. It's not something I've received a lot of in my life. Maybe that's why I struggle with the whole dating thing. I don't like being touched; I only ever seem to allow it from the O'Reilly brothers.

"What do you remember?" Sean asks. I think about it for a moment.

"I remember going to the club and being pissed off because Sophia had told her boyfriend where we were, which meant he turned up with Damien. I remember thinking I had drunk enough, but Damien insisted we had one last shot; after that, everything's a blur," I admit. I hear a deep hum radiating from Sean's chest.

"Can we agree Damien is a dick yet?"

I look up and nod. Sean sighs placing a kiss on my forehead.

"Good because he was *not* looking after you last night. I

dread to think what would have happened if we hadn't spotted you."

"He wouldn't have hurt me," I point out. Damien might be a dickhead, but he isn't a rapist. At least, I don't think he is.

"Well, whatever you think, he isn't good enough for you," Sean adds as he places a finger under my chin and forces me to look into his chocolate-brown eyes that match his twins. "You deserve someone who will show you how special you are and not just to get into your pants. They should want to give you the world and want nothing in return."

"People like that don't exist, nobody does anything without there being something in it for them. I learnt that a long time ago, Sean," I sigh as I try to turn my head away from him, but he applies enough pressure to stop me.

"Then tell me why Maximus and I spent last night watching you sleep to make sure you didn't choke on your own vomit. Rather than just dumping you on the bed and going home?"

"I don't know," I admit, feeling ashamed and embarrassed by my behaviour.

"Because we care, princess. We've always cared. What do we need to do to prove that to you?"

I look into his eyes as mine fill with tears. I watch as Sean's shoulders relax, and he pulls me back into him, holding me close.

"One day, you will believe us and see how much you mean to the four of us," he sighs before letting me go and standing up from the floor. He holds out his hand and I place mine in his so he can help me to my feet.

"Go and shower, then come downstairs for some breakfast. Maximus has gone to pick up some pastries and fruit."

Sean turns around and walks away from me as I fiddle with my dress.

"Sean?"

He stops and looks at me over his shoulder.

"Thank you for having my back."

His face softens as he lets out a deep sigh.

"Whatever you need, we are always happy to help, even if it is holding your hair as you throw up." I throw my hands up and hide behind them as Sean laughs, closing the bedroom door behind him.

I remove my hands from my face and catch sight of myself in my full-length mirror. I'm still in my little black dress, which has ridden up and is only just covering anything from my hips down. My hair is a complete mess, and my makeup looks like something I would see on a clown at a horror show.

"Fuck!" I curse as I rush towards the bathroom, planning on a long shower to try and get myself looking at least slightly human.

I walk down the stairs twenty minutes later to the sound of laughter coming from the dining area. I find all four of my stepbrothers sitting around the table, drinking coffee and eating the feast that's spread out in front of them.

Christian is dressed in his signature black suit and white shirt, the jacket hanging on the back of his chair. The rest wear more relaxed clothing, such as jeans and T-shirts.

"Hey, how's the head, Shorty?" Maximus calls loudly as Jason and Sean both laugh. I chance a glance at Christian, whose eyebrows have disappeared into his hairline.

"I thought you weren't stupid?" he remarks, throwing

my own words in my face. I walk past him and grab a crois-sant from the table as I sit in an empty chair.

"Like you never got so drunk you had to be helped home at my age!" I reply. Christian shakes his head, looking smug while drinking his strong black coffee.

"Nope."

Jason bursts out laughing as he reaches over and picks up a croissant from the table.

"Well, that's a lie."

Christian turns to face his brother, frowning.

"When did I ever need help getting home?" he asks, a smirking Jason.

"You were seventeen and had gotten into Dad's whiskey with Terry. You puked all over the stairs and your bedroom. Terry and I had to carry you to your room. Mrs Brown was ready to kill you when she saw the mess," Jason reminds his brother before winking at me. I can't help smiling at the thought of a drunk Christian. He's a control freak; he hates anything not going to plan. The thought of him being so drunk that he can't stand amuses me greatly.

"See, I wasn't lying; I didn't need help getting home; I was already there," Christian points out, lifting his cup.

"So, you aren't as perfect as you like to pretend to be," I say, grinning. Christian looks at me with one arched brow.

"I've never claimed to be perfect. My point was that you shouldn't have allowed yourself to get that drunk when there was no one around to watch your back."

I roll my eyes as I pull my croissant apart. "I had people watching my back," I protest, instantly regretting it because I know I didn't. The girls had ditched me, and I still haven't heard from them. I can't believe they left me like that with Damien, of all people. I can see from the look on Christ-ian's face he isn't impressed either.

"That idiot boyfriend of yours doesn't count."

I let out a deep breath as I reach over and steal the last strawberry from his plate. He looks up at me with his blue eyes, and I smirk as I slowly bite into it.

"Yum," I moan as I close my eyes and enjoy the sweet taste. "Do we have any more, these are delicious," I ask, turning to look at Maximus, who is smiling at me.

"Don't try to change the subject; we are going to discuss this." I hear the warning in Christian's voice and instantly want to rebel. I roll my eyes and look around the table at the other three brothers, who are all watching me.

"I know you don't like Damien. You didn't like Mark, and you *hated* Lawrence. Will you ever like any of my boyfriends?"

"No," all four answer together, and I throw my hands up in defeat.

"So, there's nothing to discuss. You don't like him, and I don't particularly after last night, so I'll probably end it at the party tonight."

"What party?" Jason asks from across the table.

"There's a house party tonight, and we're all going," I explain, leaving out the point that the house is Damien's. I quickly hold my hands up to stop anyone from shouting at me. "Don't panic. I won't be drinking much after last night; I learned my lesson!"

Maximus, Sean and Jason all look at Christian. I don't have to look at him to know he's staring at me. I can feel his disappointment radiating from me, and I hate it.

"I don't think you should go."

"Excuse me?" I ask, frowning. Christian rubs his face and looks at me with a look that makes me want to instantly rebel. I might not like that he is disappointed in me, but that doesn't mean I don't instantly hate that he thinks he can boss me around.

"I don't think it's a good idea, you going to a house party when you were so drunk last night you couldn't even stand."

I stare at him for a moment before jumping to my feet and storming out of the room. Even as I'm doing it, I know I'm being childish, but he just makes me mad at times. I stomp up the stairs and slam the bedroom door behind me as I stand seething in the middle of the room. I can hear him coming after me, and I turn to face the door with my arms crossed over my chest. I glare at it, ready for him to appear.

Christian doesn't knock; he walks straight in and stands there, staring right back at me.

"Have you finished with the dramatics?" he asks as he crosses his arms over his broad chest. His shirt sleeves are pulled tight at the top, and I can see the shadow of his tattoos through the material.

"You can't tell me what to do," I yell as it takes all my conscious effort not to stamp my feet in protest.

"No, but I can advise. If you had listened to me, you'd have realised that was what I was doing," he answers as he sighs and walks into the room. He stops and hooks a finger under my chin, forcing me to look at him.

"Do you know you fell asleep in the car last night and didn't wake up once? Even when Maximus carried you up the stairs, took off your shoes, and put you into bed, you didn't so much as moan. With that amount of alcohol in your system, anything could have happened to you, and you wouldn't have known. You could also get back to that state even quicker tonight as your body is still recovering," he explains, looking into my eyes. "Now tell me drinking again is a good idea."

I drop my head in defeat as he removes his hooked finger from under my chin. I know he's right, but I still really want to go as a few friends I haven't seen for a while will be there. When I tell him this, I hear him sigh as he sits down on my bed and pulls me onto his knees. I used to think it was weird when I sat on the guys' laps; they are my stepbrothers, after all, plus we're all adults. But there is a large part of me that likes it, too. When I'm sitting on their laps, and they have their arms around me, I feel protected. It's something I haven't felt since my father left.

"How about this? I will take you to the house party and will pick you up when you're ready to come home. That way you know that at the end of the night, you are getting home safely, and I won't worry as much about you," he suggests as he wraps his arms around my waist. I sigh as I nod in agreement, knowing that if I argue, he will find a way to take me anyway.

"Good girl. See, that wasn't so hard, was it?"

I look at Christian and smile, trying to ignore the way his praise makes my stomach knot. Christian kisses my cheek as his arms tighten around my waist for a moment before he leans back.

"Now come on, let's finish breakfast, as some of us have to work at some point today." He stands and places a hand on the base of my back to guide me to the door and back to the others, whom I can still hear laughing around the table.

Chapter Three

JASON

Christian's Mercedes pulls up in front of me as Terry, our head of securities, parks behind. I jump into Christian's passenger seat.

"What's going on that you need me *and* Terry?" I ask, tugging on the seatbelt. Christian pulls away from one of our Gentlemen's Clubs, where I've been holding a business meeting. I don't miss the way he's clutching the steering wheel so tight that his knuckles are white; he's staring at the traffic in front of us like it's preventing him from being somewhere important.

"Jasmine called, upset. I'm going to pick her up now," he replies, setting the GPS to take us to a house that looks like it's in the middle of nowhere.

"What did that prick do?" I ask through gritted teeth as I feel my hands curling into fists.

"I don't know; she wouldn't tell me what was wrong so I wanted back up," Christian explains as he starts weaving through the traffic, putting his foot down whenever he can.

"You think he's hurt her?" I ask, grabbing hold of the

handle above the door, now understanding Christian's urgency. He curses as a traffic light turns red.

"I honestly have no idea. I'll drop you off just down from the house and go to collect her. I'll leave my phone connected to yours so you can hear what happened." Christian glances at me, and I know what he wants. "The party is in his house, so that should make it easy to get to him once people start leaving."

"Make sure he never contacts her again and show him what happens if he does, gotcha. Are we going firm verbal warning like that idiot Mark? Or kick his ass like the prick, Lawrence?" I look behind us and see Terry keeping up. "Is Terry my lift home?"

Christian nods as we pull off the main road and head down a quieter one.

"The threat you issue depends on what he's done. If he's laid one finger on her, I don't give a shit if you kill the fucker." If he has hurt her either physically or emotionally, he's a dead man anyway. I broke Lawrence's hand for getting handsy with her, nothing is off-limits when it comes to our girl's safety.

After a bit of a drive, Christian pulls over to the side of the road, Terry pulling up behind him. I climb out and lean in through the door.

"Wait for my call and listen to see what he's done. I trust your judgement," Christian says, leaning towards me. I nod and look up the road to where I know Jasmine is.

"And if he isn't the reason she's upset? If he hasn't done anything wrong?" I ask to clarify.

"Then get him to end it; I'm starting to run out of patience."

I sigh as I look at my brother.

"You know you could end all this messing around she's

doing if you would just let us claim her," I point out, but he shakes his head.

"Not yet; we agreed to wait until she was twenty-one," he answers as he sits back up in his chair and faces forward. "Wait for my call and take it from there. I will take her back to hers and will be in touch." Christian takes his foot off the break and starts to pull away as I close the car door, realising I've been dismissed.

I watch his car disappear up the dirt road before getting into Terry's. At least it's warmer in here to wait for the go-ahead.

"Jason," Terry greets me as I climb into the front.

"Terry," I nod as I look down at my phone and wait for Christian's call.

"What do we know about this place?" I ask. Terry hands me a tablet with Google Maps up on the screen, zoomed in on the house.

It's an old farm, by the looks of it. I can't see any live-stock in the recent photos. Terry has found the property details on an estate agent's website. Six bedrooms, two dining rooms, kitchen, summer house and conservatory. Plenty of exits for someone to be taken from.

"He isn't going to handle it well if she's been hurt," Terry remarks next to me. I shake my head as I try to memorise the blueprints, working out an escape from each room.

My phone rings, and I answer it without saying a word.

"She's coming now and crying," Christian mutters before I hear the phone being put down.

"Hey, sweetheart. What's happened?" The change in tone when he speaks to Jasmine is such a contrast to when he speaks to anyone else.

"I don't want to talk about it," Jasmine sniffs and my anger rises.

"Okay, I take that back. Tell me what happened," his tone changing, and I know he will get it out of her. Jasmine can be a brat at times, but Christian handles her better than anyone.

"Just leave it," she whispers so quietly I only just hear her.

"I will go in there and start asking questions. Did Damien do something to hurt you?" I hear Jasmine huff before she explodes.

"What like taking my virginity and lasting less than ten seconds before telling everyone I was a shit lay!" she yells before bursting into tears. My head snaps to Terry in disbelief, and I can see he's ready to commit murder alongside me. Terry may have never met Jasmine in person, but he's well aware of her and how important she is to my brothers and me.

"Come on, sweetheart. Let's get you home, where we can talk properly," Christian sighs her sobbing becomes muffled as if something is blocking the sound. I know it is more than likely he's holding her as she cries into his shoulder. Even through the phone, I know his jaw and fists will be clenched. If Jasmine weren't his sole priority right now, he would hunt down and hurt Damien himself.

"I don't want to go home. Can we go for a drive, please?" Jasmine asks. I hear Christian agreeing before the sound of the car engine starts up.

"I'll just text Jason and let him know someone else will be taking him home," Christian explains as I hear him handling the phone.

"Don't tell him, please; he will be angry at me."

My chest hurts that she thinks I could be even slightly

27

angry with her over this. I'm furious with that prick Damien, but nothing in me could ever be mad at my Jazzy.

"Jason would never be upset with you. You know that, sweetheart," Christian says as Jasmine sighs.

"I'm angry at myself," she whispers.

"Come on, let's get out of here," Christian replies before the line goes dead.

I look out of the windscreen and wait for the lights of Christian's car to appear in the distance. As soon as I see the first signs of them, I duck down in my seat to make sure Jasmine doesn't spot me. She won't recognise the car, thankfully.

"They've passed," Terry says as he starts the car and heads towards the farm. "How are you going to play this?" he asks. I reach into the glove compartment and pull out a pair of leather gloves.

"We head up to the house and wait for him to be alone. Then I'll be having a few words with Mr Ten Second Wonder," I growl as I look at the gloves in my hand. The phone beeps, and I see a message from Christian.

Christian: Only six people are left in the house. One staying, four waiting for lifts. You heard what he did; make him pay for deflowering our girl.

Terry pulls into a sheltered area, where we hide and wait until it's time to pay Damien a visit.

Chapter Four

CHRISTIAN

I pull into our five-car garage and climb out, slamming the door behind me. Walking into the house, I'm met with silence. I know if anyone's awake, they'll be in the sitting room, where we tend to all come together in this huge house. I head straight there in need of a drink after this evening.

I check my watch as I walk through and see it's just past midnight. I can't remember the last time I was home this early on a Saturday. There's usually an issue at one of our many clubs I need to deal with or an event I need to show my face at. But tonight, I cancelled and made sure I was available for Jasmine, and I'm so glad I did.

I walk into the sitting room to find Sean in his usual spot, holding a glass of whiskey.

"Where are the others?" I ask, walking to the small bar I had installed and pouring myself a glass.

"Maximus is in the shower, and I believe Jason's on his way home," Sean replies as he looks over his shoulder at me. "Is Jasmine home and okay?"

I look at him and sigh.

"She's home, but she's far from okay," I admit as I knock back the shot in my glass before pouring another one. I expect Sean to bombard me with questions, checking on the most important woman in our lives, but he doesn't. He sits and gives me time to regroup and calm myself. I look down at my empty glass and notice how white my knuckles are from holding it in such a tight fist. I force my hand to open and wiggle my fingers as I focus on the picture of Jasmine dancing in *Romeo and Juliet* last summer, which hangs proudly over the bar. We have pictures of her everywhere in this house. My favourite, though, is one of the two of us on a beach four months ago that I keep on the desk in my study.

I'd taken her out for the day, and she'd wanted ice cream. We sat on that beach for hours, talking and laughing, and it was the first time she had leaned into me and initiated physical contact. It was a sign that I was finally getting through the protective walls she had built around herself after so many people abandoned her when she needed them.

"Is Shorty home?"

I look away from the picture of her dancing to see Maximus and Jason walking into the room together.

"How is she now?" Jason asks as he walks to me and picks up a glass.

"Been better. How did it go with the prick?"

Jason looks at me and grins.

"He had a very unfortunate accident with a flight of stairs. He will never be contacting or speaking ill of our girl again."

"He admitted to it then?" I ask. Jason shrugs as he knocks back a shot and begins to pour another one.

"I didn't give him a chance; I only had a small opening, so I did all the talking."

"Did he fucking hurt her?" Maximus demands as his face reddens with rage.

"They had sex, but he couldn't last ten seconds and then blamed her," I explain through gritted teeth.

"What?!" Sean and Maximus both yell together. Jason and I both nod and take our drinks to sit on the seats.

We designed this room so we all had a place to sit and relax together whilst discussing personal as well as business issues. In our line of work, there are constant issues of delicate matters that need addressing, and none of us want to shout those across the room.

"Tell us what happened?" Sean demands as Jason and I share a look.

I lean forward in my seat and rest my elbows on my knees. At this moment in time, I want nothing more than to get out of this fucking suit, put on some joggers and go a few rounds with a punchbag. But that will have to wait; we owe the twins an update on what's happening.

"Jasmine called just after ten to tell me that she was ready to be picked up. Straight away, I realised she was upset, and when I asked her about it, she fed me some crap about being tired. I contacted Jason and Terry, and we went to Damien's farm, where the party was being held. Jason listened in to me collecting Jasmine, and she told me what was wrong via phone. She had no idea that he was listening or in the area.

"She informed me, whilst crying, that she had lost her virginity to the guy in a ten-second fumble, and he then told her friends she was a shit lay. I took her for a drive and left Jason to deal with him."

"You heard what happened. He won't be contacting her

again, and if for any reason she makes contact or sees him, he is to head in the other direction and stay away."

"And how's Shorty now?" Maximus asks. I take a sip of my drink and lean back into the sofa whilst resting my ankle on my knee.

"She's still upset. I took her for a drive, and we sat in the car talking for a long time. I realised quickly that it wasn't just the fumble that was upsetting her. Turns out Carol arrived not long after we left there today with all her things."

"Carol's left Tommy?" Jason asks; I look at him, nodding in confirmation.

"It sounds like it. Let's face it: we knew it wouldn't last forever. I'm surprised it lasted three years."

"This is going to knock the confidence in us that Jasmine has built over the last few years. She'll be waiting for us to leave her now."

I look at Sean and nod. He's hit the nail on the head. As soon as Jasmine told me that Carol had left Tommy, she burst into tears, admitting she didn't want to lose us. It took a lot of convincing, and I still don't think she believed me when I said we were going nowhere.

"We need to show her we are here to stay," I confirm.

"As I said before, we could tell her how we feel. Show her that she is ours," Jason starts again, but I shake my head.

"Not after tonight; we need to stick to the plan. We made it for a reason, and I refuse to defer from it."

"I hope you're right, Christian, because she's going to try and push us away. We could lose all the progress we've been making, getting her to trust us," Sean says from his seat.

I sigh as I sip my drink and allow myself to feel the liquid burn as it slides down my throat.

"I know."

Chapter Five

JASMINE

Six months Later.

"I'm so glad that exam's over; it was horrible!"

"You know what you need, Shorty?" Maximus replies as I reposition my phone so I can pull my bag strap over my head.

"What?" I ask, smiling whilst navigating my way through the other students, all heading in the opposite direction.

"Lunch with Sean and me. We'll pick you up in ten," he calls out before hanging up, not giving me a chance to decline.

Crap, I need to get my shit together and meet them.

I rush towards the toilets and stand in front of the mirror. My makeup's a mess, there's no way I can meet the guys looking like this. I grab my makeup from my bag and quickly tidy myself up before letting my long hazel hair down and shaking it out. It falls in loose waves down my back after being twisted up in a bun all morning. I look at myself in the mirror and accept this is the best I'm going to achieve whilst this tired. I just hope the guys put my tiredness down to the exams and nothing else.

Rushing out of the toilets, I head towards the car park where the guys always pick me up. As I walk to meet them, I unlock my phone and read through the messages waiting for me.

Christian: Good luck with your exam this morning, sweetheart. Let me know how you get on. Xx

Jason: Good luck, Jazzy. I know you'll smash it. Message me! Xx

I quickly reply to both, telling them the exam was okay and that I'm meeting the twins for lunch.

Three years ago, the guys told me I didn't have to be alone anymore, that I had them now, and they've stuck to their word. They've never missed an event since. Whenever I'm part of a ballet production, they always come to the last night and take me out for ice cream and milkshakes afterwards. I expected that to change when Mum turned up on my doorstep and announced she had left Tommy, but it didn't. I don't know how long it will last, but I'll enjoy their company until the divorce goes through. Then I'm sure they will disappear off the face of the earth like everyone else who says they care.

I walk out of the front door and knock straight into Danielle, one bitch who instantly puts me in a bad mood.

"Watch where you're going, tramp. You'll get my clothes dirty," she mocks as I go to step around her, but her friends block my way. I'm not in the mood for this right now.

"My clothes are just as clean as yours," I sigh as I roll

my eyes and turn to face her. "Now move out of my way," I add as I sidestep them again, but Danielle steps in front of me.

"Nothing about you is like me. That's why you will never be a principal. The only reason you're a soloist is that they feel sorry for you and how poor you are," she snarls, looking me up and down. I shake my head before replying.

"Not everything is about money. Most people don't need to flash designer clothes or expensive jewellery to feel good about themselves, unlike some!" I snap as I hold my head high and storm past her before hearing a car beeping its horn. I spot Maximus and Sean both leaning against the car, smiling at me from a distance. I rush towards them excitedly.

"Hey, Shorty, you ready to grab some lunch?" Maximus greets me with a bear hug whilst kissing my cheek.

"You bet. Where are we going?" I ask, walking around to Sean, who quickly hugs me and kisses me on the top of my head.

"Your favourite place, where else," he announces, holding the passenger door open for me as I jump in excitedly.

"You usually save that for special occasions," I point out, leaning between the front two seats while the guys climb in and put on their seatbelts.

"It is a special occasion. You've finished another exam," Maximus answers as he smiles at me in the rear-view mirror. "Now sit back and put your seatbelt on."

"You're starting to sound like Christian," I sigh dramatically, sitting back.

"But you still do as you're told," Sean laughs, looking over his shoulder. I stick my tongue out childishly, which makes him laugh harder. "Now, why don't you tell me what that was about a minute ago?" he asks, turning further in his seat to look at me.

"Nothing, just Danielle being a bitch as usual," I reply quietly.

"Is she still giving you a hard time? You need to talk to someone about this, Shorty."

I look at Maximus in the rear-view mirror and shake my head.

"That will just make her worse. If I ignore her and don't rise to it, she'll get bored eventually."

"You've been saying that for the last two years, and she's not gotten bored yet. Want one of us to say something to her and her little gang?" Sean offers.

"What? No way! That will make it worse!"

"Princess, if she's getting in your face all the time-"

"Honestly, she's just a bitch, please leave it." I watch as Sean and Maximus share a look, "Please, guys, for me," I plead, watching them closely. Maximus is the first to give in.

"Fine, we won't do or say anything to her or her friends." He looks at Sean, who shakes his head in defeat.

"I don't like this, but fine," he sighs as I reach around the headrest of his seat and hug him from behind.

"Thank you, Sean."

He looks around, and I give him my sweetest smile. He rolls his eyes as he takes my hand and kisses it, which leaves a tingling feeling that races through my arm.

"You are lucky you're so damn cute at times," he sighs as I sit back, grinning.

"It makes up for the times you're a brat," Maximus chuckles, looking in the mirror at me and winking.

"Hey, be nice!" I protest before chewing on my bottom lip. "Talking of being nice, please don't tell Christian about Danielle. You know how protective he can be, and there'll

37

be no stopping him from calling the school." Again, Maximus and Sean share a look, and I know I may have a fight on my hands. The four brothers are close and don't hide anything from each other.

"We won't tell him, but we won't lie either," Maximus answers. Sean looks at him and nods before turning around to face me again.

"As much as we understand why you don't want him to know, you have to understand he only has your best interest at heart. Protecting you is his main priority."

"I know," I answer as I look at my hands on my lap. I feel my phone vibrate in my jacket pocket and pull it out to find a message from the man himself.

Christian: We're so proud of you, sweetheart. Wish we could be there for lunch, but Jason and I are on our way to a meeting. Will you have dinner with us on Wednesday evening after rehearsals? Let me know, and I'll book it somewhere. Xx

Jasmine: Wednesday's perfect. I'll be ready by seven-thirty. Xx

Christian: Great, we will see you then. Well done again. Xx

I'm still smiling when we come to a stop outside my favourite restaurant. I jump out of the car and wait impatiently for Sean to join me. I thrust my arm through his and start dragging him towards the door before Maximus can even join us.

"Princess, they're not going to run out of food in the next five minutes," he laughs as he pulls against me.

"You don't know that, come on!" I protest, tugging him

towards the door again. I feel two strong arms wrap around my waist as Maximus pulls me away from Sean, laughing.

"Shorty, if they run out of food, I will personally hunt down a chicken for you," he laughs before planting a kiss on my cheek and letting me go. He steps beside me and casually throws his arm around my shoulders as I look at him.

"Are you ever going to stop calling me Shorty? I'm only eight inches shorter than you now!" I protest. Maximus stops walking and looks me in the eye.

"Gorgeous, you could be taller than me, and you'd still be my Shorty," he says in that deep voice, which makes a knot form in my stomach and my toes curl. I stare into his chocolate eyes and fight every urge to lift and press my lips to his. Maximus grins like he knows the effect he has on me. He leans in and kisses my cheek, this time softly as if kissing a lover, before standing tall and leading me into the restaurant.

"Now come on before they really run out of food," he laughs as Sean walks beside us and we approach the front of house counter.

I have the best two hours with the twins. We laugh and drink champagne to celebrate another exam while eating so much chicken salad that I think I might burst. Of course, we make room for pudding, and they insist on me having the stickiest, sweetest chocolate cake I have ever tasted. It melts in my mouth in an explosion of flavours, and I could have easily eaten a second piece. Unfortunately, as always, our time together gets cut short when Maximus's phone rings, and they have to deal with an issue at one of their gyms.

They drive me back to the dance school and head into the car park.

"Where's your car? I can't see it anywhere," Sean asks as Maximus turns the car around.

"Oh, I got a lift this morning; my car's getting an service," I answer quickly.

"Is it going to pass? That piece of shit should have been scrapped years ago!" Maximus laughs as he pulls to a stop.

"Hey, she's not that bad!" I protest, knowing I'm lying.

"Yes, it is Shorty. Let us buy you a new one; we hate you driving that thing," he says as he looks at me, but I just shake my head, which earns me the usual eyeroll. It's an argument I have with the guys at least once a month, and will continue to do so until they get their own way. "Where do you want dropping off? Is your lift even still here?" he asks, looking around.

"She's inside practising; I've already messaged and checked," I reply, pocketing my phone before unbuckling my seat belt.

"Want me to walk you in, just in case Danielle is hanging around again?" Sean offers. I shake my head as I lean between the two front seats and kiss them both on the cheek.

"I'm fine. Thank you for lunch; it was lovely," I say, smiling.

"Anytime, princess. Will you be able to fit us into your busy schedule before next month's performance?"

I pout as I shake my head.

"You know what it's like before a show. They have us practising from morning to night and then some. Will you still be coming to watch?" I ask, looking at them both.

"Have we missed one yet?" Maximus asks with raised brows. I shake my head before opening my door.

"I'll see you the last night then," I call as I climb out. Sean opens his door and stands in front of me.

"Everything okay? Do you need anything?" he asks, as he does every time I see him. I shake my head and hug him quickly.

"Nope, I have everything I need."

"Okay, princess, as long as you're sure. We'll see you next month," he says, kissing my cheek.

"Bye, guys," I call quickly, heading towards the building. I look over my shoulder and can see them both watching me. I make a point of waving to them as I get to the door before opening it. They quickly wave back and then drive off.

I walk through the building to the back entrance, not wanting to risk them seeing me as I walk in the opposite direction of my house.

Chapter Six

JASMINE

I rush out of the rehearsal hall and instantly spot the two older O'Reilly brothers leaning against Christian's Mercedes. They are impossible to miss in their designer suits and broad shoulders, looking like the very definition of dangerous but delicious. There are women all around stealing glances at them, but when they look up and see me, it's like there's no one else on the street. I rush towards them, unable to hide the smile on my face.

As soon as I'm within reach, Christian pulls me into his arms and holds me tightly to his broad chest as he presses a kiss to the top of my head.

"Hey, sweetheart," he chuckles into my hair. I feel his hold loosen just the smallest amount before Jason grabs my hand and pulls me away from Christian and into his waiting arms as I laugh aloud.

"Hey! I'm right here as well, you know!" he chuckles as he holds me just as tightly as Christian did.

"I don't have favourites, you know that" I laugh, stepping back and looking at them both. I look down at my fitted jeans and top and realise I'm seriously underdressed. "Do I need to change?" I ask nervously. Jason shakes his head.

"You look perfect, as always, Jazzy," he says, stepping to the side and opening the front passenger door. "Now come on, we have a table booked, and I'm starving," he adds before I climb into the car, smiling.

Jason climbs into the back seat, and I turn to look at him whilst Christian gets behind the wheel.

"Are you sure you don't want to sit in the front? I don't mind getting in the back." As expected, Jason looks at me like I've gone mad.

"Put your seatbelt on, Jazzy."

I quickly do as I'm told, knowing better than to argue.

As soon as Christian pulls away from the curb and heads towards the restaurant, he starts asking about what I've been up to and how rehearsals for next month's show are going.

The guys always ask about the dance school and are fully behind me getting my degree and concentrating on becoming a professional ballerina. They will sit for hours as I talk about my next production and what I'm doing with the kids' class I'm teaching. They never tell me to stop or seem bored, no matter how long I go on about it all. It's one of the things I really appreciate about them.

I'm in full flow, talking about everything when we come to a stop. I look out of the window at the posh restaurant in front of me. I'm still staring nervously when Jason opens the door and holds out a hand to help me to my feet.

"Guys, I'm really underdressed for this place. Are you sure they'll even let me in?" I ask quietly as I look down at my jeans and feel self-conscious. I should have known better with it being these two taking me out. Jason and Christian glance at each other quickly before both shrug off their jackets and hang them up in the back of the car.

"What are you doing?"

"We won't let you feel out of place, sweetheart. The only reason we're both in suits is that we came straight from a meeting," Christian explains as he starts to roll up the sleeves of his grey shirt. I look at Jason to find he's doing the same, revealing his tattoos. He gives me a cheeky wink before holding his arm out for me. I slip mine around him, and he leads me into the restaurant, as always, making sure I'm comfortable.

Christian speaks to the Maitre D, and we're shown to our table. The guys move their chairs closer to sit on either side of me, and Christian quickly orders our first round of drinks.

As soon as our drinks are on the table, Christian pounces.

"So, school's been okay then? No issue with anything or anyone?"

I freeze with my lips against my glass of wine as I look over the rim at him.

"The twins told you then," I sigh, putting my glass back on the table. He nods, leaning back in his seat and taking a sip of his drink.

"Want to tell me what's happening in your own words?" he asks calmly, as if I actually have a choice. I take a sip of my drink and lean back in my chair, hoping to seem bored and relaxed about the whole thing.

"There's nothing to tell. Danielle's being a bitch, not like that's anything new."

"From what the twins said, she got right in your face the other day; do I need to call the school?"

I quickly shake my head. "No, I told her straight, and she hasn't been near me since."

I'm not exactly lying. She hasn't been near me. But she hasn't been to school either, and we don't see each other at rehearsals for the time being as she is practising with the principals. "She just thinks she's better than the rest of us because her father is rich and gets her anything she wants. The way she goes on, you would think he is some sort of mafia boss," I sigh, rolling my eyes and taking a sip of my drink.

"What's her father's name?" Jason asks, frowning.

"King, well, that's her surname anyway," I reply. I don't miss the look between Jason and Christian. "Do you guys know him?" I ask. Both nod, but it's Jason who answers as Christian pulls out his phone.

"He's not as big as he likes to think he is. Everything he has is thanks to us. He owes us a lot of money."

I can't stop the laugh that bursts from my lips. I quickly slam my hand over my mouth from embarrassment.

"You're serious, aren't you? And there's her giving me shit for being 'poor' all because my bag ripped once two years ago."

"Judging by what he owes, I think we're the ones paying for Miss King to attend your dance school," Christian says without looking up from his phone.

"This is priceless," I chuckle as I sit back, feeling a little smug. "Please let me throw that in her face if she starts up again?" I beg as I turn to Jason, expecting him to shake his head, but instead, he's grinning.

"Not just yet; let's see what I can dig up first," Christian replies as he puts his phone on the table and looks up at me.

"How's your mother doing since the separation?" he asks but luckily gets interrupted as the waiter comes over.

We all place our food order quickly and I hope it will distract Christian from the conversation. Unfortunately not, because as soon as the waiter's gone he looks at me and waits for an answer.

"Not great, but then I hardly see her, as I'm out so much with school and rehearsals," I say, looking at them. "How's Tommy?" I ask. Both guys just shrug. Sometimes, they are so alike in their habits and mannerisms that it's hard to believe that they aren't twins.

"We don't see or speak to him often, so who knows," Jason says as he pours three glasses of water.

"Do you think they'll get back together?" I ask but feel that last strand of hope break when both shake their heads.

"Highly unlikely. Apparently, it's been coming for a while," Christian says as he sips his water. "Did you know she had contacted a divorce lawyer?"

I shake my head slowly as I start playing with the bottom of my top nervously. If our parents divorce, there will be no reason for the guys to stick around anymore. I feel someone reach around and place a finger under my chin before forcing me to look up. I find myself looking straight into Christian's blue eyes.

"What's the matter? I didn't realise you were that close to our father," he asks quietly. I shake my head and try to look away, but he forces me to look at him. "Speak to me."

"I'm scared," I reply as I look into his eyes, feeling my own starting to burn.

"Of what, Jazzy?" Jason asks next to me as he reaches over and takes my hand under the table.

"Of losing you all," I admit as I look between the two of them. Jason's and Christian's faces soften as they look back at me.

"I told you, none of us is going anywhere, sweetheart."

"You are stuck with the four of us, if you like it or not, Jazzy."

I try to force a smile, but it's obvious neither of them is buying it.

"Okay," I reply, wishing I could believe them. When I look up at Christian, I notice a seriousness in his eyes that makes me stop.

"One day soon, sweetheart, you will understand how stuck with us you really are."

"You really don't need to drive me home; I'll get a taxi," I protest as Jason helps me to shrug on my jacket.

"There's no point in arguing; we are taking you home, and that's final," Christian replies as he hands his card to the waitress.

"Why are you so against us dropping you off? Is there something you aren't telling us?" Jason asks.

"Of course not!" I protest quickly.

"Then what's the problem? You've always let us drop you off in the past," he points out as we walk outside and towards the parked car.

"Is it Carol? Doesn't she know that you're meeting us?" Christian asks, catching up with us.

"No, she doesn't, and I don't want any arguments," I admit. "She's hurting after the separation," I add quickly. The two guys look at each other and nod, seeming to communicate without actually speaking. Jason opens the passenger door for me. I stand staring at him as my heart races. He looks at me, and I watch one side of his mouth lift into a small smile.

"We are taking you home, Jazzy. But - " he says quickly as I open my mouth to protest. "We'll drop you off at the bottom of the street and watch until you go inside from there." He reaches up and cups my cheek with his hand.

"We know the separation is hard on Carol; we don't want to make things worse for her. But we need you to tell her we are still in your life."

I nod as I look down at the floor. "I will; it just hasn't been the right time," I answer, looking up and seeing Christian looking at us over the roof of the car.

"No time will be the right time, sweetheart. But your mum needs to know that we aren't going anywhere, and although you are our priority, we are happy to help her as well," Christian adds before nodding towards the car. "Come on, let's get you home."

I get into the car and let Jason close my door. Christian reaches over and takes my hand in his.

"Talk to your mum. Don't hide us from her," he insists as he lifts my hand and places a kiss on my knuckles. I feel my breath catch in my throat as I think about what it would be like if he kissed me on the lips. I quickly shake off the inappropriate thoughts and nod my head.

"I will," I whisper. Christian smiles at me before he leans in and presses his lips to my cheek.

"Good girl." As always, his praise causes a knot to form deep in my stomach and lower, which makes me press my thighs together. I'm still in my own world of inappropriate thoughts as Christian pulls away from the curb, and we head towards my house.

We drive in silence for a short while; I'm exhausted and full after the biggest meal I've eaten in weeks. Whenever any of my stepbrothers take me out for dinner, they always make sure I have at least three courses. They say it's their way of making sure I'm eating properly so they can look after me. I think they want to make sure I'm taking care of myself; the more I eat, the more they question if I'm eating enough when they aren't around.

"Has Tommy been giving you any problems now that Carol is in the house?" Jason asks from behind. I turn to look at him, shaking my head.

"No, everything's been fine," I reply.

"Has he been in touch at all? About school or the house?" Christian asks. I shake my head again.

"Not since they split up," I answer, looking out the window at the passing streetlights rather than at them.

"If he does, let us know. We don't want him causing problems for you," Christian adds. I look at him as I nod again, not trusting myself enough to speak. I start feeling sick with nerves as we get closer to the street. The last thing I need right now is for Mum to see me with the guys; she will lose her shit.

As I see the turn to my street come into view, I quickly look at my house at the top of it to see if the lights are on or not. I can see a small amount of light shining through the gap in the front windows.

"Are you sure you don't want us to come in and speak to Carol?" Christian asks as he takes my hand again. I quickly look at him and shake my head vigorously.

"That's the last thing you should do," I say quietly before turning in my seat and planting a kiss on his cheek, forcing a smile. Christian and Jason share a look, and for a moment, I'm terrified they're going to insist on walking me into the house like they usually do. Instead, Christian shakes his head, and Jason sighs before climbing out of the car and opening my door.

"I'll see you after your show next month, sweetheart," Christian says, pulling me into a hug. "If you need anything give me a shout," he adds as he looks into my eyes.

"Thank you for dinner; it was lovely," I say with an extra smile before climbing out of the car and straight into

Jason's waiting arms. He holds me close before I feel him press a kiss on my head.

"Anything you need, just shout. I'll see you in a month, Jazzy."

I kiss him on the cheek and thank him for dinner as well, before heading towards my house.

I walk slowly in the hope they will drive off, but of course, they don't and won't until they know I'm safely inside. I get to the front door and wave before taking a deep breath and slowly opening it.

I walk in and wait for the sound of my mother shouting, demanding to know where I've been, but I'm thankfully met with silence. Slowly I make my way into the house and can see how unkempt it is. I find out why when I walk into the lounge and see Mum passed out on the sofa with an empty bottle of vodka on the floor below her. There's also an empty bottle of gin and several bottles of wine.

"Oh, Mum," I sigh, walking over and pulling the blanket from the back of the sofa before laying it over her. I consider cleaning up, but I don't want her to know I've been here. Instead, I walk to the kitchen, which is covered in dirty dishes and old food. The bins are overflowing with gone-off contents, which smell so bad my eyes water, and I have to hold a hand over my mouth and nose. I hold my breath and head straight for the back door. Slowly, I open it, not wanting to wake Mum and head out into the garden. As quickly and quietly as possible, I jump the fence and head down the alleyway, away from Mum and the house I should be living in.

Chapter Seven

JASMINE

"Jaz!"

I turn to the sound of my friend's voice to find her pushing her way through the crowd of dancers.

"Jaz! There you are! Oh my god!" Verity stops beside me and grabs my shoulder for support as she catches her breath.

"What the hell is wrong with you?" I laugh as I shove my makeup and spare clips into my makeup bag.

"What's your secret girl?" she gasps.

"What are you on about?" I ask, looking at her in the mirror.

"Four very hot men are waiting for you in the entrance hall! Who the hell are they?"

I spin around and stare at her.

"Four? Are you sure?"

"Of course, I'm sure! I can count!"

"Fuck, I didn't expect them to come!" I start throwing everything in my bag quickly and check my makeup in the mirror. Trying to ignore the fact that my stomach is now full of butterflies.

"Who are they?"

"My stepbrothers," I answer as I reapply my lipstick.

"Holy cow, you lucky woman!"

"I have to go," I snap as I throw my bag over my shoulder. "I'll see you tomorrow," I add, kissing her on the cheek before pushing my way through the crowd and heading towards the door.

I rush to the exit before taking a deep breath to calm my racing heart, slow my pace and head into the foyer.

There stood together are the four O'Reilly brothers, all talking amongst themselves. With them distracted, I take a second to look at them.

They're all in their best suits, their hair immaculate and looking amazing as always. Christian's holding a huge bunch of flowers and chatting with Sean. Jason stands with his hands shoved in the pockets of his trousers, and he talks to Maximus next to him. I love watching them all stand together like this; there's not a person around who isn't stealing glances at the four men.

"There she is, our best girl!" Maximus beams as I approach them.

"Stop it, people are looking," I hiss, embarrassed, as a few people turn to look at me.

"So they should. You were amazing, sweetheart," Christian smiles, handing me the flowers before kissing my cheek, which instantly heats from his touch and compliment.

"Thank you. I didn't think you would come," I admit, turning to Jason, who hugs me and also kisses me on my cheek.

"How could we miss you being a soloist? We told you we would be here," he says, frowning.

"I know, but with our parents' divorce now going through, you've all been quiet this month. I thought you might miss it; now you don't have to be here," I admit as I turn to Sean. He places a hooked finger under my chin, forcing me to lift my head.

"We never *had* to be here; we wanted to be. You know that, so stop doubting us."

I nod as he removes his finger and places a kiss on my forehead.

"We have been giving you space as we know how busy you are. Anyway, if we missed it, we would miss out on ice cream, and there is no way that's happening, Shorty," Maximus laughs as he pulls me into a bear hug I have come to expect and love from him.

"Maximus! My flowers!" I laugh, pulling away. He looks down at them, smiling.

"If I crush them, it gives me a reason to buy you more," he winks. I shake my head as I turn to look at them, so relieved that they proved me wrong once again and came.

"Is Carol here? I didn't see her?" Christian asks, looking around. I shake my head and look at the floor.

"No, Mum couldn't make it," I say quietly, hoping to change the subject.

"Has she been to any of the performances?" he asks. I can feel his eyes on me and shake my head before turning to Maximus. I can see the question on the tip of his tongue, so I quickly change the subject, something I'm very good at when it comes to talking about Mum.

"Are we going for ice cream? Or are we going to stand here until they kick us out?" I ask, looking at the four guys.

"Come on, princess. It's my treat this time," Sean declares as he throws his arm around my shoulder and turns me towards the door. But I don't miss the look between them. I know they are going to bring up Mum again, and I know I'm not going to be able to avoid that conversation forever.

"So, whose car are we taking?" I ask, looking around the car park.

"I've driven tonight; you can sit in the front," Jason says beside me as he presses his car fob, and the lights flash on a black Jaguar.

"Another new car?" I ask as I walk up to it. "It's gorgeous," I sigh, admiring its immaculate condition.

"You could have one if you stopped being stubborn and let us buy you a car," Christian remarks, holding the front passenger door open for me. I go to throw my bag in, but he takes it and my flowers before walking to the trunk. I roll my eyes as I get in.

"What's wrong with my baby? She might not be as pretty, but I paid for her all by myself," I point out as I climb in, and Maximus closes the door behind me.

"It's a death trap, and you know it. I hate you driving that thing," Jason replies as he climbs in behind the wheel.

"Some of us aren't successful businessmen like you lot. We don't earn hundreds of pounds a minute."

"Thousands," Sean calls from the back seat.

"What?" I ask, frowning as I turn to face him.

"We earn thousands every minute," he replies, smirking. I flip him off before realising Christian has just climbed in beside him. Christian gives me his "dad" look, and I quickly turn around, mumbling a sorry under my breath as Sean laughs behind me.

Christian hates it when I swear or do anything "unlady-like." I usually watch what I'm saying or doing a little more when he's around. The twins, however, let me get away with the odd curse word or vulgar gesture.

"Next time, we are bringing two cars," Maximus moans as he climbs in. "Or Shorty is riding in the back," he adds as the door slams shut.

"It won't be an issue if you keep slamming my doors because you'll be walking," Jason warns his brother in the rear-view mirror before he pulls out of the parking space. I chuckle to myself as I sit back and relax properly for the first time in weeks.

"I've missed you guys," I admit out loud.

"We've missed you too, sweetheart."

I turn my head and look at Christian, unable to stop the grin from spreading across my face; he instantly smiles back at me.

"Yeah?"

"Of course we have. We've had no one to pick on," Maximus says behind me before cursing as Sean hits him. "What was that for?"

"You pick on her, and you have me to answer to," Sean warns. I turn around and grin at him.

"Thank you, Sean," I say sweetly before sticking my tongue out at Maximus.

"You're very welcome, princess," Sean laughs. I glance at Christian, who's shaking his head in dismay but isn't able to wipe the smile completely off his face.

It doesn't take long before we pull up outside the ice cream shop, and all pile out of the car. We walk in together and head for our favourite booth. As always, I sit at the back with two guys on either side of me.

We're just getting comfortable when the waitress walks over.

"I take it the ballerina has finished another show?" she asks with a grin. I look up at her, smiling.

"Sure have, Hilary. How are you?"

"I'm good, thanks, sugar. All the better for seeing my favourite customers," she adds with a smile as she looks at the guys.

"You missed us, Hilary?" Maximus asks as he places his arms over the back of the booth behind me, flashing his award-winning grin at her.

"The rest of your family, yes. You, not so much, hot shot," she replies, causing the rest of us to laugh. "Now, what are you all having to drink?"

We quickly place our orders, and Hilary heads off to make them.

"So, Shorty, any idea when you will be moved up to principal?" Maximus asks.

"It can't be much longer; you looked amazing up there tonight, sweetheart. You've never looked better," Christian adds. I turn to him, smiling.

"You're biased, though. You always have been."

"No, I've always been honest. That was your best performance yet. Those extra classes are paying off."

I look away and nod before quickly changing the subject.

"When's your next fight? You got anything big coming up?" I ask the twins. Both are professional fighters and tend to win any fight they have.

They both start talking about what they are training for, and Jason fills me in on a new centre they are opening with a local youth club to give the kids somewhere to go instead of hanging around on the streets. For every two gyms they open for the gain, they open one in a deprived area for the locals to use, mainly aimed at the kids. This is one of the main reasons I have so much respect for the guys. They didn't have much growing up, not until Christian was old enough to make money fighting—everything they have now they built themselves, and they give as much as they can to others.

Hilary brings over our milkshakes and ice cream, and we all dig in, chatting away. The whole time, I feel Christian and Jason watching me more than usual. I know neither of them missed the way I changed the subject every time the conversation moved towards my mum, the house, or the extra dance lessons. But there are certain things I don't want them to know about my life, those being three of them.

An hour later, Hilary comes over and kicks us out. We are still chatting when we get back outside and head to the car. I look around and smile at my stepbrothers.

"I'm going to head off from here. My friend lives around the corner, and I promised I'd stay there tonight as her boyfriend's out of town," I say, trying to avoid looking Christian or Jason in the eye.

"I don't want you walking around on your own," Christian says as he steps in front of me. I walk to the car, open the trunk, and pull out my dance bag and flowers.

"I'm a big girl, Christian, so stop fussing. It's just around the corner," I add as I lift onto my tiptoes and plant a kiss on his cheek. "I'll be fine," I whisper, stepping away from him.

"Christian's, right, we can take you," Jason says, standing by the car. I shake my head, forcing a smile.

"It's all one way. You'll have to go all the way around to get back to that street. This way is much quicker." I walk round to him, and he pulls me in for a hug before kissing the top of my head.

"Message when you get there," he whispers into my hair.

"Will do, Dad," I reply with a wink. He nods for Christian to get into the car. I quickly hug the twins before they climb in as well, threatening to hunt me down if I don't text.

As I go to walk away, Jason steps in front of me. "Don't think we haven't noticed how odd you're acting tonight. What's going on?" he asks, looking into my eyes. "Do you need anything? If you do and don't want to admit it in front of Christian, call me, and I will meet you. I know he can be overbearing, but he worries. We all do."

I force a smile and try desperately not to let him see that my eyes are filling with tears.

"I'm fine, don't worry," I reply as I kiss him on the cheek again. "I'll message as soon as I get in," I call as I jog off round the corner with my bag on my shoulder and flowers in my arm, desperately hoping none of them follows me as I reach the front door of my secret apartment. I quickly look around and let myself in before closing the door. I lean back against it and let out a deep sigh.

"If it isn't, Miss Ballerina."

I open my eyes and look at the dickhead of a landlord, Sam Black, that lives on the floor below me.

"Look, I pay my rent, and I don't report you for all the drug dealing that goes on in your flat. Just leave me alone," I snap, storming past him and up the stairs into my dump of an apartment, slamming the door behind me as I hear him laughing. I lean against it and look around. The guys would lose their minds if they knew I was living in this shithole. There's no way they would let me stay. But I don't need their sympathy; I just need to get back on my feet, and all will be fine.

Chapter Eight

JASMINE

It's been five days since I saw my stepbrothers, and I've been avoiding their calls and text messages since. I know they picked up on my behaviour that night, and I know they have questions, but I'm not ready to answer them yet. I just need to buy myself a little more time to get a few things in place before I admit to them how bad things have gotten.

I walk into the run-down bar at the end of my street to start my evening shift. I know there are better places to work, but the guys would never be seen dead drinking in here, so there's no chance of them walking in and catching me. They made me promise to tell them if I ever needed money to survive so that I could focus on my studies and dance. But I've never asked for help from anyone; I can't start now. Let's face it: it's only a matter of time before they disappear. Everyone does eventually.

I hang my coat up and pull down my tight black T-shirt. It's short and rides up whenever I lift my arms, I hate it, but it's the uniform. I take a deep breath and push down the constant worry that lives in my gut. Plastering on a smile I walk into the bar and prepare to spend another five hours pretending I'm okay.

"Hey, Daz, where do you want me?"

My boss, who looks as old and run down as this place, doesn't bother to face me; he just points upstairs with a grunt. I sigh and head towards the top bar, hoping Dale isn't working with me tonight. It's amazing how many times one guy can "accidentally" touch your ass and breasts in a couple of hours.

As soon as I get up there my mood lifts when I see Lynsey's bright pink hair.

"Oh, thank god, I thought I'd be working with that prick," I exhale when I get within earshot of her. She turns and winks at me.

"Nope, it's me and you tonight, chick. Unless one of us gets dragged downstairs, that is," she smiles as she goes back to filling up the fridges.

I love working with this woman, her personality is as bright as her hair. I always finish the shift feeling a lot better about things.

"Want me to stock up the top shelf?" I ask, pointing to the bottles we have hanging up.

"Yeah, why not. Gets it done before the mad rush; it's student night, after all."

"How could I forget," I moan, feeling my phone vibrate in my pocket. I pull it out and look at the screen to see Jason is calling. He tried to call me when I left rehearsal and when I was getting changed to start work. I stare at it for a moment before ending the call and pocketing my phone, trying to ignore the growing guilt.

"So, it does work."

My heart stops as I slowly turn around and come face to face with a pissed-off-looking Jason.

"Fuck," I mumble under my breath. "Please don't tell, Christian," I blurt out in a blind panic. Jason's eyebrows disappear into his hairline as he looks at me. We stand staring at each other for a moment before he nods to the other side of the bar. I turn to find Lynsey watching us.

"Give me five," I sigh as she frowns and watches me follow Jason.

As soon as we are away from listening ears, Jason turns and stares at me as he crosses his arms over his broad chest.

"What are you doing here?" Jason asks.

"I could ask you the same thing!" I reply.

"Jasmine."

I hear the warning in his voice and sigh.

"Working," I answer nervously.

"Why?"

"It's a long story," I reply as I wrap my arms around myself, feeling like a disobedient child who's been caught doing something they shouldn't.

"If I told you to get your coat and leave with me now, would you?" he asks. I shake my head, chewing on my bottom lip. "Then I'll wait, and I will take you home after work so we can talk," he demands. I quickly shake my head as my eyes bulge.

"You can't," I reply, panicking.

"Why? Because you don't want me to know you aren't living at the house?" he declares.

Fuck he knows.

"How?" I ask as my stomach tightens into a knot.

"I knew you were hiding something the other night, and when you wouldn't take anyone's calls, I offered to wait for you to get home from classes last night. To my surprise, I realise you aren't going back there anymore. I spoke to a neighbour, and they said they haven't seen you for months!"

"Oh." I can't think of what else to say; it's like I've been rendered mute.

"Yes '*oh*'. So, I waited outside your rehearsal tonight and followed you."

"You followed me!" I yell in disbelief, what the fuck?

"Yes! Because if I hadn't offered to do it, it would be Christian here right now. You know you wouldn't have liked it if he found you here! You've been lying to us. Why?" he growls through his teeth, obviously trying not to shout.

"I'm fine. I don't need you guys worrying about me or following me!" I growl back. I instantly hate the way his face changes. It's like I've slapped him, and I want to apologise.

"The fact that you still won't tell me what the hell is going on tells me you are far from fine, Jazzy," he sighs, rubbing his face with his hand. "What time do you finish?" he asks, his voice and face softening.

"Midnight," I sigh, knowing there's no hiding the truth from him now. He nods as he looks around.

"Fine. At midnight, I'm going to take you home, and you are going to show me inside the building you've been living in. Then I will decide how much I'm going to tell Christian and the others."

"Prick," I curse under my breath. Jason's nostrils flare.

"Watch your mouth, Jazzy. I could change my mind and drag you out of this shithole now! I'll be over here until you finish your shift. Don't even *think* about sneaking out before then, you won't like the consequences," he warns before walking to the bar. Fuck I'm in the shit now.

The whole shift, Jason sits at a table and watches me. He only takes his eyes off the bar when he's typing on his phone or talking into it. Every time I see him with it to his ear, my heart races, panicking that he's on the phone with Christian.

I'm not scared of him, but I know if he was the one who turned up here tonight, he wouldn't have let me finish my shift; he would have thrown me over his shoulder and carried me out of here like a protective caveman no matter how much I kicked and screamed. I also hate the idea of disappointing any of them, Christian especially.

Even though I'm worried about what he will say, there's a part of me that wants him to march in here and save me. I want him to take me back to his place and tell me it will be okay whilst he holds me and puts my life back together like I know he could, as they all could. But that's one of the reasons I've distanced myself from them. The older we get, the harder it is to just see them as my big, strong stepbrothers. They are becoming the strong men in my life whom I want in a way I really shouldn't.

"Time to cash up. Want me to do it so you can get whatever you have going on with Mr Moody Pants over there sorted?" Lynsey asks. I look over at Jason and see him holding an empty glass, watching me.

I let out a sigh and grab a tray, "I'll do the glasses, he can stew for a little longer," I whisper as she gives me a cheeky wink.

"That's my girl," she replies before glancing at Jason. "I'm still not buying the whole stepbrother thing, though. If he was my stepbrother, I would have nailed him years ago," she whispers before looking at me, grinning. I roll my eyes and walk away from her, yelling 'whatever', over the music. I take my time collecting the empties and cleaning the tables purposely leaving Jason's table to last.

When I reach him, I hold out the tray for his glass.

"I'm not the bad guy here, Jazzy; we're worried about you."

"I know," I reply with a deep sigh. "I'll put this through the washer, and then I'll go get my coat. Meet me at the front door?"

Jason nods before heading down the stairs.

"You sneaking out the back?" Lynsey asks as soon as I get back to the bar.

"No point. Apparently, he knows where I live now," I sigh before filling the dishwasher. I try to take my time with it, but Daz marches upstairs.

"The guy waiting for you just told me to make sure you finish quickly," he snaps, coming behind the bar and handing me my wages for the night.

"Let me guess, he tipped you too?"

Daz nods and points towards the stairs. I sigh and say a quick goodbye to Lynsey before heading off to get my coat. I get to the front door, where Jason's waiting for me.

"You didn't need to tip my boss to make sure I finished quickly," I snap, storming past him and out of the door into the cold night.

"I wasn't waiting around in that dump any longer whilst you dragged your feet," Jason snaps back as I groan and cross the road before heading to my apartment.

"Who knows where you were tonight?" I ask, trying to ignore the growing tension between us. Dread fills me as I think about taking Jason inside my apartment. At least it could be worse; it could be Sean or Christian; both would explode, drag me out of there and never let me return.

"The guys knew I had tracked you down and that I was going to be with you until late."

"Do they know about the bar?" I ask. Jason looks at me and shakes his head; I let out a sigh of relief.

"Thank you."

"Don't thank me yet, Jazzy. That doesn't mean I won't be telling them," Jason warns.

"This is it," I whisper as I look up at the building. It's just a townhouse that has been converted into two apartments. I send up a silent prayer that Sam has already passed out and won't come out as soon as he hears me like he usually does. I take a deep breath and open the door.

It's pitch black inside, and the smell of weed and dampness hits us instantly. I don't say anything; I just head up the stairs, knowing Jason's following. I unlock my front door and switch on the light before stepping back and watching Jason's large form walk into my one-floor apartment.

Jason closes the door behind him and looks around. He doesn't say anything, and with Jason, you never know what he's thinking. He walks further into the apartment and looks at the small open kitchen and the lounge.

"Where do you sleep?" he asks. I point to the doors behind him.

"Back there's the bathroom and my room," I reply. Jason looks behind both doors. I know he'll smell the dampness that fills the whole place; no matter how many plug-in air fresheners I use, the place still stinks.

"How long have you been living here?" he asks, walking back into the lounge and looking at the bean bag and the tiny TV.

"Four months," I admit quietly. Jason nods before walking up to me and pulling me into his arms. I instantly melt into him and wrap my arms around his waist, realising how much I need him to hold me. I feel him kiss the top of my head and let out a deep sigh.

"Go and pack a bag, I'm taking you home," Jason whispers into my hair, I pull out of his arms and stare at him.

"No."

I don't want to be here; I hate this place and everything about it, but it's better than going back to the house.

"That wasn't a request. Do as you are told and pack a bag," Jason demands as he arches a brow at me. "This place isn't safe, there's more mould and damp in here than a fucking derelict building. Don't think I didn't notice the smell of weed when you opened that front door either. I'm not leaving you here, so you either come willingly, or I will drag you out kicking and screaming. Either way, you are leaving *tonight*."

"You can't take me back to the house! You don't know how bad it was!" I protest, trying to stop my voice from breaking but failing. Jason frowns at me for a moment before his face softens.

"I don't mean Carol's. I'm taking you home to ours," he says as he walks up to me and places his hands on my arms. "I don't know what the hell's happened or why you felt you couldn't talk to any of us. But right now, I just want to get you somewhere safe, warm and damp-free, and then you are telling *all* of us everything."

I open my mouth to speak, but Jason silences me with a look. "Save the arguments; you won't win. Pack an overnight bag for now, and let's get out of this shithole." Jason leans forward and kisses my forehead before stepping back and pulling his phone out of his pocket. I know he will be calling Christian, and I don't want to hear this conversation, so I quickly head back to my room and do as I'm told.

Chapter Nine

JASMINE

Twenty minutes later, we pull into a huge garage, the door automatically closing behind us. It is attached to the biggest house I have ever seen. I always figured the guys' house would be large, but this is a mansion.

Once the car is parked, we sit silently for a moment, and I try to calm my nerves as I worry about seeing the others and how disappointed in me, they are going to be. Jason turns in his seat to look at me. He reaches over and tucks a stray strand of hair out of my face behind my ear before cupping my cheek.

"I'll show you to your room and let you freshen up before we speak to the others."

I nod as I blink back the tears.

"Come on," Jason whispers before climbing out of the car. I open the passenger door and slowly force myself to get out as I walk around to the front where Jason is waiting for me with my bag in his hand.

"I've told the others to wait in the sitting room; they won't try and find you. We will go to them after you have freshened up," he reassures me as he swaps my bag to his other hand.

"Thank you," I whisper, playing with the cuff of my jumper. Jason reaches up and cups my cheek again with his big hand, but I can't help but lean into it.

"You don't need to thank me. Just tell me what you need, and I'll sort it, okay?"

I nod, chewing on my bottom lip and try desperately not to cry.

"Come on, let me show you to your room," Jason says, offering me his hand. I take it and let him lead me into the house.

We walk into a spacious kitchen. There's a large break-fast bar in the middle and at least two huge ovens.

"Is this the house you bought two years ago? Instead of all buying separate houses?" I ask. Jason turns to me and nods.

"Things changed, and we knew we needed a place we could all call home together." He looks at me as I try to work out what it could have been that changed their minds. When I met them, they were all looking forward to finding their own homes and having some sort of independence from each other. I'd been surprised when they informed me less than a year later that they had purchased this one instead.

"I will give you a proper tour of the place tomorrow when you are a little more settled in. But please help your-self to anything you want; nothing is off limits," Jason explains as he carries on leading me through the kitchen and into a large hallway, where there's a huge staircase to one side. He leads me upstairs as I try to keep up. Jason doesn't loosen his grip on my hand, which I'm thankful for.

When we reach the landing, I look around and can't

believe the sheer size of everything. There are rooms to the left and right of me, as well as another flight of stairs leading up to another floor.

"Your room is down here to the right, it's between Christian's and mine," Jason explains as he leads me down and points to a door as we pass it. "That's mine; if you need me at any time of the day or night, just walk in."

"What if you have a visitor?" I ask. Jason stops and looks at me.

"That won't happen," he replies, not breaking eye contact for a moment before leading me down the corridor again. "None of us is seeing anyone," he adds before stopping outside another door. "This is your room," he announces before opening the door and reaching around the frame to switch on the light.

Inside is the most beautiful room I've ever seen. In the middle is a four-poster bed with curtains tied to each of the posts. The bedding is white and baby blue, my favourite colours, and looks freshly made. There's a bookcase to one side of the room, next to a bay window, which is padded with cushions so someone could sit and look out to what I guess is the grounds.

Jason lets go of my hand and walks further into the room before placing my bag on the floor by the bed. He heads to a door and opens it, turning on another light.

"This is your bathroom; it has everything you need, so you don't have to share with anyone else." He turns and walks over to a door on the other side of the room and opens it. "Here's your wardrobe. There are drawers in there as well, and there is space for shoes. Someone will take you back to that flat tomorrow to get the rest of your things."

"There's not much left to get," I admit quietly. I don't look at Jason, but I swear I hear him growl a little.

"Well, either way, one of us will take you tomorrow," he says before moving to stand in front of me. He places a finger under my chin, forcing me to look at him. "This is your home now, your private space. If there's anything you don't like or want to change, let us know and we'll get it done."

I can't bring myself to reply, so I just nod. Jason leans forward and places a kiss on my cheek, which brushes against the side of my lips.

"Get sorted. I'll be back in ten minutes, and we can go to speak to the others."

"Isn't it too late?" I worry, but Jason shakes his head.

"It's never too late when it comes to you," he replies quietly before walking away to leave the room.

"Thank you," I whisper as I turn to face the door. Jason turns back to me and smiles.

"You never need to thank me for looking after you, Jazzy. Your safety and well-being are everything to the four of us. We just need you to trust us and be honest."

Before I can say anything in return, Jason walks out of the door and closes it behind him, leaving me in my new room, alone.

Chapter Ten

JASMINE

I stand staring at the door for a moment, my body frozen as panic rushes through me. My heart's racing, and I feel sick to my stomach; this isn't how I expected my day to end. I take a deep breath, reminding myself I'm safe with the guys. I've always been safe with them.

I slowly turn to look at the room. Everything about it is perfect, from the white walls and the bed to the decoration. I pick up my bag to place it on the bed before stopping myself. I'm scared to mark the bright white crisp bedding. I notice a chair on the other side of the room and quickly walk to it for somewhere to rest my bag. From inside, I pull out my pyjamas and wash bag before placing them on the bed, ready for later.

I walk into the wardrobe with my remaining items and freeze. My jaw drops at the sheer size of it. My whole apartment would fit in here; there is so much storage space. I place my bag on the bench in the middle of the floor; yes, it's so big in here it fits a freaking bench! How much stuff do they think one person needs? There again, knowing the guys, they probably have enough clothes to fill this space and more. Christian definitely will with how many designer suits I bet he owns.

I quickly hang up the one change of clothes I brought with me, before closing the doors on the monstrosity. I grab my wash bag, head into the bathroom, and again stop in my tracks. Is anything about this house small or even average size?

The bath stands alone in the middle of the room; I'm not short by any means, but even at five foot nine, I bet I could stretch out in it, and my toes would only just touch the end. What I would give to sink into it right now and forget everything that's happening.

I force myself to turn away from the bath and shower on the one side of the room and walk over to the twin sinks. Everything in here is white marble, and I'm terrified of dirtying anything. I quickly wash my face and dry it carefully on the softest white towels when I hear Jason call my name.

"Coming," I call back before carefully folding the towel and placing it on the side where I found it.

I open the bathroom door to see him standing in my room, watching me as I walk out.

"You ready to go down?" he asks as he offers me a small smile. I start chewing on my bottom lip and can't quite manage a nod. Jason walks up to me and pulls me into his arms. Leaning my cheek against his chest I inhale the smell of his aftershave to calm my racing heart.

"You're not in any trouble, Jazzy; we aren't mad. We've been worried about you. But no matter what you tell us, we will not get angry. We just wish you had come to us, rather than hide how you were living."

I nod because I know I should have come to them from

day one. A part of me has picked up the phone every day since everything started going wrong to ask them for help. But I'm too stubborn and couldn't bring myself to admit that I was failing, that I needed someone other than myself.

"Can we get this over with?" I whisper into Jason's chest. I feel him nod and kiss the top of my head.

"Come on, everyone's in the sitting room downstairs." Jason steps away from me and holds out his hand. I take it, and he interlocks our fingers as he leads me out of the room.

On the way Jason points towards Christian's door and the twins' rooms on the other side of the building, he also informs me that there are more rooms upstairs.

"Who used to use the room I'm in?"

"It has always been your room," Jason answers before glancing at me as he carries on walking. "We've been asking you to come for years, but you've never accepted. But we always hoped you would eventually," Jason offers me a quick smile as we reach the bottom of the stairs. I don't pay much attention to anything else around us; all I can think about is the fact that the guys decorated that room for me.

We come to a stop outside of a large dark wooden door and I suddenly feel like I'm going to be sick. I take a step back, and Jason looks at me.

"Jazzy, do you think any of us would do anything to hurt or upset you?" he asks quietly. I shake my head and step back beside him. "Good girl, come on," he whispers, opening the door. I grasp both my hands around his, desperate for any support as he leads me inside.

As we walk into the room, I spot Christian, Sean, and Maximus sitting on two leather couches in the centre of the room. Between them is a coffee table the same colour as the couches. Across the back wall is a bookcase that covers the whole width of the room. I see Christian go to stand as they all turn to face us, but Jason holds out his hand to stop him. Christian looks down at our joined hands and nods before leaning back into the sofa.

All three of them are holding glasses of what I'm guessing is whiskey, their go-to drink. I see a fourth on the table as well as a glass of rosé.

"I figured you could probably use a drink," Christian says to me softly as we approach them. I force a nod and follow Jason who sits on a third sofa between the other two facing the table in the middle. He sits, pulling me down, so I'm next to him. Leaving very little space between us.

Jason leans forward, picks up the glass of wine, and holds it out for me. As my fingers close around it I nearly spill the contents because I'm shaking so much. Jason quickly takes the glass and looks me in the eye.

"Take a deep breath, Jazzy, and remember what I said upstairs. You're not in any trouble; we aren't mad at you."

I nod and close my eyes before taking a deep breath, followed by another one before looking back at him.

"You, okay?" he asks quietly. I nod and reach for the glass. This time when Jason lets go my hand doesn't shake as much and I feel him squeeze the hand he's holding, before giving me a small reassuring smile. He reaches over to pick up his glass and sits back on the sofa. Our hands, still linked between us as I cling to him for support.

I look up and see Christian watching me.

"*Are* you okay?" he asks softly.

"Not really," I answer, chuckling nervously.

"Want to tell us what's been going on?" he asks. I quickly glance at the twins, who are both watching me carefully. I take a sip of my wine before letting go of Jason's hand and holding the glass with both of mine.

"I don't know where to start," I admit, looking down. I feel Jason's hand rub the bottom of my back.

"Why don't you start with why you're no longer at the house," he says softly.

"I had to leave," I admit.

"When?" Sean asks, quietly.

"Five months ago," I answer, not looking up from my glass, scared to see any signs of disappointment or anger on their faces.

"You told me you had been living in the flat for four months," Jason points out next to me.

"I have."

"So, where were you sleeping?" he asks.

"The first week, I stayed with friends, but that didn't work out, so I started sleeping in my car."

I hear Maximus and Sean both curse under their breath as Jason's hand stops moving against my back. I can feel Christian's eyes on me, but I can't bring myself to look up at him. I know if I do, I'll cry, and I really don't want to break right now.

"Your friends let you sleep in a car? Even Amber and Sophia?" Jason asks. I don't need to look at him to know he's angry. I take a deep breath as I think of the people I used to think were my best friends.

"It's amazing how quickly people show their true colours when you need them for once."

"Why did you move out of the house?" Christian asks. His voice not portraying anything, but I can't shake the feeling of his eyes boring into me.

"It wasn't safe there anymore; she's drinking and using again."

This time all four of them curse. They know Mum's history with drugs and alcohol and that I was taken into care for short periods whilst I was younger.

"Is that why she and Dad split up?" Maximus asks.

"I don't know. No one would tell me anything," I answer before taking a sip of my wine. Jason's hand moves against my back, and I relax a little from his comforting touch. "I moved into the flat as soon as I saw it was available. I used the last of my savings to pay the bond and three months' rent. The day I moved in, I went over to the pub and asked for a job; they hired me on the spot. I've been working every night I wasn't at rehearsals or performing. Some nights, I went to the pub afterwards and cleaned."

"How much was the pay?" Christian asks.

"Not enough. I had to make cutbacks, like the extra classes. This last month has been the toughest as the dance school said I had to make a payment towards my fees, or they would remove me from the school. They let me pay a little at a time. I guess Tommy stopped paying my fees when I stopped paying rent."

"What do you mean you paid rent? On the house?" Jason asks. I look at him and nod. His head snaps to Christian, who looks angrier than I've ever seen him.

"How much were you paying him?" Christian asks through gritted teeth. I want to sink into the chair and never come back out.

"Six hundred pounds a month, it included rent and bills. The only other thing I had to pay for was food," I explain. Maximus jumps to his feet, but Christian quickly looks at him before he can say anything.

"Sit down. We will discuss it later. Jasmine has been through enough," he says firmly as Maximus does as he's told.

"Where did that money come from? I'm guessing you

weren't struggling until you needed to pay for tuition fees as well?" Jason asks. I shake my head.

"I could earn enough for the house, but the rent on the apartment and the school fees together was too much, so I sold things," I answer, quickly taking another sip of my drink.

"What did you sell?" he asks. I finish my drink, and Jason takes the glass from my hand. "Jazzy, I asked you a question. What did you sell?" he asks firmer this time.

"Nothing illegal or myself!" I snap, staring at him. I would never be desperate enough to sell myself. "I sold some clothes, DVDs, CDs, old costumes, my laptop, and my car. Anything I didn't immediately need, basically."

"Why didn't you come to us?"

I look up at Christian and watch as he sits forward, leaning on his knees. His look intensifies, and I can't help feeling bad. I've disappointed him, and I've hurt him by not coming to him when I needed help. I messed up.

"Why didn't you come to us and tell us what was going on? You know we would have helped you in a heartbeat. We'd have never let things get this bad."

"I couldn't," I whisper as I look into his blue eyes, trying desperately to stay calm. "I couldn't face telling you I was failing, that I was hanging on by a thread and couldn't see a way out on my own. I was ashamed and scared of what you would think of me. I hate that you would be disappointed in me." I take a deep breath and look down at my hands, which are fiddling with the cuff of my jumper. "It's not like I'm even your problem anymore," I whisper.

"When are you going to realise you matter to us, Shorty? That we're not your parents or those arseholes you called friends. We actually give a fuck!" Maximus snaps. I lean back, putting more space between us, surprised by his outburst. Jason's hand moves with me; he doesn't try to move away; if anything, he moves closer. I've never been more thankful for him than at this moment.

"Look, it's getting late. Everyone's exhausted, physically and emotionally. Why don't we call it a night? We can carry this conversation on when everyone has rested and calmed down," Jason suggests next to me as he looks over at Maximus. I look up and see Christian nodding before Sean and Maximus agree as well.

"Do you have class in the morning?" Christian asks. I shake my head.

"We aren't back until Monday. I have three days off," I answer. "I have an evening shift in the pub tomorrow. I start at six," I add nervously.

"No, you don't. I told that prick you quit tonight," Jason replies quietly. I turn to say something, but the look on his face tells me I'll be wasting my breath. Plus, I'm too tired to argue right now.

"Then tomorrow, we will sit down and come up with a game plan. You need to be honest and tell us what you really need, and we will get everything right again."

I stand to leave, knowing I've been dismissed and needing some time to clear my head. Jason and Christian get to their feet, too, but it's Christian who steps in front of me.

"I'm sorry you've been going through all this alone, but we are here now, and like Maximus said, in his undignified way, you matter to us more than you will ever know."

I look up at Christian, and he smiles softly at me. I take a step forward and wrap my arms around his waist, resting my face against his broad chest. Christian holds me tightly in his arms whilst he rests his cheek against my head. It's like he is holding me together, and it's just what I need at this moment.

"Thank you."

"Anything for you, sweetheart, you know that," he whispers before pressing a kiss on the top of my head. I step back from him.

"Do you remember where your room is?" Jason asks. I nod as I force a small smile. "You head up then. I'll come and check on you in a bit," he says before kissing me on the forehead.

"Okay," I whisper before walking around the two of them and heading towards the door. As I reach the other sofa, Sean stands up and pulls me into his arms, placing a kiss on my cheek.

"Night, princess, get some rest," he says with a small smile. I nod as I turn to see Maximus standing in front of me. He pulls me into one of his bear hugs, and I instantly relax against him.

"Sorry for getting worked up, Shorty," he sighs into my hair.

"It's okay," I whisper. Maximus stands back and cups my face in his big hand.

"No, it's not. I wasn't mad at you, just the situation. I could never be mad at you; you know that, right?"

I don't trust myself to answer, so I nod and start chewing on my bottom lip. Maximus looks at me for a second before kissing me on the cheek.

"Good night, Shorty."

"Night," I manage to whisper back before rushing from the room as the tears burn the back of my eyes and my throat contracts. I only just manage to get in my room before the floodgates open.

Chapter Eleven

JASON

The second the door closes, Maximus curses under his breath.

"Calm down. Wait until she has time to go upstairs," Christian warns quietly. He looks over at me and nods towards the empty glass on the table. "Want a top-up?"

I nod, passing him the glass before sitting back down on the couch and running my hand over my head, letting out a deep breath. Christian goes about pouring the four of us fresh drinks as I try to calm myself. I watch Maximus pace for a moment before he also returns to his seat.

"How bad was it?" Christian asks as he hands me my glass and sits.

"Her place or the bar?" I ask, shaking my head, still unable to get around everything that has happened this evening.

"Both. I want to know everything," Christian replies. I let out a sigh and take a sip of my drink whilst leaning back on the couch.

"The pub was a typically cheap, run-down bar. The

owner was a dick, and the people drinking there weren't much better. I couldn't tell if Jazzy enjoyed the job or if she was just faking it. The uniform was revealing, and every time she lifted her arms, the top rode up her back and stomach. Left very little to the imagination. That was obviously by design, as it was student night, and I had to stop myself from punching nearly every male kid that went in there because all eyes were on Jazzy and the girl she was working with."

"You should have dragged her out," Sean growls as Christian hums in agreement.

"What good would that have done? She'd have just gotten her defense back up and refused to even talk to us. I had to give a little to get a little. But I'm surprised I didn't crack a tooth as my jaw was clenched the whole time watching her, knowing she was a million times too good for that place."

"What about the flat?" Christian asks. I look at him and shake my head in disbelief.

"Don't even get me started on that dump. I'll be finding the landlord of that place personally; it was a fucking shit-hole. Whoever lives downstairs obviously smokes a lot of weed, as the smell's overpowering as soon as you stand outside the building. How it's not been raided yet I don't know. But that will change as soon as we get the last of her things out of there. I don't want her associated with that shit."

"You sure she hasn't been using anything?" Maximus asks, and all three of us protest instantly.

"No matter how things have gone for her, I know our girl would never use drugs. She's seen what it does to her mother," Sean argues.

"Don't get me started on Carol; that'll be dealt with

another time," Christian replies as he leans forward and looks at the three of us. "I want to concentrate on getting Jasmine safe and settled first. I'll take her tomorrow to get the rest of her things," he adds.

"Remember to wipe your feet on the way out," I growl under my breath, still angry at the conditions Jasmine was living in.

"Was it that bad?"

I turn to look at Sean and nod. "There wasn't a wall that didn't have some form of mould or mildew. I could smell the dampness and weed, even over all the air fresheners she had around the place. The shower and toilet might as well have been on top of each other, and the bedroom wasn't much better," I sigh before continuing. "There's just a tiny single bed, with a broken wardrobe where she kept her things. Not that she has much, which showed in the rest of the place.

"In the lounge, there's a small beanbag and the TV you got her for her small room when she was eighteen, Christian. The kitchen was bare, with maybe two tiny pans and a couple of chipped plates. The cupboards were pretty much empty, as well as the fridge. I looked in the bin, and it doesn't seem like there was much thrown away, which means she hasn't been eating properly, if at all."

"That explains why she demolished her ice cream and cake the other night as well as half of mine," Maximus pipes in.

"Probably. She's certainly lost weight, and I don't think it was due to the dancing," Christian sighs. "That's another thing to sort tomorrow. I'm going to take the day off and spend it with her. I want her to feel like she is in a better place mentally by the evening at least," Christian adds.

"I will stay here for the morning and then go to your

meetings for you in the afternoon. I should be home by dinner time for us all to spend some quality time with her," I suggest as Christian nods in agreement.

"You need to contact Tommy too; if I do it, I'll hunt the fucker down," Maximus growls.

"He will be handled, mark my words," Christian replies.

"I'll go and check on her in a minute and see that she has everything she needs for tonight. I have a feeling she will sleep in tomorrow; she looked exhausted a moment ago. She probably hasn't slept well in that place. It wasn't safe; anyone could have gotten in with minimal effort."

"So, is this it then? Are we keeping her here with us?" Sean asks as he looks from me to Christian. We both look at each other and nod.

"We always knew she would end up here; it's just sooner than we thought," Christian says, looking at the twins.

"She needs us more than she's willing to admit. She has been alone for as long as she can remember, and now it's time for us to step up and look after her the way we all know she needs," I add.

"Do you think she will fight us?" Maximus asks. Again, Christian and I look at one another and shake our heads.

"No, the second I told her I was bringing her back here and we would take care of her, every muscle in her body relaxed. She has clung to me, and you saw the way she walked straight into Christian's arms. She never used to hug us; we always initiated physical contact, but slowly, she's come to trust us and let us in, and I truly believe she knows how we feel about her."

"It's decided then, we start showing our girl how much she means to us and caring for her in the way she has always deserved," Christian announces. We all nod in agreement.

"Well, I'm going to check on her and then go to bed. We'll meet in the office at nine to arrange the day. We need to let Jazzy sleep as long as possible."

I say a quick goodnight to my brothers and head up to Jasmine's room to check on her, quietly hoping she will already have fallen asleep.

She looked so exhausted and frail this evening, the bags under her eyes so dark that her makeup couldn't cover them. Her lifestyle needs to change. She needs to put on some weight and get a decent amount of sleep each night. These are all things we can help her with, and we will.

I come to a stop outside her room and knock softly. There's no reply, so I slowly open her door just to check if she's asleep. Even through the darkness of the room, I can see that the bed is empty. I look further into the room and see Jasmine sitting on the windowsill with her legs pulled up to her chest as she looks out into the night.

"Hey, what are you still doing up?" I ask softly. Jasmine jumps and quickly starts wiping her cheeks. I walk over and sit down next to her. "Are you crying?"

Jasmine tries to hide her face, but I place my hand over her damp cheek and make her look at me. My heart breaks when I see so much pain and fear in her eyes. "Come here, angel," I whisper as I pull her onto my lap. She instantly curls up into my chest, and her body shakes as she starts to cry again.

I hold her against me as I run a hand over her damp hair. Realising she must have showered, I reach forward and pull the throw from the back of the chair and wrap it around her so she doesn't get cold. I continue to hold her close and occasionally kiss the top of her head, hoping to reassure her.

"Talk to me, angel. I can't help you if you don't tell me

what you need," I whisper after a few minutes as her tears subside.

"I don't know what to feel, what to do, nothing," she whispers into my chest.

"You don't need to do or feel anything, Jazzy. We've got you, and we are going to look after you," I try to reassure her.

"But what about in the long run? I can't stay here forever. Eventually, I will need to find another place and I can't ..."

"Hey, enough," I interrupt. I lean back so I can look at her face and into her bright blue eyes, which always remind me of a clear summer sky. "You are not going anywhere; this is your home now. It will always be your home," I tell her forcibly. "You never have to worry about finding a new place. You are staying here with us, and that's final."

"Yeah, until you have a girl with you and realise that you don't want your 'once stepsister' next door."

I sigh and hate her parents more than I ever have. All this woman has ever known is abandonment. She has looked after herself since her dad left and never came back when she was eight. She has never had a parental figure to take care of her, and that changes now.

"What did I tell you? I'm not seeing anyone. I haven't seen anyone for the last two years when I realised that no one compares to you."

"What?" Jasmine asks as her eyes bulge. I smile at her and tuck some damp hair behind her ear.

"I care for you, Jazzy. I have since the moment I met you. There is nothing that will ever change that," I whisper as I look back into her eyes. "I know that deep down, you knew that. Same as deep down, you know that the guys and

I aren't going anywhere," I add. I can tell from the look on her face I'm right.

"Now, you're going to go back into the bathroom, wash your face, and use the hair dryer under the sink to dry your hair properly. Then, I will tuck you into bed, where you will sleep for as long as you need." I lean forward and press my lips to hers softly before smiling at her when she doesn't fight me.

"Go on, do as you are told. I'll be right here when you are finished."

I help her to climb off my lap and watch as she walks into the bathroom, looking a little dazed. I quickly pull out my phone and fire off a text to the group chat my brothers and I have.

Jason: I've told her how I feel. She was upset and thought we would be kicking her out in a few weeks.

Christian: How did she take it?

Jason: she didn't argue the fact, so time will tell. I didn't mention you guys.

Sean: We can deal with that tomorrow. The last thing she needs is to be overwhelmed late at night.

Maximus: Agreed. We will speak in the morning.

I lock my phone and climb off the windowsill to make sure Jasmine has everything for a good night's sleep, probably the first one in a long while.

Chapter Twelve

JASMINE

My head's reeling. Did Jason just tell me that he cares for me and not as a stepsister? I know he kissed me. He pressed his lips to mine. But I can't help thinking I might have misunderstood something.

I absent-mindedly finish drying my hair and run a brush through it one last time before heading back into the bedroom, where I find him folding the bedcovers back for me.

"What time is it?" I ask nervously, looking around for a clock.

"It's after two; you need to get some sleep," Jason whispers as I walk up to the bed. He signals for me to climb in. I do as I'm told and turn on my side, facing him before he pulls the covers up to my shoulders.

"I'm just next door if you want me; you know where the others are, too. Our doors are always open to you," he whispers before leaning in and kissing me on the top of the head. "Night, Jazzy." I watch as he starts to walk to the door.

"Wait," I call out as I sit up, my head racing.

"What's the matter?" Jason asks, looking over his shoulder at me. I chew my bottom lip, and I look down at the bedcovers.

"Would you mind staying with me? I don't want to be alone right now," I admit as I look up at him. Jason's face relaxes as he gives me one of his warm smiles.

"Of course, let me get changed, and I'll be right back," he replies before leaving the room.

I sit back on the bed and wait. It's not long before Jason walks in wearing a pair of grey sweatpants and his chest bare. It's not the first time I have seen him topless, and as always, it's a sight worth seeing.

All four of the guys have tattoos, and Jason's are across his chest, shoulder, and neck, as well as down his arm. They are all beautiful, and I realise I have never looked at the designs they create before. Whenever I have seen them topless, I always try to avoid looking at them too much, scared they will notice.

Jason walks around the bed before climbing in. He flips a switch to turn the lights off before turning on his side and facing in my direction. I roll so I'm facing him, placing my hands under my head.

"You, okay?" he asks softly, as he brushes my cheek with his knuckles.

"I'm getting there," I admit quietly. "Thank you for looking after me."

As my eyes adjust to the darkness, I see the slightest smile on Jason's lips.

"I would do it all again in a heartbeat; you mean the world to me, Jazzy."

I realise that I'm starting to believe him. I guess, in a way, I have for a while, but that nagging voice in my head stops me from relaxing completely when it comes to the guys. There will always be a tiny part of me waiting for them to leave.

I look at Jason and know that I'm safe with him, that I haven't been alone with my growing feelings for him. I don't stop to think about what I'm doing; I reach up and cup his cheek like he has done to me so many times, feeling braver than I probably should, I lean forward and press my lips to his before slowly moving back. My heart's racing knowing there's a real chance he'll reject me.

"You don't have to do that. I didn't tell you how I feel so you would act on it," Jason says firmly as he places his hand over mine. Oh god, I misunderstood what he meant.

"I know," I admit my voice shaking as my heart continues to race. I wait for him to get up and walk out. Instead, he kisses my palm before cupping my cheek and kissing me back.

His lips are soft against mine and I move so I'm pressed up against him. he runs his tongue over my lips, begging for entry which I grant hungrily. As the kiss deepens, I lift my head so Jason can place an arm underneath it. He threads his fingers into my hair as his other hand slides down my side and comes to rest on my waist, his grip tightening as he tugs me closer against him. I freeze as I realise I can feel his hard cock against my stomach. Our lips part as I gasp with surprise. Jason leans back a little smirking.

"Do you feel how hard I am for you, and only you?" His lips crash into mine again as he grinds against me, making me moan into his mouth. I grind back against him as his grip on my waist tightens, and he pulls his lips from mine.

"There's no going back from this. I hope you're aware of that."

"Good," I reply, before kissing him again.

Jason's hand slides between us and cups my sex before sliding up and into my shorts.

"Fuck, you're so wet," he growls against my mouth, as his fingers find that special spot, causing me to instantly moan. His fingers work me in a way I haven't been touched before. I've been wanting this for so many years. With the slightest touch, I'm right on the edge, and he seems to know it.

Jason slides one finger into my core and instantly growls.

"Fuck, you're so tight."

"Jason, please," I beg as my whole body seems to come alive, every little touch is pushing me closer to that release I so desperately need. Jason seems to realise as I feel his finger working in and out of me, as his thumb rubs me in just the right spot.

"You like that, Jazzy? You going to cum on my hand like a good girl?"

Jason starts kissing my neck as I arch back into the bed, moaning.

"Cum for me, angel. Show me how fucking good you feel with my hand between your legs."

I instantly gasp as his finger and thumb work me together, and I fall apart. I swear Jason works my body, making the orgasm last longer than I ever thought possible.

As I come down from the most incredible high, I feel Jason slide his hand out of my shorts and watch as he lifts his fingers to his lips before sucking my juices from them.

"You taste even sweeter than I dreamt you would," Jason groans with the most devious grin on his face. "I can't wait to taste that directly from the source."

"Jason," I moan as I press my body against his, bringing my lips to his. Jason kisses me gently this time, and there's no more hunger there. He pulls away from me slightly and smiles.

"As much as I want to make you cum again and again, you need to sleep. Be a good girl and get some rest because I promise you, you're going to need it as I plan on fucking you until you beg me to stop very soon."

"What if I don't want to sleep," I ask, grinning. Jason leans forward and kisses me softly on the lips before lying on his back and pulling me with him so I'm resting my head on his bare, muscular chest.

"Sleep. You will learn quickly to do as you are told," he chuckles as he places a kiss on the top of my head. I want to argue with him, but the orgasm he gave me has wiped me out, and I feel my eyes close as I listen to the steady beating of his heart.

"Night, Jason," I whisper as I drift off to sleep as he strokes my head.

"Sweet dreams, angel."

Chapter Thirteen

JASMINE

I wake as someone kisses the top of my head. I jump up, nearly head-butting the person as I scramble away from them.

"Fuck! Sorry Jazzy. It's only me."

I look around the strange surroundings and, for a second, have no idea where I am.

"It's okay, Jazzy, you are with us," Jason says softly as he sits on the side of the bed and cups my cheek. I instantly relax as the last twenty-four hours come back to me.

"Shit," I sigh as I slump back onto the bed, throwing my arms over my head. I hear Jason chuckle as he takes my arms and pulls them away from my face. I open my eyes to see him smiling down at me.

"You need to get your lazy ass out of bed," he says before leaning down and pressing a kiss to my lips.

"I don't want to. Can't we stay here?" I ask, wrapping my arms around his neck and pulling him back in for another kiss. Jason moans against my lips before pulling back.

"As amazing as that sounds, Christian's waiting for us. Plus, you need to eat something." Jason kisses the tip of my nose and sits back up as I pout.

"You're no fun," I sigh, moving so my back is against the headboard, Jason smirks as he stands and heads into the bathroom.

"Trust me, I have plenty of fun planned for us. But first, we have to get a few things sorted," he calls. I sigh and throw my legs out of bed, stretching. I look to my left and see a plate of toast and a latte glass of coffee on the cabinet.

"Is this for me?" I call out as I pick it up and smell the latte.

"No one else here drinks that vanilla shit," Jason calls as he walks out of the bathroom with a thick dressing gown over his arm. He places it on the bed next to me and lifts the small plate of toast before taking the coffee out of my hand.

"Hey, I was drinking that!"

"You can have it back when you eat some of this. Coffee isn't food," he declares with an arched brow.

"Yes, Dad," I sigh as I roll my eyes. Jason puts the plate back on the side before leaning over me, forcing me to lie back with his arms on either side of my head.

"I warned you; you will learn to do as you are told quickly because you need a keeper to take care of you, someone willing to discipline you when you don't look after yourself."

I bite my bottom lip as I feel a tingling between my legs.

"You wouldn't discipline me," I reply quietly as I look into his eyes, but a smile spreads across his face as he moves until his lips are only millimetres from mine.

"Oh, I most certainly would, but I think you would respond better if it was Christian taking you over his knee."

I gasp as Jason's smile turns into a full smirk. His lips crash into mine as the tingling between my legs turns into an inferno. Jason's arm moves from the side of me, and I feel him cup my sex and squeeze, causing me to gasp against his mouth. He lifts, ending the kiss, grinning down at me.

"I thought as much," he whispers before standing up and pulling me back into a seated position. "Now eat your toast, drink your coffee, and get washed and dressed. I'll be back in twenty minutes to take you down to Christian, who's waiting to get a few things sorted," he winks before leaving the room and me to a million very explicit thoughts.

Twenty minutes later, on the dot, Jason walks into my room as I pull on my jumper. He looks at me for a second before walking over and tugging me to him by my jean belt loop.

"You've lost more weight than I realised. We need to rectify that," he says before kissing me on the lips once and pulling me from the room. "Come on, Christian's waiting in his office."

I follow him silently, gripping his hand as we head down the corridor. We pass a picture, and I freeze, pulling him to a stop.

"That's me!"

Jason looks at the picture of me dancing in Swan Lake three years ago.

"That's Maximus's favourite. There are pictures of you all around the house. Didn't you notice last night?" Jason asks. I look at him, shaking my head.

"Why?" I ask, amazed. My mother doesn't even have pictures of me dancing.

"Why not? You're beautiful, even more so when you dance."

I look at him as he turns and starts walking down the corridor again, leading me past two more pictures of myself.

"We are very proud of you, Jazzy. We love watching you dance; we have never missed a single performance. Every night, at least one of us will be there, if not all four. We only make a point of meeting up with you on the last night as we know you will let your hair down and relax. But we watch every single one."

I pull him to a stop, forcing him to look at me.

"Why didn't I know that?" I ask. Jason smiles and cups my face.

"There's a lot you don't know, but you soon will," he answers as he kisses me quickly before pushing open the door in front of us.

We walk in, and I hear Christian's voice from the side of the room. I find him standing in front of a large mahogany desk, a phone pressed to his ear. He looks up at us and signals for us to take a seat on the coach against the far wall. Above it is another large picture of me dancing. Jason sits on the sofa, and I go to sit next to him, wondering if Christian knows that something has started between us. Jason pulls me onto his lap at the last moment. I turn and stare at him wide-eyed, but Jason winks as he kisses me quickly on the lips. I guess if he didn't know, he does now. I turn to see Christian looking at us, his face giving nothing away. Whoever's on the phone seems to restart the conversation as he frowns and his jaw clenches.

"So, you did listen to the voicemail I left you?" he asks as he pinches the bridge of his nose. "Let me get this straight: you knew of the situation and didn't feel the need to check in on her? You left her to deal with her mother on her own?" Shit, he's on the phone with Tommy. I feel my body tense; Jason notices as he tightens his hold on me, making me lean into him. He places a hand on my thigh and rubs the fabric with his thumb.

"Do you want to explain to me why Jasmine was paying you rent on a house we own and cover all bills for? … Oh, cut the bullshit, she told us everything. You will return every penny to her, understood?" I sit up and stare at him before turning to Jason, who nods.

"As I said, there are a lot of things you don't know but soon will," he says as he tucks a section of hair behind my ear.

"And the money that was meant to be for her school fee, where's that gone?"

I turn to look at Christian again, but he's looking at the picture on his desk, which I realise is another picture of me. It's one we took on a day out last year when it was just the two of us.

"But you haven't been paying it, have you? I phoned the school today and found out they haven't received a single payment from you this year, and Jasmine has been giving what she could when she could, as well as cleaning and teaching the kids to help pay her tuition fees."

Fuck they do know everything now; I didn't want them to know that part. Jason's hand rubs up and down my back again as my heart starts to race.

"We are so proud of you for trying to do this on your own; don't ever think we aren't. But you should have come to us," Jason whispers into my ear.

"Well, you were happy for her to be your problem when you were with Carol and receiving our money," Christian states as he looks at me and Jason. I see Jason's head move out of the corner of my eye but miss what he says. Christian nods and focuses on me as he answers his father.

"Well, she isn't your problem anymore as we are taking over Jasmine's care and anything she needs we will give her direct," Christian snaps. I see Jason holding his hand out, and Christian hands the phone over to him without saying a word to his father. Jason takes the phone and lifts it to his ear as his hand on my hip tightens protectively.

"It's me," he says as I watch his face change. "What Christian's saying far too politely is that we will no longer need to transfer money to your sorry ass, you're no longer our problem and in turn no longer have access to anything we own. If you don't like it, you should have done as we asked and not left Jasmine to deal with your wife on her own. Don't bother trying to fight this; you won't fucking win. Goodbye, Tommy."

Jason hangs up the phone and holds it out to Christian, who takes it, shaking his head and putting it into his pocket.

"You own the house?" I ask as I look between the two of them. Christian nods as he sits on the edge of the coffee table in front of me and Jason; he reaches over and takes my hand.

"We own the house and thought we were paying for the dance school. If we had known what was going on, you would have ended up here a lot sooner. You certainly would have never been left to deal with all this shit on your own," he says as he looks at Jason, who nods when I look at him.

"But why didn't you tell me?" I ask, looking back at Christian.

"We were going to eventually. We wanted to know that you were safe and cared for, but we weren't paying as much attention as we should have. But that changes, now."

"What if I don't want your help," I ask as my stupid,

stubborn streak comes out. Christian gives me a look that tells me it isn't a choice. I stare back at him as I feel my eyes filling with tears. "I'm not a charity case," I add under my breath.

"No, you are not. But we want you to have the best of everything and are in a position to offer that to you. Is it such a bad thing?" Jason asks as he runs his hand down my back. I know it's not, and I shake my head as I start chewing on my lip and blinking back the tears.

"Now that's settled; I need to go over a few things with you before we go get the rest of your things from this apartment," Christian says as he stands up and walks over to his desk.

"Don't fight this. You will not win," Jason whispers in my ear. I turn to look at him and find him smiling at me. "I know that look, Jazzy. You need to learn to do as you are told and learn that we *will* be looking after you. Like I said, you need a keeper, someone to have your back and make sure you take care of yourself properly."

I look to where Christian's walking back to us. I picture myself over his knee as he spanks me. The inferno between my legs roars back into life, and I swear Jason chuckles under his breath behind me as I squirm.

"I need you to sign this letter, which is informing your landlord you are vacating the premises with immediate notice," Christian explains as he places a piece of paper in front of me and holds out a pen. I take it before turning myself so I'm no longer sitting across Jason's lap and instead straddling it with my back to his front. Jason grips both my hips as I lean forward and sign the letter, not bothering to read it. Jason pulls my hips back as I sit up, and I feel his hard cock press into my ass, which just heightens my arousal.

"I also need you to sign this. It's for the bank. This way, you will have full access to any funds you need," Christian explains as I look up at him. My jaw drops open, and he holds out a bank card. "The pin is your date of birth; it's all set up and ready to go."

I take the card and look at it. It has my name on it; there's no way this has only been organised today.

"What is this?" I ask as I sit up and stare at him. Christian looks at me like everything he's just said is perfectly normal.

"You heard that is your new bank card," he repeats, but I shake my head.

"Did you just happen to have this lying around? It takes days to get a bank card, not hours," I exclaim as I hold out the card in question. "Plus, why would I need access to your money? It's not mine."

"Everything we have is yours. As Jason said, we are in the position to make sure you have the best of everything, and before you start arguing, this is non-negotiable. You can refuse to use it; that's your choice, but we *will* still buy you what you need and want. Either way, the money will be spent on you."

"And what if I say I don't want your help, that I don't want to live here? Then what?" I ask as I stare at Christian. I feel Jason's grip tighten on my hips again.

"I told you last night, there's no going back from this now. You can fight it and argue all you like, but you won't win."

Chapter Fourteen

JASMINE

I look out the passenger window at the building beside us. It's dark and dingy even in the warm afternoon sun.

"I hated this place the moment I saw it," I say quietly. I feel a hand take mine, and I turn to see Christian looking at me.

"Why didn't you come to me? To any of us?" he asks as I turn to look back out the window, unable to face him.

"I was scared."

"Of us?"

I shake my head, "Of losing you all." I turn and look at him before continuing. "Every person in my life has left me; I'm used to that. But the thought of you four telling me I didn't matter anymore scared me more than living in a dump and losing everything else." I look back out the window as Christian sighs and lets go of my hand. I hear him undoing his seat belt and exiting the car without saying a word. I let out a deep breath and undo my seatbelt. As I reach for the door, Christian opens it and holds his hand out. I take it, letting him pull me to my feet and into his arms in one swift move. Christian holds me against his chest as I wrap my arms around his waist, needing the comfort.

"You need to get it into that head of yours; we aren't going anywhere, no matter what you do or ask of us. None of us wants to live a life you are not a part of."

But all I hear is one of the last things my dad ever said to me. *"I love you, flower. You make my life worth living."* Less than a week later, he was gone, and I never saw him again.

I swallow the lump in my throat and nod into Christian's chest, wishing I could believe him. He lets out a deep sigh and steps back from me. "One day, I'm going to make you see how much we care about you," he declares before turning around and looking up at the building. "For now, I'll settle for getting your stuff and you away from this dump."

I walk past him and open the door. As usual, the smell of weed is overpowering and causes me to cough. Christian growls under his breath as we walk into the building. I glance behind to find him glaring at Sam's front door. I haven't told him that's the landlord yet as I don't trust him not to confront him. Christian may not fight anymore, but I know he still trains, and his physique shows how fit he is. I also know how intimidating he can look at times, put the two together, and I have no doubt he could cause some real damage if he wanted to.

I walk up the stairs and unlock the front door to my apartment. The smell of dampness is stronger after spending some time away from this place, and somewhere as clean as the guys' place.

"This is where you've been living?" Christian asks as he walks into the kitchen. He looks so out of place in his pristine designer suit, crisp white shirt, and smart shoes.

This man always looks like he should be walking the red carpet, not in a place as dark and depressing as this. It's no wonder my moods have been so low recently; this place can suck the happiness out of anyone.

"It's not much," I whisper as Christian walks around and looks in the cupboards. He turns and gives me that look he gets, which now makes me think about him taking me over his knee. Fuck, what is the matter with me?

"Sweetheart, a hole would be better than this place, you deserve so much more," he replies before walking into the bedroom. I follow him in and walk over to the tiny bed. I reach underneath and pull out a small rucksack and suitcase.

"Where are all your things?" Christian asks as he looks around. I shrug as I open the bag.

"Most of it I had to leave at the house. I only picked up the essentials when she was out one day. I haven't risked going back to get the rest," I admit. Christian walks up to me and hooks a finger under my chin, forcing me to look at him.

"Tonight, you are going to tell me what happened, and then we will go in the next couple of days to get your things."

I shake my head. "I'll go on my own; she'll be vile. You don't need to see that," I protest, but Christian's brows arch as he argues.

"All the more reason for you not to go on your own. I will be with you or one of the others. I won't risk you getting hurt."

"You can wait outside. If it's just me, then she won't be so bad," I continue to protest. Christian shakes his head and kisses me on the forehead.

"Let's just get your things out of this place first. We will decide what to do about the rest later."

I nod, knowing there is no point in fighting it right now.

"Thank you." I turn around and start piling stuff into the bag. Christian is just passing me a photo of the five of us I keep on the bedside table when his phone rings. He looks down at it and curses.

"I need to take this. I'll be right back," he says before heading out of the apartment.

He's only gone for a minute before I hear the front door open again.

"That was quick!" I call as I hear footsteps heading towards the bedroom. I turn to find not Christian but Sam standing in my doorway. "What the hell? Get the fuck out of my flat!" I yell, standing tall. He looks down at the bag by my feet, and I see his face change.

"You haven't given me a month's notice, you little bitch. Don't think you can move out without paying a month's rent!" he growls as he steps towards me.

"I'm paying you fuck all," I growl back as I take a step away from him. I can see from his eyes he's high, and after my upbringing, I know how quickly a high person can turn nasty.

"You'll pay me what you fucking owe bitch," he hisses. I can see him looking me up and down before an evil smirk appears on his face. "Or if you haven't got the money, you could pay another way? I hear you ballerinas, are very flexible. I know a few people who would pay good money for a night with you." He walks slowly into the room, heading straight towards me with a sick smile on his face. And I have no doubt what he has on his mind. He stops just in front of me and runs a finger down my arm. "If you don't want to be shared around, I'm sure you and I could come up with our own agreement on how you can pay for this place."

I move away from his touch and watch as his face changes.

"Stuck up bitch."

As he steps forward to grab me, I react on instinct and bring my knee up, hitting him between his legs. As soon as he crumples over, holding himself, I run from the room desperate to get to the front door and crash straight into Christian's broad chest.

"What-?" he doesn't get any further when Sam comes rushing out of the bedroom.

I watch as Christian's eyes darken. He looks down at me in his arms and then at Sam whose face has drained of colour.

"Fuck!" Sam curses as he runs back into the bedroom, slamming the door closed behind him. Christian storms towards it, and with one hard kick, the door flies open, and he charges into the bedroom. I hear Sam grunting from inside before he comes flying out, landing in a heap on the floor. Christian storms up to him and has him pinned against the wall in one move like he weighs nothing.

"Did he touch you?" Christian growls as he looks into my eyes. I shake my head, unable to speak.

"Who is he?" Christian asks as he pulls a flip knife from his pocket and holds it against Sam's cheek.

"My landlord, he lives downstairs."

Christian turns back to Sam.

"Do you know who I am?" I watch as Sam's eyes widen further, and he gives a small nod, as he moves the knife edge cuts into his cheek. Not deep, but enough to draw blood. I watch as Christian makes a point of making sure the blood doesn't touch him.

"Good, because you have just put yourself on my shit list. You upset *my* Jasmine, you upset me and my brothers. Do you know what we do to people who upset us?"

Sam quickly nods.

"Well, that's nothing to what we do to people who upset that woman right there. If you want to live, I suggest apologising right now."

"I'm sorry, forget what I said. You owe me nothing. I'm sorry," Sam splutters before looking back at Christian, who slowly lowers him.

"Now go downstairs, lock yourself in your little shithole of a drug den and stay out of my way whilst I get Jasmine's things out of here. Don't even think about leaving until we are gone. Is that understood?"

My landlord nods and bows his head.

"Yes, sir. I'm sorry, I didn't know she was yours. I won't bother her again, I swear," he stammers before rushing out of the room, not even looking in my direction as he runs past me.

"When we get back, I want you to tell me everything you know about him," Christian demands, walking over to the sink and washing his hands. I stare at him, unable to move or speak as my mind races from all I just saw and heard.

Sam knew who Christian was. How? Christian had a knife in his pocket! Does he always carry one? He made it sound like I was his. Why?

Christian turns to look at me as he dries his hand on my tea towel before throwing it in the sink. He stares at me for a moment before his face softens and he walks towards me slowly holding his hands up.

"You are okay, sweetheart. I would *never* hurt you," he says quietly as he takes another step towards me, expecting me to bolt for the door as Sam did.

"I know," I whisper. Christian relaxes a little and pulls me into his arms. I wrap my arms around him and hold him tight as my heart beats dangerously fast.

"I thought I had scared you," he whispers. I shake my head and pull back from him. I'm not scared. But I am confused.

"Can we get out of here?" I ask, wanting to put this place and Sam as far behind me as possible.

Christian looks down at me and nods.

"Is there much left to get?"

"Only the bag I was pack - oh shit, wait!" I spin around and grab a knife from the drawer as Christian tells me to mind my language.

"Sweetheart, I would rather I did the stabbing," Christian laughs behind me as I rush towards the lounge with the big knife in my hand. I go to move the cabinet the TV is resting on.

"What are you doing?" Christian asks as he takes over and moves the cabinet with ease. I kneel on the floor and pull the carpet up from around the radiator pipe.

"If you want to blow the place up, I know a better way," Christian offers. I shake my head and use the knife to lift one of the floorboards.

"I didn't trust that creep not to break in and steal anything he might be able to pawn. I learnt when I was a kid to hide my valuables," I explain as I lift the floorboard I had cut and pull out my jewellery box. I sit back on my heels and smile down at it. Almost everything that means anything to me is in there, including gifts from the guys I know my mum would have sold.

"Is that everything?" Christian asks behind me. I nod as I climb back to my feet, not bothering to put the floorboard or carpet back. I head back into the bedroom and place the box carefully in the bag before closing it up. I double-check my room to ensure I have everything before walking out and heading into the bathroom.

"Don't worry about all that, you have new at home," Christian points out, from behind me where he is now holding my bag. I nod as I look around the lounge.

"My TV," I say as I go to take it but Christian places his empty hand on my arm.

"Leave it, sweetheart."

"But you got it for me," I protest, causing Christian to smile.

"There's a bigger one in your room; it's just hidden away until you need it."

I stare at him for a moment, before he places an arm around my shoulders and kisses me on the top of the head.

"Come on, I'll show you when we get back."

Chapter Fifteen

JASMINE

As soon as we get home, Christian takes my hand and leads me to his office. As he grabs a pen and paper, I stand in front of his desk, watching him.

"What was your landlord's name?"

"Sam Black," I reply, fidgeting with the cuffs on my jumper. Christian writes the name down and makes a note of my old address. "Are you going to hurt him?"

Christian looks up and sighs before walking around the desk and standing in front of me as I turn to lean back against the cool wood.

"Not straight away. I want the word to get out that you are under our protection and what will happen if anyone tries to harm you." He looks at me, and I can see him trying to work out what I'm thinking. "Did what you saw today scare you?" he asks. I slowly shake my head.

"Then what's going on in that head of yours? You've been quiet since it happened," Christian asks as he looks me in the eye.

"You called me yours," I whisper.

"Sweetheart, is that what upset you?" Christian runs his knuckle over my cheek as he looks deep into my eyes. I slowly shake my head, not wanting his hand to leave my face.

"I'm not upset."

"Then what?" he asks as his head cocks to one side.

"It confused me," I whisper, stopping myself from leaning further into his touch.

"Why?"

I swear Christian moves closer to me, and my breath catches for a second.

"Because I liked the idea of being yours," I finally admit quietly. My heart's racing. I never planned on the guys knowing how I feel about them, but here I am, admitting to another of my stepbrothers that I feel more than I should.

"And you like the idea of being Jason's, too?" Christian asks. I nod slowly, unable to find my voice. "Good, because you might have cum on Jason's hand last night, but you don't just belong to him."

I gasp, shocked that Jason would tell him what we did, but there is also a part of me that likes that he knows. I know it shouldn't, but it stokes the fire that's been burning slowly within me since Jason mentioned Christian disciplining me.

I stare into Christian's eyes for a moment as they darken. He leans forward as if to whisper in my ear, bracing his hands on the edge of the desk; he traps me in his arms.

"Did you like the fact that I made a man bleed for disrespecting you?" Christian whispers as his lips brush against my ear. I nod as I close my eyes, and my toes curl into the soft carpet. His scent overwhelms my already stimulated senses as every nerve in my body seems to come alive in his proximity. "I need you to say the words, sweetheart. Always use your words with me," Christian demands as his lips brush my neck, causing me to grip the desk for support.

"Yes," I gasp as his lips brush against my skin again, leaving a trail of fire in their wake.

"Good, because I will gut *anyone* who disrespects you." My whole body comes alive as Christian's lips crash into mine.

Unable to hold back, I throw my arms around his neck as he wraps an arm around my waist and pulls me tightly against him. I can feel him everywhere as his tongue forces its way into my mouth, and the kiss deepens. He takes what he wants from me, and I am powerless to stop him, not that I want to. He's right; him making Sam bleed for upsetting me did turn me on. Does that mean there's something wrong with me? Right now, I don't care.

Christian breaks the kiss and steps back from me.

"Undo your jeans."

I obey instantly, which causes a smug smile to appear on his face.

"Now take them off, I want to see that tight pussy."

I quickly take them off, leaving me completely naked from the waist down. A tiny voice in my head is telling me this is wrong; I shouldn't be giving myself to him so easily. But I'm too drunk on him. I need him. I've always needed him.

"Good girl," he whispers. The praise causes my stomach to tighten as I start to throb between my legs, desperately needing him to touch me. He grips my hips and lifts me with ease before placing me on the edge of the desk.

"Spread your legs and let me see you," Christian growls as his eyes darken further whilst he shrugs off his suit jacket. For a second, I'm very aware that it's Christian, my step-brother, asking for access to my dripping wet pussy. I obviously take too long as Christian looks at me with that one arched brow as he starts taking off his tie. "Don't make me repeat myself. Do as you are told."

I instantly open my legs, making Christian smile before he looks down at me.

"It's more perfect than I ever imagined," he whispers to himself as he devours me with his eyes. I'm on fire waiting for him to touch me, to do something, anything. Instead, he slowly unbuttons his cuffs and starts rolling them. It's like he's deliberately slowing every move to tease me to the point of despair until I'm willing to beg for his hands on my body.

"Christian, please," I plead as my core aches to be touched. I swear I could cum from the way he's looking at me alone.

"Please what, baby girl?" he asks as he steps forward. Closing the gap between us a little.

"Touch me," I beg as I bite my lip. Christian steps forward so he's between my legs.

"Like this?" he whispers against my mouth as he runs a finger through my pussy lips, making me moan out loud. When he does it a second time, my eyes close, and my head rolls back.

"You're so wet already, so responsive, I need to taste you."

I open my eyes just in time to see Christian drop to his knees and feel his tongue run across me, replaying what his fingers had just done.

"Fuck," I gasp as my head rolls back, and he does it again. Suddenly, I feel a sharp slap against my sex. I lift my head to look at Christian, who is looking at me from between my legs.

"Language. Don't make me stop again."

"Sorry," I whisper, trying to look innocent.

"You will be if you swear again," he replies before his tongue finds my core once more.

He positions himself so my legs are over his shoulders before tugging me to the edge of the desk, giving him better access. His tongue starts massaging my entrance as his finger rubs my clit as Jason had done last night. I have to bite my bottom lip to stop myself from swearing as he starts to lick that sensitive bundle of nerves and slides one finger into me.

"You're so tight," Christian groans as he stands up and moves to kiss me. As soon as his lips are against mine, the kiss instantly deepens. I can taste myself on his tongue, and I groan as his finger slides in and out of me slowly.

"Other than that selfish prick who took your virginity, has anyone been where my finger is now?" He asks as he wiggles his finger as emphasis.

"Only Jason's hand," I reply before grinning, "and mine."

"You have us now, and you are not to touch yourself without permission. Is that understood?" Christian growls against my lips. I nod and quickly yelp as he nips my bottom lip. "Remember what I said about using words."

"Yes, I understand," I answer quickly.

"Good girl." He hooks his finger and catches that spot inside of me, causing me to moan and grind against his hand. "Does my girl want more?"

"Yes," I gasp. Christian starts kissing my neck.

"So greedy; can you take it?"

"Yes! Please!" I beg as he kisses me on the lips before pushing things from his desk.

"Lie down, baby," Christian orders, and I quickly do as he asks. "Good girl, stay just like that," he adds before I feel his tongue on me again as he slides his finger out of me and adds a second.

"Christian," I gasp, as for a moment it feels too much, I'm too full.

"I know, but you are doing so well, sweetheart. It will ease in a minute, I promise." Christian's tongue rubs over my clit again as I feel the discomfort ease a tiny bit.

"Breathe, sweetheart," I want to please him. I let out a deep breath, and suddenly, the pain dissolves, and I am overcome by the pleasure his fingers and tongue are giving me.

"That's my good girl. Just think how good we could make you feel if we can just stretch you a little more."

"Please, don't stop," I beg as I get closer and closer to climaxing.

"Cum for me, baby girl. Flood my tongue with your sweet juices."

I scream as I climax hard.

"Fuck."

In my orgasm haze, I look to the side and see Sean standing in the room.

I know I should be embarrassed; he just witnessed his brother giving me an intense orgasm, but I'm not. I want him as much as I want Christian and Jason.

I don't just want two of my stepbrothers; I want them all.

"Can you take more, sweetheart?" Christian's voice pulls me out of my trance, and I realise I've been staring at Sean, who's holding his obvious hard-on through his jeans. I look back at Christian and nod.

"Yes," I croak. My voice is hoarse from screaming.

"Good girl, come here." He helps me to sit up on the desk and tells me to lift my arms. He pulls off my sweatshirt, quickly followed by my top and bra. He looks over at his younger brother, and a smile creeps across his face. I can see the way he's watching me looking at Sean.

"Do you want him as much as you want Jason and me?" he asks. I turn back to Christian, and for a second, I panic.

Will he get mad if I'm honest?

What will he say?

But as always, he reads me like a book. He hooks his finger under my chin and forces me to look at him. "There's nothing wrong with it if you do. You can't deny the connection you feel with us, and we will never deny the one we feel with you," Christian says before kissing me softly on the lips. "So, I ask you again, do you want Sean and Maximus the same way you want me and Jason?"

I look back to Sean and nod. I don't even recognise my own voice when I finally answer.

"Yes."

"Good," Christian replies as Sean moves forward until he's next to the desk. He steps between my legs and threads his fingers into the hair at the back of my head.

"Can I finally kiss you, princess?" Sean asks softly as his brown eyes look deep into mine.

"Please," I sigh as his grip tightens on my hair and his lips crash into mine. Being in his arms feels so natural, even knowing that his older brother is standing right there next to us.

"Lie down, sweetheart, let him see this sweet pussy properly," Christian says as he runs a hand over my head. Sean loosens his hold on me and smiles as he cups the back of my head until I'm lying back against the desk. "That's it, sweetheart, well done."

Christian's praise instantly relights the fire in me, and I start to throb again.

"You like to be praised, princess?" Sean asks as he presses his lips to mine, leaning between my legs.

"Yes," I gasp as he reaches down and runs his fingers between my pussy lips.

"Fuck, you are so wet, so perfect," he gasps as he runs his fingers down until he slides one finger in. I instantly arch my back as he plays with me. He leans down and kisses me again. "You're so tight," Sean growls through gritted teeth.

Christian's face appears above mine as he moves to the other side of the desk. I reach out to cup his cheek as Sean works me towards another orgasm.

"Scoop some of your juices onto your finger and offer them to Sean, sweetheart. Let him taste how sweet you are," Christian orders. I quickly do as I am told, and as soon as Sean's lips are around my wet fingers, he moans.

"Fuck, I need to taste that direct." Before I know what's happening, I can feel a tongue on my clit as two fingers slide into me. I moan, a little from pleasure and a little from discomfort.

"Gently. She's going to need lots of stretching before we can fuck her," Christian warns, but I cup his face and smile.

"I'm okay," I whisper as I look into his blue eyes.

"You enjoying that, baby?"

"Yes!" I gasp, heading towards another orgasm. Christian kisses me as he plays with my breasts.

"Cum for Sean, baby girl. Let him feel how tight you contract around his fingers as you climax."

It's as if my body has to obey him, to do as it's told because, in seconds, I climax hard as Sean continues to lick me through my orgasm.

Slowly, I open my eyes to see Sean leaning over me and pressing his damp lips against mine.

"You are so beautiful and delicious when you cum,

princess," he whispers and kisses me again before pulling me up into a sitting position and wrapping me in his arms.

I lean my cheek against his chest and look to see Christian smiling at me as he reaches up and runs a hand over my head.

"You okay, baby girl?" he asks softly.

"Is Jason going to be mad?" I ask quietly as the guilt and worry start to set in. Christian shakes his head as Sean lets go of me and hooks his forefinger under my chin, forcing me to look at him.

"Jason knows how we all feel about you, and we all guessed how you feel about us. Jason won't be mad at all; he'll be pleased," Sean explains. I look at him and then look at Christian, and I feel him run a hand over my head again.

"I know it's a lot to take in, and we'll discuss it with you together when the others get back."

"Okay," I reply quietly, not sure what else to say. Christian walks forward, and Sean moves out of his way. Christian stops before me and ensures I'm looking at him.

"I can see you overthinking this, and you need to stop. You have four of us all wanting to look after you and give you everything you need. I know it's a lot, but we have known for a very long time that you would be ours."

"Really?" I ask, amazed. Christian nods, and I see Sean smiling behind him.

"You have no idea how long, princess."

Christian smiles down at me and tucks a stray section of hair behind my ear.

"Why don't you go upstairs and have a shower? By the time you get dressed, Jason and Maximus will be back, and we can all have a chat," Christian says as he picks up my jumper and pulls it on over my head.

I stand up from the desk and get dressed. As soon as I'm

about to leave, Christian wraps an arm around my waist and tugs him against him.

"Everything will be fine, I promise," he says before pressing his lips to mine and moving out of the way so Sean can pull me into his arms.

"I'll get Jason to come and see you when he returns so he can tell you himself that you have nothing to worry about," Sean says, kissing me gently. I nod before walking away from them and heading back to my room as my head spins and my heart races.

Chapter Sixteen

JASMINE

I walk out of the bathroom with a towel wrapped around my body to find Jason in my wardrobe. I stop in my tracks, wondering if he knows what occurred downstairs between his brothers and me. Jason turns to place something in the drawer and spots me standing aimlessly behind him.

"Hey, Jazzy. I've picked you up some new clothes. If you don't like anything, we can take it back and pick something else," he says, smiling over his shoulder. I chew on my bottom lip as the guilt consumes me. Jason turns to face me with a soft smile. "I've spoken to Christian and Sean. I'm not upset, Jazzy," he says, walking up to me and pulling me into his arms.

"Really?"

"Come here, angel." He takes my hand and pulls me onto his lap as he sits on the bench, holding me close as I rest my head on his chest.

"I promise you; I am far from upset. In fact, I'm relieved," he starts as he runs a hand over my bare arm.

"Why?" I ask, confused.

"Because it means none of us needs to hide how much we care about you anymore. It's been the hardest few years waiting for this day to come. We've cared about you for so long, and now we can finally show you. We can hold you, kiss you, and worship you, just as you deserve."

"This is a lot to get my head around. It doesn't feel real," I admit as I look at him. Jason smiles and kisses me gently on the lips.

"I can imagine. Get dressed, and the five of us can sit down with some food and talk it all through. Hopefully, we can help put your mind at ease. Maximus is home, and I know he can't wait to finally hold you," he says standing up and placing me on my feet. I quickly grab some clothes and head back to the bathroom to get dressed and dry my hair. I am still feeling a little confused but relieved Jason isn't angry.

I'm just running the brush through my hair when someone knocks at my bedroom door.

"Come in."

I watch the door open, and Maximus walks in, smiling.

"Hey, Shorty," he says, grinning as he walks to where I'm standing and pulls me into his arms before leaning in and kissing me. I instantly melt against him as I wrap my arms around his neck, still unable to believe that after all this time of wanting him to kiss me, he actually is. As he pulls away from me, smiling, I can't hide my own.

"I just wanted a moment with you to myself, as the others have all gotten one," he winks. "How are you feeling?" he asks, running his hand down my face before cupping my cheek.

"Confused, excited, a little overwhelmed and hungry," I chuckle. I feel Maximus's thumb stroke across my skin.

"I can imagine." He leans down and softly presses his lips to mine before looking deep into my eyes. "Come on, the others are all in the sitting room waiting for us. There's even some food in there as well." Maximus takes my hand and leads me out of my room and towards the sitting room where we all chatted last night.

As we walk into the room, I see the others sitting around with plates of food. My stomach flutters with anticipation as to how this is all going to go.

"Breathe, Shorty, we've got you," Maximus whispers into my ear before kissing my cheek. Christian must hear us because he looks over his shoulder and smiles.

"Sweetheart, sit and eat, please. You haven't eaten since you woke up."

I walk over to the sofas and sit down with Maximus next to me. He passes me a plate from the table, which is filled with chicken Caesar salad, one of my favourite meals. I thank him and start eating instantly. As my nerves settle a little, I realise how hungry I am.

We sit eating as Jason and Christian talk business, and Maximus fills me on the guy he's been training with today. Sean sits on the other side of me and asks about the next production we are putting on at the dance school and when my next exams are. I relax further as it's like any other meal I've had with them all.

Nothing ever feels forced when it's just the five of us. The guys are the only people I have ever truly relaxed around, and tonight is no different. I've never had to try to be someone I'm not. It's something that took a little getting used to, even with my mother a simple conversation is forced. We've spent more time silently disliking each other than we have talking. But since that first night, the five of us sat on the beach, it's been easy.

I hear Christian clear his throat, and I turn my attention to him.

"I hate to rush everyone, but there are a few things we need to discuss before anyone gets called away," he says as he gives me a soft smile. I have to force myself to swallow the last mouthful of food before I place the now empty plate on the table in front of me.

"I know Jason's spoken to you, and you're struggling to get your head around the four of us wanting to be with you."

I nod and look around at the guys.

"I don't understand how this would work, the five of us together," I admit. Maximus places a hand on my back, and I lean into his touch, thankful for the moral support.

"It works however you want it to work. You don't have to choose one, two or three of us, you get us all. We want to take care of you and be with you in a romantic, sexual relationship. There doesn't have to be a schedule or plan we just go with the flow. You're not obligated to just pick one of us at a time. We are all here for you, no matter what you want or need," Maximus explains as he runs his hand up and down my back.

"Have you shared a woman before?" I ask nervously.

"No. The twins have had threesomes, but this is different. It isn't something we've even contemplated until you," Jason answers. I look over at him and frown.

"Why me?" out of all the gorgeous women I've seen staring at them and near enough throwing themselves at their feet. Why would they choose the girl her own parents couldn't even love?

"Why not? You're funny, caring, intelligent, and beauti-

121

ful. We all fell for you the moment we met you," Sean says next to me as he takes my hand.

"Isn't it weird though? With you being brothers. Is it even legal?"

I watch as the four of them share a look before their attention returns to me. They all have smiles on their face, and I can't help but wonder how long they have been considering this arrangement if that's even the term for whatever this is.

"We are in a relationship with you, Jazzy, not each other. It's perfectly legal as long as you don't marry more than one of us. That's when it becomes a problem," Jason explains.

"It's called a reverse harem, sweetheart, where one woman is in a relationship with multiple men," Christian adds.

"Will you be seeing other women as well as me?" I ask nervously as I chew my bottom lip. I hate the thought of sharing them, even if they are happy to share me. To my relief, all of them instantly start protesting.

"No, princess. None of us will be with anyone by you," Sean reassures me.

"That also means that no man will ever touch you again. You belong to us, and even if we are happy to share you with each other, that's it. It's the five of us, no one else," Maximus declares as I look at him.

"I don't want anyone else. I haven't for a long time," I answer. Maximus leans in, pressing his lips to mine.

"I know I, for one, am very glad to hear that, Shorty," he replies with a cheeky grin.

"We all are," Christian chimes in from his seat. I look at him and smile.

"Anything else you want to know, Shorty?"

I look at Maximus and nod. "What about sleeping arrangements?" I ask.

"Your room is your private space. You can sleep in there alone or with any of us; if you ask for privacy, you will get it. You sleep anywhere you want, with whoever, and as many of us as you want," Jason explains.

"I wasn't sure if you would be up to more than one of us at a time, but you seemed to enjoy it with Sean and me before," Christian says with a grin. I can't stop myself from smiling as I nod.

"Do you think you could handle all four of us?" Maximus almost growls in my ear. I turn to look at him, smiling as my whole body heats with the thought of all four of the guys touching me together, but it also makes me nervous.

"I'm not very experienced. I've been touched more in the last twenty-four hours than I ever have."

"We will take it slow, sweetheart. We won't rush you into anything. We can keep it to foreplay until you are ready for more," Christian says before pulling out his phone as it starts ringing. "Excuse me." He quickly stands up and leaves the room with his phone to his ear.

"Do you feel better about it all now, Jazzy?" Jason asks. I look up at him and nod. "Good," he replies, relaxing into his seat as Christian walks back and grabs his jacket from the back of his chair.

"Sorry, Jason, we're needed at one of the clubs," he announces as he walks over and cups my cheek while kissing me. "It's been an emotional couple of days; get some sleep. We'll continue to get you settled in the morning," he adds as he moves out of the way of Jason, who kisses me before walking away.

"When will you be back?" I ask, but Christian lifts his

phone to his ear and starts talking as he leaves the room again.

"Not until the early hours, probably," Jason answers as he picks up a tablet off the table on the other side of the room and hands it to me.

"This is yours. I figured you sold your last one. It's all set up and linked to the bank card, so download whatever you want. I've already signed you up for Kindle Unlimited."

I look down at the newest version of the Kindle Fire in my hand and smile. I love to read and will always choose books over TV any day. It's something Jason and Christian have always encouraged, constantly gifting me new books or vouchers to pick my own.

"Thank you so much. I've missed mine." I jump up and throw my arms around his neck, hugging him.

"I thought you might have," Jason laughs, hugging me back.

"Change of plan. Sean, you're with me. Maximus and Jason, you're needed at The Highway Gym. There's been an incident," Christian says as he walks back in. Both the twins curse as they stand. Sean walks up to me and pulls me in for a kiss.

"Be good, princess. If you want any of us to come and see you when we get back, leave your door open," he winks before following Christian out of the room, both waving as they go.

"Get some rest, Shorty," Maximus says, leaning down and kissing me.

"Come on, Maximus," Jason calls from the door before looking at me.

"You are perfectly safe here, Jazzy. No one can get in, and security is on-site. If there are any issues, just shout, and they will come to you, okay?"

I nod nervously. He gives me a wink before following Maximus out of the door.

I stand alone in the sitting room for a moment, not knowing what to do. I look at the clock and see it's nearly nine in the evening. I'm tired, but I'm not sure if enough to sleep. I look down at the Kindle in my hands and smile as I rush up to the huge tub in my bathroom, planning a long soak whilst reading a new book to relax for the first time in months.

Chapter Seventeen

JASMINE

I wake up as someone takes the Kindle from my hand. The scent of Maximus's aftershave fills the air, and I find myself reaching out for him, a moan slipping past my lips. He chuckles as he kisses my head.

"Sorry, I didn't mean to wake you."

"Will you stay?" I open my eyes and look at him. Maximus smiles, nodding before stripping down to his boxers and climbing into bed with me.

"Go back to sleep, Shorty," he whispers as I rest my head on his shoulder. He kisses the top of my head again as he wraps his arm around my shoulder and holds me against him.

"What time is it?" I ask, placing my hand on his chest, savouring the way his smooth skin feels under my fingers.

"Just gone two."

"Are the others back?" I enquire, continuing to draw against his firm pec with just the tip of my fingers.

"Only me and Jason. Christian and Sean will be out for another hour at least," Maximus whispers into my hair as he sucks in a deep breath. I smile realising my touch is what caused the change in his breathing.

"Okay," I whisper before lifting my head and kissing him on the lips. Maximus instantly kisses me back and tightens his hold on me as he rolls his body so I'm pressed up against his front. I feel his tongue on my lips and quickly open my mouth a little.

He keeps kissing me as his hand runs up and down my back. I tighten my arms around his neck and grind against him. I can feel how hard he is in his boxers; the feel of him rubbing against me causes me to moan.

In one swift move, Maximus rolls us so he is lying over me. He nudges my legs with his knee, and I make room for him to lie between them. He breaks the kiss, and even in the dark room, I can see the smile on his face.

"You are meant to be sleeping," he points out before brushing some stray hair off my face and placing a soft kiss on the tip of my nose.

"Then stop kissing me," I grin.

"I don't think I can, gorgeous," Maximus replies before kissing me again.

He starts by kissing my lips, then moving across my jaw and down my neck. As he does, I feel him grind against me in just the right place, and I arch up to meet him.

"I've been walking around with a semi ever since they told me how tight you are and how sweet you taste. Can I taste you, gorgeous? Can I play with your sweet pussy until you scream my name?"

"Yes," I gasp as he kisses my collarbone. Maximus sits back on his heels and tugs me into a sitting position. He grabs the bottom of my top and pulls it off before throwing it across the room as I giggle. Maximus leans forward, forcing me to lie back. Leaning across, he turns the bedside lamp on.

"I need to watch you as I make you cum for the first time," Maximus growls before taking hold of my shorts. "Lift those hips for me, Shorty."

I obey instantly, and Maximus strips me. I watch him as he looks down at my naked body.

"You are so fucking gorgeous," he groans as he runs his hand down between my breasts, over my stomach, until he reaches the apex of my thighs. His finger slides between my lips, causing me to moan as he brushes my swollen clit and down to my entrance. A one-sided grin spreads across Maximus's face.

"Make that sound again," he demands as he repeats the move, causing me to moan a little louder. "Fuck, I could cum from that sound alone," he groans as he rubs me again. He leans forward and takes my right nipple between his teeth as he slowly slides one finger into me.

"You feel even more perfect than Sean told me you would," he growls, his finger wiggling, making me moan loudly.

"Maximus." His name slips off my tongue as I ache for more of his touch. I reach for his boxers to pull them off, but he moves my hand away.

"If I remove them, I will end up fucking you. We swore this evening we would all be present the first time one of us makes love to you," he whispers as he keeps teasing me. His kisses slowly move from my breasts down my stomach until he stops just above where I want him. I hear Maximus take a deep breath and groan as he uses his other hand to grasp my thigh.

"I know you can open those legs wider, gorgeous; spread them for me."

I smile down at him as I slowly do as he asks. Maximus devours me with his eyes, he looks up, and I swear his eyes have darkened.

"You have the most beautiful pussy I have ever seen," he growls before he slowly licks from where his finger is still in me to my clit. I moan loudly as he does it again, just as slowly, teasing me to the point I'm groaning with pleasure and frustration. He torments me as I grab hold of the sheets, feeling like I'm on the verge of an orgasm but not quite getting there. It's as if he's pushing me to the brink and then pulling me back.

"Maximus, please," I beg as he licks me over and over again.

"Does my girl need to cum?" he asks, grinning up at me from between my legs.

"Yes," I plead loudly. Maximus grins as he goes back to licking and fucking me with his finger. It feels too good; I start grinding against his hand and face.

"Stay still, gorgeous. Stay perfectly still, or I will stop," he warns, and I quickly do as I'm told. Maximus grins, "Are you going to be a good girl for me, gorgeous? Are you going to stay just like that and let me pleasure you?" I nod as my hands tighten in the sheets. "That's my gorgeous girl." I instantly warm from the praise. Maximus must notice as his grin widens.

"You going to be our good girl, Shorty? You going to let us look after you and trust us to take care of all your needs?"

"Yes. Please."

Maximus chuckles before I feel him add a second finger and slowly starts rubbing something inside of me that makes me gasp.

"How can I say no to that gorgeous sound." Maximus

starts to devour my pussy like it is the last thing he'll ever eat. I throw my head back and moan embarrassingly loud. It's like every nerve in my body is bursting to life. Every tiny little touch makes it harder to stay still, but I somehow manage it until Maximus picks up the speed with his tongue, and I curse as my whole body explodes and I have the most intense orgasm yet. I squeeze my eyes so tight that when I open them, I swear I see stars.

Maximus continues to lick me and move his fingers in and out of me, but slower and softer until I become over-sensitized, and I beg him to stop as I try to move away from him. He chuckles as he kisses the inside of my thigh and slowly withdraws his fingers before moving back up the bed and kissing me gently on the mouth as I wrap my arms around his neck.

"You taste even better than they said when you cum," he smirks before whispering in my ear. "I can't wait to feel you clamp around my cock like you did my fingers."

"Maximus," I gasp as he starts nibbling on my ear lobe. He chuckles and rolls to the side before pulling me to him. I rest my head back on his chest and feel more relaxed than I was before I fell asleep.

"Get some rest, Shorty," he whispers as he tightens his arms around my shoulders, holding me close to his chest, before kissing the top of my head. I close my eyes with a smile on my face as I breathe in his masculine scent as he holds me safe in his arms.

Chapter Eighteen

JASMINE

I groan as I open my eyes and look up, wanting to know who's dragging me from a wonderful dream.

"Come on, Jazzy, you need to get up," Jason says as he gently shakes my shoulder. I feel Maximus's arm tighten around me, and I realise he, too was asleep, my head still resting on his chest.

"Dude? What time is it?" Maximus groans as he rubs his face with his free hand.

"It's nearly nine," Jason answers as he stands up and crosses his arms over his broad chest. I look at the tight black t-shirt he's wearing and, for a moment, consider asking him to join us.

"Why have I got to get up?" I ask as I go to roll out of bed, but Maximus tightens his hold on me.

"You haven't; I'm keeping you here," he declares as he kisses the top of my head. I relax into him, smiling, closing my eyes.

"No, she's not. Christian's waiting for her. We have to go

131

and see your mother, Jazzy," Jason says as he pulls off the covers, revealing my naked body.

"Jason!" I pull back the covers but groan as he stops me. "She won't even be up yet!" I protest.

"That's why we're going now. We need to catch her when she's sober," he explains. Maximus groans as he gets out of bed.

"He's right; now's the best time to go. But I'm going back to bed. I'll see you later, Shorty," he kisses me quickly before disappearing out of the room. I groan loudly as I climb out of bed and take the dressing gown Jason holds out for me before heading to the bathroom.

"Give me twenty minutes, and I'll meet you downstairs," I huff, turning away from him.

"You have ten, and I'll wait," Jason replies as I spin around to face him.

"Do I need a babysitter now?"

"Yes, I don't trust you not to stall. I know you don't want to do this and will drag your feet."

I groan again, throwing my hands up in the air and storm into the bathroom, slamming the door behind me.

"Lose the attitude, Jazzy," Jason calls as I flip him off behind the closed door and head into the shower for a quick rinse, knowing that if I take too long, he'll storm in here and drag me out.

Twenty-five minutes later, I'm sitting in the passenger seat of Christian's car with Jason in the back, tapping away on his phone. My heart starts racing as he pulls onto my old street and stops outside the house.

"Please let me go in on my own? She will be in a vile

mood, and I can handle her better without an audience," I beg, turning in my seat to face Christian, who shakes his head.

"We are coming with you. You don't know who's in there, and we won't risk you getting hurt. Plus, we want to offer Carol our help."

"What do you mean?" I ask. Jason reaches forward and places a reassuring hand on my shoulder.

"We know a very good rehab facility and want her to know that option's there if she wants it," Jason explains as I turn to look at him, shocked.

"You would do that? Help her get sober again?"

Jason nods as Christian takes my hand.

"Sweetheart, we might not agree with everything Carol has done, but she's still your mother, and we can see what her substance abuse has done to you."

I look between these amazing men and then at the dark house.

"She won't take the offer. I appreciate you trying, but I think this time she's too far gone," I sigh.

I look out the window and want to cry. I loved this house when I moved in. Everything about it was perfect. The guys had come around and helped me decorate. Jason and Maximus helped build all the furniture, and for the first time in years, it felt like I had a real home. That was until Mum and Tommy started having problems, and Mum moved in. She took my room, as it was the biggest, and I moved into the smaller one. Mum started drinking heavily until I had no choice but to leave. Tommy warned me that I wouldn't like the consequences if I told the guys about the rent and financial agreement. It was one of the reasons I could never bring myself to phone them and ask for help, even though I knew it was the logical thing to do.

I hear one of the car doors open and look up as Jason opens mine and holds out his hand.

"Come on, angel. The sooner you get this sorted, the quicker you can move forward and stop looking back."

I look at his hand and nod before taking it and letting him help me out of the car. As he closes the door, I feel Christian's presence as he walks up beside us. I quickly look between the two of them.

"Please don't mention our relationship in there; she'll just use it as ammunition," I ask as the guys share a look.

"We won't hide that we care about you, but we will leave out the fact that all four of us are with you, for *now*," Christian replies, but I don't miss the way he emphasises 'now'. I take a deep breath and look back up at the house. I don't say anything; I just start heading up the path through the overgrown garden to the front door and take one last deep breath before opening it, knowing it wouldn't be locked.

We walk into the house and are hit with the smell of rotting, stale garbage, drugs and alcohol. I retch and have to stop for a second before I can take another step, but as I go to move, I feel an arm blocking me.

"Let me go first; something doesn't feel right," Jason whispers, walking past me and turning to look at Christian, whose arm wraps around my waist from behind.

"I've got her. Shout, and I'll get her to the car before coming back," Christian says over my head. Jason nods and heads into the house. "Don't panic; he's just checking who's here," Christian whispers into my ear. I nod and heave from the smell again. "Breathe through your mouth; it's easier," he adds, holding me a little tighter. I do as he suggests. I'm about to tell him I can taste the smells when I hear a thud and someone curses.

Christian moves so quickly that I nearly fall as he places

himself between me and the entrance to the rest of the house. I hear what sounds like someone falling down the stairs before a body flies into view.

"Think you can jump me, you piece of shit! Get the fuck out of my house!" Jason growls loudly as he comes storming into view.

"Your house? Who the fuck are you?" The guy curses as he tries to get to his feet, and I realise he's naked. I move so I don't have to see the state of his skeleton-thin, abused body.

"Jason! Get the hell out of my house!" I hear my mother scream, and my back straightens as Christian tightens his hold of me and stops me from stepping around him. Jason doesn't even acknowledge her; I can't see what's happening as Christian won't let me move from the safety of his back, and for a moment, I'm grateful when I hear someone curse and the sound of flesh hitting flesh.

"Leave him alone!" my mother screams, and I hear Christian curse. As he turns, I can see from his face that he's getting me out of here.

"No!" I protest, quickly ducking past him and rushing into the lounge.

As I get to the room, I see Mum behind Jason, who has the other guy by the throat. Jason has blood coming from the side of his mouth, and looks like he is about to kill someone.

"Stop! Everyone, just stop!" I scream as I hold my hands up as Christian holds me from behind, ready to get me out of the way of danger. Everyone turns to look at me, and I see the shock on Mum's face before it changes to a look of pure evil, and she launches herself at me, snarling.

"You!"

Christian pushes me out of the way before restraining her.

"Carol, stop, we're here to help," Christian warns as she fights against him. He looks up at Jason and looks towards the guy he has hold of. "Is he the only one here?"

Jason nods and looks at the guy.

"If you want to leave this place alive, get dressed and fuck off. Try and fight me again, and you will end up where we put all drugged-up fuckers like you," Jason drops the guy, who grabs his clothes from the floor and rushes out of the door.

"Kyle, stay!" Mum screams as she starts fighting Christian again. "Get your fucking hands off me, you prick!"

"Mum, let him go so we can talk," I say calmly as I step in front of her so she can see me. "We just want to help you get the care you need. If you calm down, Christian will let you go, and we can talk properly."

I keep eye contact with her as my heart breaks. I've never been overly close to my mother; she has never been the type of mum I wish she'd been, but she's the only one I have, and to see her looking so thin, unkept and just plain broken is too much.

She stops fighting Christian and stares at me with her bloodshot blue eyes, and for a moment, I think I see the mum who danced with my dad when I was three, who made cookies with us at Christmas and who smiled at me on her wedding day three years ago like she finally had everything she needed in her life. She'd been the happiest I've seen her since before my dad left, and she was happy for a while afterwards.

"Please, Mum, just talk to me," I say quietly as I take a step towards her and try to hide the fact that her smell is assaulting my nose and making me feel sick to my stomach.

Jason steps next to me and puts an arm out, stopping me from getting any closer to her.

"Carol, Christian will let you go, but if you try to hurt Jasmine, we *will* intervene. We just want to help you," he says, keeping his arm across my front. Mum looks at him for a moment and bursts out laughing.

"Of course, you will protect *her*! It's always been about precious Jasmine. Make sure she has everything she needs: the house, the expensive dance school, and everything that goes with it," Mum snarls as she glares at me. "No one gives a shit about Carol. No one wants to help her because they care; it's always because of Jasmine. *Jasmine needs a mum who is sober. Jasmine needs a healthy home.* Maybe Jasmine just needs to stop being a spoilt brat and realise that everything doesn't fall from the sky and land perfectly at her feet!" she snarls. Not once losing the evil look on her face. I feel my anger rise, and for the first time, I don't attempt to pull it back.

"Are you for real right now, Mother? Do you really think I don't know how hard things were or are? Who was it that was cleaning up your sick and covering up for you at the age of nine? ME! Who saved your life on three separate occasions because you had overdosed? ME! I've bailed you out when dealers came looking for payment and put a roof over your head when you left Tommy? IT WAS ALL ME!" I scream as all the anger I have felt towards her my whole life starts rushing to the surface. Jason holds me back as I try to get close enough to hit her.

"You didn't help me last time someone came knocking for money, though, did you? You turned around and ran like the fucking bitch you are! Leaving me to deal with them!" Mum yells. I freeze as the last tiny thread of control snaps, and I jump forward, screaming.

"YOU BROUGHT FOUR MEN INTO THIS

HOUSE AND TRIED TO SELL MY FUCKING
VIRGINITY TO THE HIGHEST BIDDER!"

Silence fills the room. Jason and Christian both stare at
me with their mouths hanging open. I look Christian in the
eye as I point to my mother. "That's right, I lied when I told
you I had lost my virginity that night. I tried to, god, I
wanted to, just because I knew she was back on the drugs
and would use me as payment if she knew I was still one.
But the stupid prick Damien didn't even get it in me! It
doesn't fucking matter, as she found out and tried to sell it
anyway! That's why I ran and didn't come back because I
knew if I did, she would stand by and let me get raped as
payment for her drugs!"

"You fucking bitch!" Mum snarls as she surges forward
again.

"Lock her in the kitchen. I'm getting Jasmine's stuff, and
we're leaving," Christian growls as he throws Mum at Jason,
grabs my hand, and drags me up the stairs.

He heads for the main bedroom, but I pull my hand
from his and storm into the smaller room Mum forced me
to move into. Trying desperately to ignore the state of my
once beautiful house. I barge into the small room I called
mine for less than a month and freeze.

The place is trashed. There's nothing left intact. The
curtains have been ripped down, the wardrobe emptied,
and the contents destroyed. The mirror and picture frames
on the walls are all smashed, and I don't want to even think
about what is covering my sheets.

"Sweetheart, leave it," Christian whispers softly as he
places his hands on my shoulders. I step away from him as I
walk over to a double picture frame that's lying on the floor
upside down and pick it up. I hear the glass rattling and
falling onto the floor as I turn it around and see my two

favourite pictures. One of my grandparents and I taken the summer before they died from a gas leak in their home. As well as a picture of the guys and me taken the night of the wedding when we sat together on the beach and talked until dawn. I'd fallen asleep there, and one of them had carried me up to my room. That was the night I knew I was going to fall for the four men beside me, and I knew I was going to be the one hurt when they walked away, just like everyone does.

I pull the pictures from the frame and look at the damage on the one of the five of us and run my fingers over the slash made from the broken glass.

"I have that picture and more from that night. We will get as many as you want printed," Christian's voice comes behind me as his hand rests on my shoulder. All I can do is nod as I blink back the tears whilst looking around my room. "Do you have a hidey hole here?"

I look up at Christian and nod, pointing to the radiator. I watch as he pulls on some leather gloves and walks over before squatting down. He pulls back the carpet, runs his fingers over the floorboards, and finds the right place to pull it up. I watch as he retrieves a shoe box wrapped in a plastic bag.

"That's everything I put in there," I say quietly. He turns to look at me and nods before standing up and putting the floorboard and carpet back in place. He picks up the package and walks over to me.

"Just so you know, you never need to hide anything at home."

I nod as I already knew that. The guys would never take from me like my mum and her friends have.

Christian places a hand on the bottom of my back and leads me towards the door.

"Whatever is left, leave; we'll replace it," he whispers as he applies pressure and leads me back downstairs, where we find Jason standing over Mum, sitting on the sofa, in nothing but a dirty dressing gown.

"Kitchen door won't close, but she knows not to move," Jason declares, not taking his eyes off her as he stands with his arms crossed over his chest. Mum rolls her eyes and leans back on the dirty sofa with her hands up in the air.

"Don't worry, I won't touch your precious, *Jazzy*," she turns and looks at me, grinning. "I always knew you would end up fucking one of them, which one is it? Christian or Jason?" she asks as she turns her nose up at them. She looks back at me, and an evil smirk appears on her face. "They will get bored of you soon enough, and when they are done, who will look after you then? No grandparents, your father's gone, I don't give a shit, and your four rich stepbrothers will leave you in the gutter just like their father left me. Enjoy the fun whilst you can, as it's all downhill from here, girl."

"That's enough, Carol!" Jason snaps as he turns to look at me and Christian. "Is that everything?" he asks, looking at the package in Christian's hands. I avoid looking at him or my mother as I feel myself beginning to shake and my eyes burning. I refuse to let them see me cry. "Then let's get out of this dump," Jason growls as Christian turns me around and guides me towards the front door. I don't fight him; I just let him lead me.

We walk to the car in silence, and I stop next to the front passenger door, waiting for Christian to unlock it, but instead, I hear keys being tossed through the air.

"You drive; she rides in the back with me." Christian takes my hand and pulls me into the back seat with him, but when I sit next to him, he pulls me into his arms and positions me across his lap with my head resting on his shoulder.

Part of me wants to pull away and put some distance between us. But when I try to move, he tightens his arms around me as Jason starts the car and pulls away from the house and out of the street. I try to move again once we are moving, but Christian tightens his grip once more.

"I'm not letting you go, baby girl. Not now, not ever."

Chapter Nineteen

JASMINE

Christian holds me the whole way home. He doesn't say or do anything other than occasionally run his hand up and down my leg as if reassuring me that he's there. But the words my mother snarled at me before we left kept going around in my head, the same thing that I'd been scared of since the day I met the guys. One day, they will leave me, and I'll have no one.

We park in the garage and Jason opens the door so Christian can climb out with me still in his arms. He carries me through the door that leads into the large kitchen where Sean and Maximus are both drinking coffee. They look up, and I force myself to look away, not wanting to see their faces.

"What happened?" I hear them both ask as the sound of the chairs scraping across the floor fills the air. Christian places me on a chair and squats down in front of me.

"We are going to talk, all five of us. We will discuss what just happened after you eat some lunch," he says, forcing me to look at him.

"I'm not hungry," I whisper, but it just earns me a raised brow.

"I didn't ask if you were. You will eat if we tell you to eat. You will learn to do as you are told," he warns. I frown as I look at him.

"Why?"

"Because we know what is best for you, and we will look after you and all your needs. That includes making sure you eat and look after yourself.

"Unlike what your mother just stated, you are wanted and loved, and the four of us will prove that to you every day until you believe us. We certainly will not 'kick you to the curb'. You are stuck with us whether you like it or not. We are no longer your stepbrothers; we are going to be your Daddies and will always put your well-being above all else."

I look into his blue eyes, confused. "What does that even mean?"

Jason takes Christian's place as he cups my cheek and looks at me with his soft grey eyes.

"It means you need to trust us to do right by you and to push you to achieve all you can. But as I warned, you need to learn to do as you are told and not to fight us. Everything we do is for you, not us." Jason takes hold of my hands and cups them with his.

"You no longer need to worry about anything, Jazzy. Not where the next payment for school is coming from, rent, or your next meal. We will take over all of that. We'll make your decisions for you when needed and look after you like you should have been looked after your whole life," he explains further.

"But we will be in a relationship?" I ask, frowning. Jason smiles at me as he nods.

"Nothing could make us give you up. I know it's a lot to

take in, but this is what you need, you need someone to take care of you, and there are four of us more than happy to give you the best of everything. You just have to let us and not fight it. Trust us to know what you need, whether it's with your life or in the bedroom. You are what's important. You don't look after yourself properly because you have never been shown how. Let us do that; let us help you."

I look from Jason to Christian and then the twins behind them. All four men together in front of me saying they want to look after me, protect me and all I have to give back is my trust.

My inner voice is begging me to protect myself, to realise that there is no way they would all pick me forever. But they have shown me over and over again that I'm important to them; they have had so many chances to run, but they are still here. They are the only ones who have stuck by me since my grandparents died. I look up at Christian and start chewing on my bottom lip.

"Okay," I whisper. Christian's face softens as he walks up to me and pulls me up onto my feet before wrapping his arms around me.

"You finally ready to be ours, baby girl? Are you going to let the four of us look after all your needs?"

I look into his eyes and nod nervously.

"Remember what I said about using your words, sweetheart. *Always* use your words with us; it's important," he warns. I quickly swallow and look into his eyes.

"I want to be all of yours," I reply as I look from Christian's chest and see Maximus, Sean and Jason smiling at me. Maximus walks up to me and leans in to press his lips to mine. I feel Christian's hold on me loosen as Maximus pulls me into his arms and deepens the kiss. A second pair of arms wrap around my waist from behind, and as I feel lips against my neck, I groan, knowing it's Sean behind me. Maximus moves his lips until he is on the opposite side of my neck as his brother. As they kiss my neck and shoulders Jason smiles at me before leaning around his brothers and kissing me.

"You ready for us to make you ours?" he asks.

"Please," I gasp as a hand lands between my legs and squeezes my hot wet wanting pussy.

"Let's take this to your room, angel," Jason grins as his brothers let me go. Jason picks me up in his arms before carrying me out of the kitchen and heading straight up the stairs.

As soon as we are in my room, he places me on my feet next to the bed and kisses me before stepping back, grinning.

"Take your clothes off, angel. Let us see you."

I don't stop to think. I instantly do as he asks, and the four of them watch me. I can't miss the way their eyes burn into my skin, heating everywhere they land. I find myself chewing on my lip as the intensity of their hungry eyes causes my stomach to knot and my pussy to flood.

"Lie down in the middle of the bed, baby girl, and place your hands above your head."

I do as Christian asks and watch as the four gorgeous men strip in front of me. I always imagined them as being well-hung, but now, seeing the four of them naked and hard, I realise they are even bigger than I thought.

Sean and Maximus walk to each side of the bed and crawl on until they are on either side of me. Sean kisses me on the mouth as Maximus takes my nipple between his teeth. I close my eyes and moan as I feel featherlight kisses on my ankle that slowly move up my leg as Sean moves his lips from my mouth and takes my other nipple, sucking and teasing with his teeth just as Maximus does. There's a mouth on my leg and each of my nipples. I moan as I arch my back, trying to get my breasts closer to the twins as they play and suck on them.

"Open your eyes, baby girl."

I open them to see Christian naked by my head as he strokes his hard cock. The sight of him turns me on further, and I can't tear my eyes away from him or how he strokes himself slowly, over and over again. Christian picks up one of my hands which is still above my head, and places it around his cock. With his hand around mine, he shows me how hard to grip it and how fast to stroke him. The feel of his silky-smooth foreskin in my hand feels amazing. Christian closes his eyes and groans.

"After I licked you on my desk yesterday, I had to go to my shower and relieve myself. I pretended it was your hand, and I came harder than I have in years, but fuck, it didn't feel half as good as this," he groans as he tips his head back, letting go of my hand and leaving me to pleasure him. Just as I'm thinking about moving so I can take him in my mouth, I feel a tongue against my clit, and I moan at the same time as Jason.

"Fuck, you taste even better than you did the other night on my fingers," he groans as he starts licking me. He slides a finger into me, and I open my legs further to give him better access.

The assault on my pussy as well as my breasts, is sending me closer and closer to an orgasm. My breathing speeds up as I moan loudly.

"Add a second finger, Jason. Our girl can take it," I hear Sean say before Jason does as his brother says, and I moan even louder.

"Cum for us, princess. Let Jason savour how amazing

146

you taste when you cum," Sean whispers before his lips land on mine, and I fall apart drastically.

"Want to know a secret, sweetheart?" I look back up at Christian as I come down from my orgasm. "I was gutted when you told me that little prick took your virginity; I wanted it to be me. I wanted to be the one you gave yourself to for the first time."

I stare up at Christian for a moment, then smile.

"Then take me. Please? He couldn't do it. I was relieved because I wanted you to be my first."

Christian stares down at me before his lips crash into mine.

"You giving yourself to me completely?" he asks as his brothers bring me closer and closer to the edge again.

"Please, Christian, be my first," I beg. The thought alone of him taking me has me rushing towards that second release I desperately want.

"You heard her, Christian, be the one to take our girl for the first time. It was always going to be you anyway," Jason says as he removes himself from between my legs.

"Fuck," Christian swears as he moves off the bed and moves around until he's kneeling between my legs. He lifts my hips and gets as close as possible to me. "There's no going back from this, sweetheart. Once I take you, I'm going to have you whenever I want. You belong to all four of us, no one else."

"I don't want anyone else; I never have," I gasp as I see Christian's large penis back in his hand. He's so big I have no idea how that's going to fit in me, but I don't care; I want it.

"Come here, princess," I look to the left of me and see Sean's face. He kisses me as his hand finds my breast; at the same time, I feel another set of lips on my neck and hand on my breast.

I feel two fingers press into me and stretch me before I feel the tip of Christian's dick. Christian starts rubbing my clit with his fingers as he slowly starts easing into me.

"That's it, relax for me, baby girl," he coaxes as he continues to slowly move inside me. Maximus and Sean continue to give me pleasure in any way they can, attempting to distract me from the discomfort of Christian's dick entering my tight pussy. I cry out, and he stops.

"No, keep moving! Please!" I beg as my virgin pussy stretches to accommodate him.

"That's it, angel, you can take him," I look up and see Jason kneeling above me, grinning as he leans down and kisses me. "You look so fucking hot, lying there for us all. So fucking gorgeous," he praises me, and I find myself pushing against Christian to take him further. Jason's grin widens as he kisses me again.

"You like to be praised, don't you, angel? Do you like it when we reward you? Are you going to be a good girl for your daddies?"

"Yes," I scream as I orgasm, and Christian pushes the remaining cock into me.

"That's it, baby girl, you took it all. Fuck you are squeezing me like a vice. You feel so fucking good," Christian growls through gritted teeth. I've never felt so full, and it feels so good and painful at the same time.

"Please, move. Please," I beg as I look at Christian; he looks at me before glancing at Jason and grinning.

"Please, what?" Christian asks, looking back at me.

"Please, I need more," I beg as I try to move my hips, but Christian holds me still as Jason grins down at me.

"Please, what?" Christian asks again. Jason leans in, and I feel his breath tickle over my ear.

"The words you are looking for are 'please *Daddy*'."

I instantly lift my head and look at Christian. "Please, Daddy, please take me," I yell as the twins both restart their assault on my nipples, and Christian starts to play with my clit and grins at me.

"What daddy's girl wants, daddy's girl gets," he responds before he slowly starts moving in and out of me, and I gasp with pleasure.

"So fucking beautiful, angel," Jason growls as he starts stroking himself. I reach out and take it in my hand like I did Christian's. "Fuck," he hisses as I start stroking my hand up and down his manhood. I watch as a small amount of pre-cum leaks from him. I wipe it off with my finger and lift it to my mouth. I keep eye contact with Jason, and I slowly lick it.

"Fuck, princess, you are hotter than I ever dreamt you would be," Sean curses next to me.

"You ever sucked a cock, angel?" Jason asks. I look up at him and shake my head before closing my eyes and losing myself in the feeling of Christian easing in and out of me as he picks up speed.

"Think that will have to wait, Jason. Our girl's getting fucked for the first time," Maximus chuckles next to me. I look over and see him stroking his cock to the left of me. To the right, Sean's doing the same. I reach out and take both in my hands and stroke them as I moan loudly.

"Fuck, I'm going to cum so fucking hard in you, baby girl," Christian moans as he picks up speed, and I lose all sense of what's going on around me. I feel the twins take control of my hands as they use them to chase their own release.

"Oh god, it feels too good," I scream as I get closer and closer to coming.

"Fuck, cum for us, angel; let us see what we do to you," Jason says as he kneels over me, stroking himself vigorously.

"Cum for us, baby girl, cum for your daddies," Christian calls as he slams into me hard and sends me over the edge.

"Daddy, yes!" I scream as I feel myself contract around Christian's huge dick as he thrusts into me hard again.

"Fuck," he curses as I feel him filling me with his hot release. In seconds, I feel both my hands covered by Maximus's and Sean's own deposits.

"Open up, angel." I open my mouth just in time for Jason to shove his dick into my mouth as he cums hard, I have to swallow a couple of times to stop myself from choking on his load, but I take it all.

"Fuck you are so hot," Jason smiles down at me before kissing me on the lips.

I let go of Maximus's and Sean's dicks and feel them both taking hold of my wet hands. I look over to see them grinning at me as they wipe up their mess with some tissues.

"It's a good job, Mrs Brown put these in here," Sean says, smiling at me. I hiss a little from the sting as Christian's now soft dick falls from me before Maximus helps me to sit up. I lean against Christian's chest as he kneels in front of me.

"I didn't think you could look more beautiful than you do on the stage, but that was something fucking else," Maximus says as he comes around and plants a kiss on my lips.

"Thanks, I think," I chuckle as Christian's arms tighten around me. He kisses me on the top of the head before moving away and standing at the end of the bed. He holds his hand out for me, and I move so I'm sitting on the edge of it.

"Put your arms around my neck, baby girl," he whispers as he places an arm under my knees. I do as I'm told, and he lifts me with ease.

"Meet us in the sitting room in thirty minutes," he says to his brothers before walking out of the room and carrying me into my bathroom.

"Where are we going?" I ask, leaning against his chest with my eyes closed.

"You and I are going to have a soak in the bath," he replies softly.

"That sounds like heaven," I sigh contently as I smile to myself.

"I couldn't agree more," Christian replies as he places me on the stool and starts running the huge bath.

Chapter Twenty

JASMINE

I lean back in the warm water as Christian wraps an arm around me, his lips brushing against my neck and down my shoulder.

"How are you feeling, sweetheart?" he whispers into my ear as he kisses my shoulder again.

"A little sore, but okay," I admit as I close my eyes and enjoy the feeling of his gentle touch as he washes my skin with a washcloth.

"I need to ask, sweetheart, are you on the pill or anything?"

"Yeah, I am," I answer as I feel myself relaxing further against him. Christian kisses my shoulder again before tightening both arms around me.

"You did so well earlier; you certainly seemed to enjoy it."

I turn my head to find him smiling at me before leaning down and kissing me on the lips.

"Are you going to tell me why you lied to me about not being a virgin? I understand why you lied to Carol, but why me?" he asks as he looks into my eyes. I don't know how to answer, so I shrug and go to look away, but he lifts his hand and twists my nipple.

"Ouch, Christian," I protest as I go to move away from him, but he traps me with his arms.

"Firstly, I know I told you to use your words with me. That's an important rule, baby girl. You will be punished for ignoring it.

"Secondly, did you just call me Christian? Because I'm pretty sure you just agreed for us to be your daddies.

"Now, why did you lie to me?"

I look at him for a moment before curling up so I am across his lap rather than leaning against his front. Christian goes to twist my nipple again, but I grab his hand.

"Hang on, I'm just getting comfortable; then I will address all your questions, Daddy," I answer. Christian huffs under his breath but helps me move so I can lean my cheek against his smooth, tattooed chest.

"Firstly," I start with a smile which earns me a raised brow, but I continue. "I'm getting used to using my words; please give me time to adjust after being told to be quiet most of my life." Christian's jaw clenches, but he doesn't say anything. I take it as my cue to continue.

"Secondly, I didn't realise that you being my daddy included when we aren't having sex. Can you explain it to me a little more, please?"

"The guys and I will do that together," Christian answers, nodding. I go to nod but quickly remember and stop myself.

"Thank you, Daddy," I reply with a smile. Christian rolls his eyes, but I can't miss the pleased look on his face.

"And the third thing? Why did you lie to me, Jasmine?" As soon as he uses my name, I know I'm in trouble, and I quickly decide honesty might be the best policy.

"I honestly don't know. I had gone there with the intention of letting him sleep with me. We even got as far as putting the condom on, but he couldn't keep it up and blamed me. He told everyone I wasn't hot enough to arouse him, and I left. I nearly told you the truth, but then I wanted you to notice I wasn't a little seventeen-year-old girl anymore," I admit as Christian looks down at me.

"I wouldn't have treated you any differently if I thought you were a virgin or not. We have always planned for you to become ours. We were just waiting for you to turn twenty-one, then we were going to claim you, and this," Christian says as he reaches between my legs and runs a finger between my slit. I moan as soon as he touches me, and Christian's grin widens. "You are so gorgeous when you make that sound," he whispers, touching me again, and I melt in his arms. He removes his fingers, and I open my eyes to look at him.

"You need to tell me if any of the men your mother brought back ever touched you," Christian says as he looks at me. I bite my bottom lip before sighing.

"Not since I was taken from her when I was younger," I admit quietly as Christian's arms tighten around me. I told him a long time ago about the guy who snuck into my room and put his fingers between my legs when I was ten. I'd screamed so loud for him not to touch me and for him to get out of my room the neighbours heard and called the police.

"None of them tried?" Christian asks as he kisses my forehead.

"I didn't give them a chance," I admit. Christian nods as he rubs my leg. "I'm sorry I lied to you about not being a virgin. I won't lie again," I promise as I look up at Christian through my lashes and hope he drops the subject. He hums deep in his throat before relaxing against the back of the bath and holding me tighter to his chest.

"Fine, I'll ignore it this once. From this point, though, if I ever find out you lie to me, you will be punished." I hear the warning in Christian's voice and swallow deeply.

"Define punished," I ask cautiously.

"I will go over the rules properly with the others, but punishment will depend on what you do to deserve it. It could vary from time out to withholding your orgasms, spanking, or even testing your pain threshold."

"You would purposely cause me pain?" I ask as I sit up to look at him.

"To a point, yes. This is why you need to always use your words with us. We would never push you past what you can endure. If we were to ever push you until you couldn't take anymore, we'd expect and trust you to tell us so we could put the situation right," Christian explains. He cups my cheek to make sure I'm looking into his eyes before continuing. "We would never cause you any type of pain you couldn't handle, nor would we cause any permanent damage to your body or mind. But we need to trust you to always communicate with us."

"Okay," I answer, unsure of what else to say.

"Good girl," Christian praises me as he runs his hand up my inner thigh and cups my pussy in his hand. "Don't forget if there is punishment, there are also rewards," Christian whispers as his lips brush against mine, and he squeezes me below. "Do as you are told, and we will reward you in more ways than you could ever dream of," he adds as the tip of his finger brushes lightly against my clit.

"How can I want more?" I gasp as he plays with me, and I open my legs to give him better access.

"Because you know how good I can make you feel," he whispers. He continues rubbing my clit, before running his finger down and sliding into my slightly sensitive hole. I push against his finger so he enters me further. "So ready for Daddy to make you feel good, baby girl? Do you trust me to give you what you need?" he asks, smiling.

"Yes, Daddy," I gasp as I grind against his finger, moaning as he adds a second. Suddenly, I feel a finger against my back passage. I instantly stiffen as Christian chuckles.

"Shush, baby girl, I'm not taking that just yet." I relax as he rubs it gently whilst two of his fingers slide in and out of my pussy. I moan as the sensation of him at both my holes causes me to have many deviant thoughts.

"Would you like that? Would you like one of your daddies to take your ass as another takes your pussy?" Christian asks as he kisses my neck and shoulder. I lean my head back to give him better access.

"Yes, Daddy," I whimper as he applies a little more pressure at my back passage, but not enough to enter. "Please, Daddy, just a little," I beg as I push against his finger and the tip slides in.

"Baby girl, are you ready for me to take you again? Do you want to feel my hard dick in your pussy as I finger your asshole?"

"Yes, please," I beg as I grind against his hand, feeling him everywhere. Christian removes his hand completely and grabs my hips. He helps me turn around so I'm straddling his lap. I look down and see his huge penis standing to attention. He grips the base of it and strokes it slowly.

"Do you see how hard you make me, baby girl? Do you see what you do to me?"

"Yes," I reply, looking down at it in his hand, "I want to feel you in me."

"Lift," Christian orders, and I quickly do as I'm told. He moves down the bath and positions himself at my entrance. "Slowly lower yourself down; if it gets too much, lift up slightly, wait, then try again," he instructs. I slowly do as I'm told. Christian, holding my hips the whole time, supporting me. I place my hands on his chest and moan as he starts to stretch me again.

"That's it, you are so fucking amazing," Christian curses as he leans his head on the back of the tub with his eyes closed.

"You are so big," I groan as I take him a little further.

"But you are taking it all," he growls as he lifts his head and looks at me with a look that I feel in every fibre of my body. I swear my pussy floods as the rest of him slips in from the wetness. Christian curses as I take all of him.

"I don't know what to do," I admit just before Christian's lips meet mine. I feel his hands on my hips tighten as he helps me to grind against him.

"Just like that baby girl, ride Daddy's cock," Christian growls as I follow his lead. I can feel him rubbing me in just the right spot inside, and I move so his hard cock rubs against it again. I rock repeatedly, chasing that orgasm that's right there. I can hear Christian groaning, and the fact I'm bringing my big, strong daddy to the point he can't even keep his head up brings me close to that big release.

"You look so perfect there riding my cock," he growls as I feel something push against my back hole before sliding in and filling me back there; as Christian's dick fills my pussy, I moan with pleasure. It's nothing like I thought it would feel; it's so much better.

"One day, I'm going to watch as the other three fuck each of your holes. I want to see you with a dick in your pussy, one in your ass and one in your mouth." Christian growls as his finger moves in and out of me, and I start rocking harder and faster against him.

"I'm going to cum, Daddy." I cry as I throw my head back. I scream as I cum as hard as I did in my room. Christian holds my hips and pushes into me hard as he finds his release.

"Fuck," he yells, pulsating in me as I fall against his shoulder, gasping for breath. We stay there for a moment in the lukewarm water, Christian holding me close.

"You are amazing, sweetheart," he sighs as he kisses my shoulder before forcing me to lift and look at him. "We need to get out of this bath and downstairs," he says as he presses a kiss to my lips.

"I know," I sigh as I lift off him and feel him slide out of me.

"Sit back there a moment," Christian orders. I scoot to the other side of the large tub and watch as he climbs out of the bath and wraps a towel around his waist. I look up at the tattoo on his back, which goes over his shoulder.

"Turn around a minute."

Christian frowns at me as I stand up and move so I'm standing in front of him. I take his shoulder and look at the tattoo from the back before moving him so I can see the front. It's a mixture of rose thorns twisting together with occasional roses, moving up his shoulder and over towards his chest, where it blooms into a mixture of jasmine flowers and runes. I run my fingers over each rune individually.

"It says '*until I die*'," Christian whispers. I look up at him, frowning.

"When did you get that tattoo done?"

"The week I met you and realised one day you would be mine," he explains as I look up at him.

"How did you know my middle name?" I ask as I trace the roses. Christian picks up a towel and wraps it around my chest before helping me out of the bath.

"You told us when we were all sitting on the beach talking after the wedding party. You told us your full name and all your dreams. That's why we support your dancing financially as well as never missing a show. We know how much it means to you," Christian explains as he leads me into the bedroom.

"We all have various versions of tattoos that represent you; you probably didn't notice before as you were preoccupied." He winks at me whilst smirking. "Jason has your star sign over his heart. Maximus has a swan because Swan Lake was the first performance we ever came to watch a month after the wedding. He watched every single performance, and it's still his favourite. Sean has a large ballerina on his back. We all got them within a month of meeting you. That was when we realised how much you meant to us all," he explains as he wraps the dressing gown around me and ties the cord around my waist before leading me through to my wardrobe.

"Did it cause arguments between you?" I ask. Christian takes my chin between his fingers and lifts my head.

"No, and it won't. We always knew we would share you. You have nothing to worry about when it comes to our relationship with you. It will only ever cause issues if one of us was to put you in danger. Now get dressed," he declares before kissing me and walking out of the wardrobe. "Meet me on the landing in ten minutes," he calls, disappearing out of sight.

Chapter Twenty-One

JASMINE

Ten minutes later, I walk out of the bedroom and find Christian on the large landing adjusting his shirt cuff. He looks up at me and stares for a moment before stepping forward, wrapping an arm around my waist and pulling me against him.

"You're so fucking gorgeous," he growls before his lips crash into mine. He pulls away from me, takes my hand and leads me to the stairs before I've even caught my breath.

"Who washed my things from yesterday? My jewellery box and everything else are in my room, too. Do you have a housekeeper?" I ask only just managing to keep up with Christian.

"Mrs Brown is the best housekeeper we could ask for. She's efficient and quick at her job. If you need anything done, just ask; she will happily help," he explains as we get to the bottom of the stairs and head toward the sitting room.

"How haven't I seen her yet? Jason said there's security as well?" I ask as I look around to see if I can spot anyone else before freezing and pulling Christian to a halt. "Have you got cameras everywhere?" I demand.

"Yes."

"So, security could see us on your desk and in my room!" I ask in a panic. Christian steps forward and cups my face.

"They know what would happen to them if any of us found out they were watching anything like that. They have been given instructions to shut off any camera at the slightest hint of sexual activity."

"But they can watch me when I sleep?"

Christian shakes his head. "The only time that camera is ever on is if the four of us are out and you're completely alone in this building. *If* they saw that you were undressing, they would turn them off to give you privacy."

"And if they didn't and watched me?" I demand.

"Then I would kill them," Christian says calmly before turning around and walking towards the sitting room again, with me trying to keep up beside him.

"How haven't I seen anyone?" I ask, looking around again.

"Because we only hire the best. I will introduce you to everyone in a couple of hours when we call a staff meeting," Christian explains before opening the door to the sitting room. Inside, the guys are together on the couches with cards in their hands.

"It's about time you two turned up; Maximus is wiping me out here," Sean moans, not looking up from his cards. Maximus winks at me.

"What do you reckon, Shorty, we take my winnings and go to get pizza?"

"Pizza sounds amazing," I sigh. I haven't eaten since some toast this morning.

"That will have to wait; there are things that need to be sorted first. There's food over there under the plate covers, Jazzy," Jason says as he looks up at me and nods towards the table at the side of the room. I let go of Christian's hand and quickly grab the plate. It's warm, and when I lift off the cover, I see my favourite chicken and roasted vegetable salad. My mouth starts watering as soon as the aroma hits my nose, causing me to moan aloud. I turn just in time to see Maximus win another round as Jason and Sean throw their cards on the table.

I pick up the plate and the cutlery next to it before heading over to the couches where everyone is sitting. I go to sit down in the empty seat, but Maximus grabs my hips and pulls me onto his lap.

"My food!" I yell, holding my plate up. Luckily, Sean's next to us and grabs it before I lose its contents. I quickly thank him before taking it back once I'm comfortable.

"Just making sure Christian doesn't try keeping you to himself any longer," Maximus says with a smile before pressing a quick kiss to my lips. I roll my eyes before taking a fork full of food and shoving it in my mouth. I moan as all the flavours explode on my tongue.

"Good?"

I glance over at Jason and nod with a mouth full of food. I quickly look over at Christian and point to my mouth as I chew. Jason and Sean laugh out loud as Christian rolls his eyes.

"Yes, you are fine not to speak when your mouth is full," he says, smiling.

"I can think of other things to fill your mouth with," Maximus whispers into my ear. I look at him wide-eyed as I force myself to swallow.

"Don't say things like that when I'm eating; I nearly

died!" I cough, smacking Maximus's chest. He laughs as he reaches down and steals a piece of my chicken. "Hey!" I protest, moving my plate out of his reach.

"That's amazing, just one more piece," Maximus reaches over to take more of my food, but I move it out of the way.

"Daddy!" I moan, looking at Christian, who's shaking his head in dismay.

"Maximus, pack it in; Jasmine needs to eat," Christian warns his brother. I turn to Maximus and stick my tongue out at him. "Jasmine, behave and eat your food."

I turn to Christian and smile sweetly before shoving a fork full of food into my mouth.

"Now Jazzy's eating. Can we discuss everything that's happened before we get side-tracked by her pussy, again," Jason looks up at me and winks as I stare at him open-mouthed.

"I think we need to discuss what will be happening from now on," Christian explains as he sits back in his seat with a glass of whiskey in his hand before turning to look at the twins and me.

"Have either of you heard from our father since yester-day?" he asks. The twins both shake their heads. "Good, we have cut him off, so expect him to try and weasel his way in through you guys," Christian explains.

"So, he did know the whole situation?" Sean asks as I feel Maximus tense underneath me.

"Yes, he's been pocketing the money he should have been paying the school, and he's been ignoring the fact that Jasmine is no longer living in the house. Don't get me started on him charging her rent; that will be returned. Jason and I agreed that he would no longer get anything from us. If you guys want to give him anything, then that's up to you, but personally, Jason and I are done."

"I'm happy to ignore the prick. He's never done anything for us anyway," Sean answers before looking at Maximus, who nods.

"He only ever gets in touch when he wants something. I'm sure he will try soon enough," Maximus adds.

"That's decided then; Tommy gets nothing from any of us anymore," Christian confirms, and the three other brothers agree. Leaving me stunned.

"Just like that? You're going to cut him off because of me?" I ask, looking at Christian. I feel Maximus's hand on my back, but I'm focused on his older brother.

"Tommy has been a pain in our sides for a long time, sweetheart. He treated our mother like trash and didn't even wait for her body to be cold in her grave before running off with someone else. Carol wasn't the first person he was with after Mum passed. Everything he has is because of us," Christian says calmly.

"We have only kept him around as we wanted to be sure you were looked after," Jason says from his seat. I turn and look at him, frowning.

"I thought he was the one who started your company? He told me he paid for your first gym?"

Sean laughs next to me. "He paid for a few boxing lessons for Christian, that's it. After Christian's first fight, he knew he could make money off of him, so he purchased the first property with the winnings. Everything that man has ever paid for has been from money that we earned. If it'd been left to him, he would be living in a gutter somewhere or dead from the number of people he owes money to."

"But Mum and him were never home; they travelled all

the time. If he has no money, how did he pay for that?" I ask.

"Us. It's always been us," Maximus states behind me.

"What an arsehole," I sigh as I lean into his chest.

"Language, baby girl," Christian warns from the other sofa. I turn to him, frowning.

"You swear, why can't I?"

"Because it sounds wrong coming out of that sweet mouth," he replies with arched brows. I open my mouth to reply but quickly think better of it and shove some food into it instead. "Wise choice, sweetheart," Christian chuckles before looking back to Jason.

"Speaking of the gyms, we need to tell Jasmine a little more about the *business* as she may have caught a glimpse of what we sometimes do yesterday."

"Why, what happened?" Jason asks as he stays leaning forward in his seat.

"There was a bit of an incident with Jasmine's landlord whilst I was talking to you on the phone." Christian turns to face me and gives me a soft smile. "Can you fill us in on what he did or said that scared you so much?"

"Do I have to? You dealt with him," I answer, but one look from Christian, and I know I have no choice. Maximus's hand starts rubbing up and down my side, as I put my fork down and focus on my food.

"He was mad about me moving out without giving him a month's notice or payment and then made a suggestion or two on how I could pay him," I answer, not looking at anyone as Maximus's hand stops moving.

"What did he suggest?" he growls as his hand tightens on my side.

"You're hurting me," I whisper, placing a hand over his, which quickly loosens.

"Sorry, but what did he suggest?" He asks, loosening his grip further.

"He said that people would pay a lot of money to sleep with me. Or we could come to our own arrangement if I didn't want to be shared," I reply quietly as I start pushing my food around on my plate. I quickly place it on the table in front of me and risk looking up at the guys. All four are staring at me, looking like they are ready to hunt down Sam and kill him.

"I hope he isn't still breathing, Christian," Sean growls, not taking his eyes off me.

"He is, but not for long," he replies.

"You cut the guy's face with a knife; isn't that enough?" I ask.

"I should have gutted him for speaking to you like that," Christian growls before getting up and walking over to the small bar.

"Can I have a drink, please?" I ask as he pours himself a big measure of whatever he's drinking.

"Not until you finish your food."

"I wasn't asking for your permission," I snap. That gets Christian's attention as he turns around and stares at me.

"Good, because I wasn't giving it. You have hardly eaten all day, if not for weeks, and I won't allow you to drink hard alcohol on an empty stomach. Finish your chicken and veg, and we will discuss it then."

"But I'm thirsty," I argue. I watch Christian reach into the tiny fridge under the bar and pull out a bottle.

"Sean," he calls as he throws it. Sean catches it with ease and hands it over to me.

"I don't want water," I sulk.

"It's that or nothing until you have finished your dinner.

Keep arguing with me, baby girl, and we will be discussing punishments quicker than planned."

I turn and stare at Jason, who is holding his hands up.

"Don't look at me; I agree with him. I saw the state of your fridge and cupboards. You can't tell me you have been eating properly."

I turn to Sean and Maximus, but neither of them argues.

I pick my plate back up and force a fork full of food into my mouth before glaring at Christian.

"Good girl," he says with a smile which I feel deep in my gut and lower. Damn my body for wanting to please him.

"As I started to explain to you before we got a little carried away on the desk yesterday," Christian starts with a smile as he walks back to his seat. "I would gut anyone who disrespects you. As I'm sure you have figured out, there's a lot of things you don't know about what we do and how we became so rich. As you saw by your landlord's reaction to seeing me, the O'Reilly name is something that is feared and not just in the ring." Christian sits forward and leans his elbows on his knees, holding his glass between his two hands. I can tell there's a real chance I'm not going to like what I hear.

"We have built what we have from the ground up. There were people that our father was in trouble with before we were rich, and we had to do things to pay off his debts. Over time we have gained power and taken over the businesses we once worked for.

"Yes, a lot of what we do is illegal; we have also had to kill and hurt people to get to where we are. None of us will apologise for that. Especially when who we are could keep you safe."

"What do you do?" I ask. Not looking anywhere but at Christian.

"We deal in many things, firearms, illegal fights, loaning out large sums of cash but there are certain things we won't touch. Women and children are a no-go for us; if we get wind of sex trafficking or paedophile rings, we end them. That doesn't make us saints, though. We've killed people for crossing us, we have killed by request, and we all would kill for you."

"What about drugs?" I ask.

"We only deal in drugs at our underground fights. We do that as a way of making sure only clean stuff is used, and we can't be held accountable for anyone dying from a dirty batch on our premises," Jason explains as he sits forward, looking at me.

"Do you fix fights?" I ask as I look at the twins smiling at me.

"Do you think we need to fix the fights to win? I'm wounded, princess," Sean says, placing a hand over his chest.

"Why are you telling me all of this now?" I ask. Christian lets out a deep sigh as he sits up a bit.

"Because now you are here, and we're going to be open about how much you mean to us, you could be exposed to that side of our lives."

"Could it put me in danger?" I ask nervously.

"In theory, yes, but we will never allow any harm to come to you," Maximus says as he runs a hand down my back. I place my empty plate on the table and curl up on his lap. Maximus wraps his arms around my shoulders and holds me tight.

"What are you thinking, sweetheart?" Christian asks as Maximus runs a hand over my head.

"It's a lot to take in," I admit.

"I know, but I can promise we will always do everything in our power to make sure you are safe and nothing that we do interferes with you," he says, watching me. I take a deep breath and nod.

"I know," I add quickly.

"That being said, there are a few things you will need to know and do if the situation ever calls for it," Christian says as he continues to watch me. I feel my body tighten as I shake a little.

"Can this not wait, Christian? It's been a mad couple of days for her. She must be exhausted and scared. I can feel her shaking," Maximus says as he runs a hand over my head again before planting a kiss on it. Christian shakes his head.

"When I threatened your landlord yesterday, I announced you as ours, and the word will be out already, which could make you a target."

"So, what do I need to do?" I ask, but I'm not sure if I'm processing everything as my mind is in overdrive. Christian gives me a reassuring smile before starting.

"Until we get you your own car, one of us will drive you around. If none of us is available, you will have a member of our security team drive you and wait for you," Christian says before taking a sip of his drink.

"That doesn't seem too bad," I admit.

"You will also always have someone close by. Terry, our head of security has already designated someone to you."

"I can't have a babysitter!" I protest as I sit up from Maximus's chest.

"You will, and watch your tone," Christian warns.

"I'll be the laughingstock of the school!"

"They will be discreet; no one will know they are there or why," Jason says from his seat.

"But I will!" I argue. I look back at Christian. "Please, I will do anything you say, but I already stand out at school; don't make it worse for me. Please, Daddy." I throw in a little extra pleading with the 'daddy' in the hope it works. I watch as Christian looks from me to Jason, who shrugs.

"Speak to Terry and see what he suggests; I trust his judgement."

"Wasn't he meant to have eyes on her, and they failed to notice she was living rough!" Maximus says as he looks at Jason. Jason shakes his head.

"Tommy had cancelled her security and given them other assignments. He told them to tell Terry they were still checking on her."

"What? I had personal security?" I ask, and all four guys nod.

"See, you didn't know then, so now won't be any different," Sean says, offering me a small smile. I climb off Maximus's lap and start pacing around the room. I can't sit still whilst my mind is in overdrive like this. I wrap my arms around myself, needing some kind of comfort.

"You okay, Jazzy?"

I shake my head and quickly mumble a "no" before Christian can give me hell.

"What are you thinking, sweetheart?" I hear Christian ask. I hold up a finger as I need a moment to process.

"Let me get this straight: you guys have been paying for the dance school for the last three years. You've had security follow me until four months ago, and you own the house I thought I was renting from your dad? You are also some kind of what? Mafia Dons who have hurt and killed people? What else don't I know?" I ask as I turn and look around and look at the guys who are watching me.

"That's everything, I promise," Christian whispers as he

stands up and looks at me with those warm eyes which usually calm me. But not right now. So much has happened and changed in such a short space of time, but it's all becoming too much.

"This is a lot. I need some air," I whisper as I go to walk past Christian, who steps in my way.

"I know it is, but I know you can handle it. You are stronger than you give yourself credit for, sweetheart," Christian says as he cups my face. I look into his eyes as I feel mine starting to fill.

"I just need a minute," I whisper before heading out of the room.

Chapter Twenty-Two

JASMINE

I walk out of the room and realise I have no idea where to go. I need to be out in the open to clear my confused and overwhelmed mind. Bonus points if there's room for me to move.

Ever since I put on my first leotard all I've ever wanted to do is dance. It helps me clear my mind and focus.

My grandmother was the first person to take me to a dance class, and my grandparents have funded my ballet for as long as I can remember. It's one of the reasons my mother has resented me so much. She always said her parents loved me more than they ever loved her, as they never gave her anything. In truth, she took and took until they had no choice but to stop, as it was funding her substance and shopping addiction.

It heightened my mother's hatred for me when my grandparents died in a freak accident and left everything to me. They wanted to ensure I could fund my ballet until I was able to do it myself. My mother made my life hell, and I ended up giving her a lot of the money. Which in turn meant I'd struggled to pay for the dance school and lessons.

I was so happy when Tommy said he would happily fund it as long as I paid for my accommodation. He said he had the perfect property for me and would rent it to me for a reasonable price. I thought he was trying to help me stand on my own two feet, but I guess I was wrong.

I enter the kitchen and stop when I see a lady with short black hair standing at the breakfast counter chopping vegetables. She looks up and gives me a warm smile.

"Hi, you must be Miss Connors," she says, wiping her hands on her apron and offering me one. "I'm Mrs Brown, the housekeeper."

I walk towards her and shake her hand.

"Hi, it's a pleasure to meet you," I reply nervously before taking my hand back.

"Oh, the pleasure is all mine! It's so nice to finally meet you, I have heard so much about you from the O'Reillys," she continues as she goes back to the stove and starts stirring whatever is in the pot.

"They've talked about me?" I ask, wondering if that will ever stop shocking me.

Mrs Brown looks at me and rolls her eyes, the smile still plastered on her face.

"Only every single day. I'm glad you have finally joined them; it will be nice having another female around the place." She turns to face the other counter where I can see some pecan plates on a cooling rack. "It's beef stew and dumplings for dinner. I hear it's one of your favourites," she calls over her shoulder as she places a pastry on a paper napkin before turning around and holding it out to me. "I also hear these are your favourites; please let me know what you think."

174

I take the pastry from her and lift it to my mouth. As soon as I take a bite, my eyes close, and I'm sucked into food heaven.

"Mmmm, this is amazing," I open my eyes and look back at Mrs Brown, who's grinning widely.

"I'm so glad you like them." she turns around and grabs a pad of paper from the side. "Now I know you don't like mushrooms, liver, kidneys, kidney beans or cauliflower. Is there anything else I should avoid?"

I stare at her wide-eyed and shake my head slowly.

"How did you know?"

Mrs Brown laughs as she puts down the notebook. "The O'Reilly boys have made sure to let me know all your likes and dislikes. But please let me know if there is anything you fancy, and I will happily make it for you." She claps her hands together and looks around. "Now, is there a reason you came in here? Would you like a coffee? Tea? Anything at all?" she looks so happy that for a moment I forget why I'm here.

"Oh, I was, umm, looking for a way to get outside for some fresh air to clear my head," I reply as I look around.

"Of course. Just through the door there, dear, and you'll be in the garden. There are some benches dotted around, which are always good to sit on and reflect."

I nod as I turn to walk towards the door, quickly stopping to look at Mrs Brown.

"Thank you for the pastry, it was lovely."

She looks at me with her bright green eyes, and I can't help but feel a little relaxed.

"You are more than welcome. Anything you need, anything at all, just come and find me. I will be here or in my annex behind the garage." With that, she turns and walks away before I can say anything else. I turn back to the door she pointed to and walk out with the half-eaten pastry in my hand.

Opening the door, I find myself on what looks like a driveway that leads to a second garage. I slowly walk out and look around.

The grounds are beautiful, and there are so many different flowers, trees, and hedges planted. The guys must have a gardener because I can't imagine them doing all this work themselves. They don't seem the gardening type. There again, they didn't seem like the killing type either, but I guess I was wrong.

I follow the path down into the garden as I finish the amazing pastry from Mrs Brown and find a clearing. I look around and can't see anyone. I'd half expected someone to follow me or to find one of the security team behind me. I guess if I haven't seen them already, then they aren't going to suddenly appear now.

I walk over to a bench and sit down before pulling off my trainers and socks. Placing my bare feet against the damp grass, I close my eyes and enjoy the feeling of the blades between my toes as I wiggle them. I pick out a routine and listen to the music in my mind. As the music plays, I stand up and slowly walk into the middle of the clearing as if walking onto the stage. I take the starting position and I start to dance.

Even on the grass, I perform as if on stage. With my eyes closed, I picture the bright lights, scenery, and other dancers. I know the routine like I know my own body, each move practised to perfection, following smoothly on to the next. It all flows perfectly. Even with the restriction of my tight jeans and my missing pointe shoes, I'm still able to perform the majority of it. I adjust the moves accordingly and, for a brief moment, attempt to forget the chaos that has become my life.

This is why I dance; I can pretend for a short while that the problems in my life no longer exist. It's just me and the music as I escape into the world I'm dancing in.

As I move, I ignore all thoughts of the guys and how we all came together upstairs. I pretend that they haven't been hiding things from me. Or that their father, who I thought cared, hasn't been ripping me off. That last point hurts more than I'm willing to admit. I trusted Tommy; I trusted that he had my mother's and my best interests at heart. I believed that he had accepted me into his family. But everything from the last few years has been a lie and I can't forget that.

I force that last thought from my mind and continue to dance. However, I can feel the stray stones under my feet and miss my pointe shoes. I force myself to try and continue, but I nearly fall as I attempt a jump, thanks to the restriction of my jeans stopping me, and I find myself huffing in defeat.

"I'm sure it would be easier on a harder floor."

I spin around to find Sean sitting on the bench, his legs stretched out in front of him, crossed at the ankle, and his hands resting beside him. I smile at the sight of him looking so relaxed and comfortable in jeans and a hoodie.

"I wasn't sure if any rooms in your mansion were big enough to practice," I tease, walking over. He stands and closes the distance between us. As soon as he's within reach, his fingers thread into the hair at the top of my neck, and his lips press against mine. I instantly melt into him as he wraps an arm around my waist and tugs me tighter against him. As his lips leave mine, he smiles down at me.

"You have no idea how great it is to be able to kiss you

freely at last," he whispers. He looks into my eyes whilst tucking a stray section of hair behind my ear.

"How did you know where I was?" I ask. Sean smiles and points towards the side of the house where security cameras are pointing towards me. "Of course, there's CCTV," I sigh.

"How are you doing?" Sean asks as I walk over to the bench and sit down before lifting my foot to dust the stray grass from it.

"I honestly don't know," I admit, looking around. "It's been a mad couple of days, to say the least," I sigh, pulling on my sock and trainer before cleaning my other foot.

"Do you need more space?" he asks, squatting in front of me. I shrug, pulling on my sock.

"I don't know what I need. You've given me a lot to work through."

He takes my trainer from my hand and slides it onto my foot.

"You know that we would never, *ever*, hurt you, don't you?"

I look into his brown eyes and nod slowly.

"I know," I reply honestly. There has never been a time that I thought the guys would hurt me. I always knew there was a part of them that would hurt anyone else who did, but I've always been safe with them.

Sean reaches out and takes my hands.

"If you weren't here and you needed to clear your head, where would you go? What would you do?" he asks gently.

"To the school, I always dance until I can start making sense of whatever's weighing on my mind," I reply as I look around us. "But I don't suppose going there's an option right now, is it?" I flutter my eyelashes at him playfully. Sean laughs as he stands up and looks around.

"Probably not, as Christian is sorting out security. Jason and Maximus have gone out and will be out for a while. But I have a good idea where you can practice." He holds out his hand; I take it and let him lead me back to the house.

"I thought Christian would already be dragging me into the meeting with security," I confess, looking at the flowers that we pass.

"He's put it off to give you time and for the others to get back."

"Where are they?"

Sean looks to the side for a moment before letting out a deep breath and looking at me.

"Maximus has struggled with the fact Tommy was taking your money; he's gone to confront him."

"And Jason has gone with him?" I ask in a panic. He stops and cups my face again.

"Jason has gone to make sure he doesn't go too far."

"Do you think Maximus is okay?" I ask as he steps back beside me, and we walk back into the house. Sean looks at me with an arched brow as he lets go of my hand and places his arm around my shoulder, tugging me against him.

"It's not Maximus you need to worry about. There's a real chance he will kill Tommy for taking money from you."

"I didn't mean to cause any problems," I whisper as guilt eats away at me. I always knew there was tension between the guys and their father; the last thing I wanted was to make matters worse. Sean leads me to a door by the stairs and opens it, revealing steps that go down.

"You've done nothing wrong, don't ever think that you have. Tommy saw a way to make money and took it. We're just angry that it has been going on for so long, and none of us have realised it. We should have."

As we get to the bottom of the stairs, I realise we're in a

large gym. There is every type of equipment you can think of here, from free weights to rowing machines, bikes, treadmills, and machines that work every type of muscle.

"You can come in here whenever you want. I'm not sure if you ever use the gym, but it's here if you want it," Sean explains as he leads me through. He points to a door at the far back wall. "There are punching bags, a ring and other sparring equipment in there. If you need anyone to train with, just say, and one of us will happily hold the pads for you," he says with a smile that widens as we reach another door. He stops at it and turns to face me.

"This room should be spacious enough for you to dance in," he announces as he opens it and allows me to step in first.

As soon as I walk into the room, he switches on the lights, and my jaw nearly hits the floor. I'm standing in a large room with mirrors on every wall from floor to ceiling. There's a long dance railing against one wall, which is the perfect height for me to hold to stretch, and the wooden floor is perfect for dancing on.

"There is a stereo in the cabinet in the corner there. The sound has been checked, and you can hear everything perfectly from every point in the room. We have been ensured that the room has everything you will need to practice, but if there is anything we missed, please don't hesitate to tell us, and we will get it for you." Sean says as I walk into the middle of the room and take in the perfection of everything.

"You all did this for me?" I ask, overcome with gratitude. Other than my grandparents, no one had ever done anything for me before the guys, but this leaves another spark in my heart to remind me how much they care.

"Of course. We all know how much you love to dance,

and we knew one day you would be here with us. We wanted to make sure that you had everything you could need available to you."

I turn to look at Sean as the excitement of the room becomes too much. I squeal as I run up, launching myself into his arms and wrapping my legs around his waist. He laughs as he holds me tight.

"Thank you, it's perfect," I squeal into his neck before lifting my head and kissing him.

"I'm glad you like it, princess," he chuckles as he cups my ass and kisses me again. "Anything you need, whether it's for your dancing, clothing, absolutely anything, you just need to ask, and we will sort it for you. It's not just Christian and Jason who want to be your daddies; it's all of us, and we want to look after you and give you everything you need."

I sit up in his arms and smile. "How will it work? Won't it get complicated and confusing if I call you all Daddy?"

Sean shakes his head as he smiles back at me.

"No, princess. We will work something out, and I'm sure you can find a way to distinguish between us all," he says before kissing me on the lips and squeezing my ass playfully as he places me back on my feet. "Now, why don't you go and get your shoes? You can practice until Christian needs you."

I don't say anything in reply I just rush for the door squealing excitedly heading for my room to get changed into my gear. Eager to get back to my own studio to dance.

Chapter Twenty-Three

JASMINE

I've been dancing for at least an hour. I don't know how many dances I've done, but each one has helped me to clear my mind, and I'm starting to feel a little better about everything.

Sean's right; no matter what the guys may do outside of this house and away from me, I know that they will never hurt me. Does it surprise me that there is more to their *business* than the gym, various clubs, and fighting skills?

No, not really.

I guess part of me always wondered how they made as much as they do. Tommy had hinted more than once that he could hurt me if I was to ever tell the guys about our arrangement, and I believed him, so I guess the rest makes sense, really.

I also believe that the four guys are only in this kind of business thanks to their father. I could just see him being the type to find himself in trouble. I push the thoughts of him and the guys' confession to the back of my mind. I don't want it to ruin the good mood I am now in. I'm so happy after dancing in my studio that I need to see Christian to thank him personally. I can't remember the last time I was this excited about anything.

I grab my towel and wipe my face and neck. Picking my cardigan off the floor, I turn everything off and head out, promising myself I'll be back shortly to finish the routine I'm working on.

Rushing through the gym and up the stairs, I pull on my cardigan and tie the wrap around my waist, heading to Christian's office. I'm sure that's where I'll find him.

I still can't believe I have my own space to practice. I couldn't wait to get to my room and pull on my pink leotard, tights and leg warmers. Now, as I rush up to the main part of the house, I realise I've left my pointe shoes on in my eagerness to see Christian, as well as Jason and Maximus, if they are back.

I reach the office and rush in without knocking with a smile on my face.

"I've been in my ..." I come to a stop when I see two guys I don't recognise with Christian. Christian is just shrugging his suit jacket on as he turns to look at me.

"Sorry, I didn't realise you had company," I apologise, quickly turning to leave, but Christian's voice calls out.

"Where do you think you are going? Baby, come here, please."

I turn and look at him, trying to read his mood, but as usual, his face is giving nothing away. I quickly walk to him and try not to look at the other guys in the room.

As soon as I reach him, Christian places a hooked finger under my chin, applying pressure until I'm looking at him.

"Never apologise for being in a room I'm in. I don't care

what I'm doing. If you want me, you can come and find me. You are always my priority, understood?"

I nod before quickly remembering his golden rule.

"Yes."

Christian looks at me with a cocked brow, "Yes, what?"

I look nervously at the guys in the room who are watching us.

"Who am I, baby girl?" I can hear the impatience in his voice.

"Daddy," I reply quietly, not risking looking at the guys again, as I'm sure this is highly amusing to them. Christian forces my head up higher as he leans down and kisses my lips.

"I don't care who is around us. I am your daddy, and you are my baby, and if anyone wants to pass comment, I'll kill them, understood?"

I swallow deeply as my toes curl in my shoes.

"Yes, Daddy. Sorry." I reply, forcing a smile.

"Good girl. Now, what did you come in here to tell me?" Christian asks as he starts doing his jacket up.

"Oh! I've been in my dance studio, and I love it. Thank you," I reply, showing him a more genuine smile. Christian looks me up and down, smiling before pulling me close against him.

"You are more than welcome, baby," he says before pressing a kiss to my lips. "I'm glad you're here," Christian starts before turning me around to look at the other people, face on. Christian nods towards the guy in the front. He has black hair in a military cut, short back and sides and looks like he could kill anyone with just a look, but when his eyes fall on me, his whole body and face soften.

"This is Terry, our head of security,"

Terry steps forward, holding out his hand. "It's a pleasure to finally meet you, Miss Connors; my daughter is a big fan."

"Oh, goodness. Don't think anyone has ever said they are a fan of mine before," I reply, blushing. I hear Christian clear his throat behind me. "You are biased, and don't count," I reply, quickly throwing a wink over my shoulder as he squeezes my hip playfully. "Does she dance?" I ask.

"Yes, ma'am. Day and night, she has auditions for the dance school next year."

"I hope she gets in. It's a fantastic school with the best teachers. I'd be happy to meet with her and give her some tips," I offer with a smile.

"She would love that, thank you," Terry replies, smiling. Suddenly, I remember a Terry being mentioned before.

"You aren't the same Terry who drank Tommy's whiskey with younger Christian, are you?" I ask eagerly. Terry bursts out laughing as I feel Christian pinch my hip again. "Ouch!" I spin around to look at him, only to find him frowning at me.

"Thanks for bringing that one up." I can't miss the playfulness in his eyes, which makes me laugh and puts me further at ease.

"Yes, the very same. I've been friends with the guys for many years," Terry answers with a smile.

"You will be seeing a lot of Terry from now on, Layton, as well," Christian says as he places a hand back on my hip and nods towards the guy behind Terry.

"He will be your personal security most of the time. Christian has said you are reluctant to have him with you when you are in the school, so one of us will always be in the car park. We'll give you a panic alarm, so if there's ever an issue, all you have to do is activate it, and we'll be able to track you instantly. The school has permitted us to be on-site and anywhere you are," Terry explains with a smile. I quickly nod and thank them.

"Do I know you?" I ask Layton, as his blonde hair and square face looks very familiar, but I can't place him. He steps forward with his hand out, and I shake quickly.

"Yes, miss, but I didn't think you would remember me," he answers, smiling.

"Layton was the bouncer who was looking out for you the night you got drunk, and the twins had to take you home," Christian answers behind me. I hide behind my hands as I remember him now.

"Oh god, I was nearly sick on your shoes. I'm so sorry!" I declare, looking at Layton, who laughs.

"It's fine, miss. To be honest, I should be thanking you. It was that night I was given the details for this job."

"Maximus was so impressed with the way he looked out for you; he near enough hired him on the spot. Layton has been training with Terry since knowing he would be your personal security," Christian adds as I feel his thumb running up and down my hip.

"At least something good came out of that night," I sigh, rolling my eyes.

"If either of them ever tells you to do something, you do it without question," Christian says as he looks at me.

"Yes, Daddy," I reply before smiling at him. "Thank you for listening to me," I add quickly.

"I'll always listen, but you need to remember that what I say and do is always for your protection. So, if I tell you something is happening, you listen until we have time to discuss it," I don't miss the warning in his tone, but I smile as I reply.

"Of course, Daddy."

Christian looks at me for a moment like he doesn't believe me, and to be honest, I'm not sure I believe myself. I know I don't always listen, but I do promise to try at least.

"I need to pop out for a bit and deal with a situation. But Sean's around somewhere. Make sure you get something to eat and rest up. You had a busy day, and I don't want you overdoing it," Christian says with that look that relights the fire between my legs.

"When will you be back?"

"I don't know, baby. I probably won't be here for dinner. But I'm sure you can find ways to keep yourself occupied and out of trouble whilst I'm gone," he says with a grin. I smile back before turning to leave.

"I'll be in my studio!"

"Umm, excuse me!" I hear the warning in Christian's voice and stop in my tracks before slowly turning back to face him.

"Yes, Daddy?" I ask sheepishly. Christian calls me over with one finger. As soon as I'm in front of him, he hooks my chin and lifts it so I'm looking up at him. He leans over and whispers against my lips.

"Never leave without giving your daddies a kiss first."

I grin as his lips press into mine, and his arm wraps around my waist, pulling me flush against him. As he breaks the kiss, he grins down at me. "Go and dance. I'll try to catch you before you go to bed," he says, letting me go and heading towards the door.

"It was good to meet you, ma'am. I'll come by tomorrow to give you your panic alarm and instruct you on how and when to use it," Terry says as he smiles at me before following Christian out of the door.

"Thank you, Terry. Maybe you can give me some more stories of Christian causing trouble," I call out.

"Baby girl!" I hear Christian growl out in warning, but I just giggle as they all walk out of view, leaving me alone in the office. I look around and smile to myself before heading back to my studio to dance a little more.

Chapter Twenty-Four

MAXIMUS

I stand over two guys tied to chairs in the middle of the ring we use for underground fights.

"Christian's here," Jason calls as he climbs through the ropes. One of the guys starts fighting against the restraints and trying to talk through the duct tape over his mouth. I move so I'm in his line of sight, and he fights harder.

"Carry on fuckface, and I'll be sure to break your jaw so you can't speak at all," I warn with my arms crossed over my bare chest. I'd removed my shirt before jumping these two fucks and bringing their sorry asses here.

"Is this them?"

I turn to see Christian walking to the ring.

"Yep," Jason confirms as he holds the ropes for Christian to enter. He comes to a stop in front of the guys and looks at me. I step forward and rip off the duct tape from their mouths, causing them to curse as it pulls at their facial hair.

"We were just following orders!" The blonde one, Wade, calls out.

"You weren't following *my* orders," Christian points out, and both guys go quiet. Christian walks closer. "When Terry hired you to watch over Miss Connors and do the odd guarding of my father, he warned you what would happen if you crossed him, or more importantly, us, did he not?"

"Yes, sir, but Mr O'Reilly said-"

Christian holds his hand up, and Wade stops talking instantly.

"To save confusion, refer to him as Tommy, and I know what he said. That your employment had changed, that he was now in charge of your assignments and to keep what he had you doing to yourself. Does that sound right?" Christian asks, and both men nod. Christian turns and looks at Jason, "You would think they'd double-check with their actual employer, wouldn't you?"

"Especially when they know who pays their wages," Jason adds. Both men look at each other before the bald guy, Henry, speaks.

"Terry told us that we had to do what Mr - I mean Tommy said!" Henry protests.

"Even if that meant lying to us?" Christian asks.

"Yes!" Henry and Wade agree. Christian nods as he turns his back to the guys and looks to the entrance of the makeshift arena. "Did you hear that, Terry?"

Terry walks into view followed by two of his other guards Layton and Calvin behind him.

"I sure did." Terry approaches the ring and climbs in. The other two stay outside but don't take their eyes off the guys tied up.

"Did you tell your men to lie for my father?" Christian asks. Terry shakes his head and stops right in front of the guys.

"I did not."

"You told us to do whatever Mr - Tommy said."

"And to report back to me. Not once did I suggest that you should lie to me or your employers," Terry answers as he stares at them. If I was those men, I would be shitting myself right now. Terry didn't get where he is by being calm.

Terry has worked for us for at least ten years, and I know Christian and Jason trust him implicitly. He was a childhood friend of theirs who joined the Marines but was injured whilst deployed. His friend Calvin was injured a little while later, and Terry asked my brothers to hire him, too. I personally hired Layton after seeing what he was like with Jasmine when she was intoxicated. I saw something in him I liked, and after hearing how much he had put into his training, I believe I had made the right choice.

"Please, sir, we were just doing what Tommy said. He told us he would hurt us if we didn't." I can see the pleading in Wade's eyes, and for a moment, I actually feel a little sorry for beating the crap out of him. I know how my father can be, and I know what it's like to be at the receiving end of his fists. But then I remember the way my Shorty looks, so frail from the weight loss and her bright spirit dimmed. No, they played a huge part in that and deserve everything that they get in return.

"Because of you, our woman was in danger daily, and we had no idea, purely because we trusted that you were reporting the truth," Christian growls as he walks up to Henry and leans over him. I can see the fear in the arse-holes' eyes as they both look at Christian and wait to see what their fate is going to be.

Christian is the eldest, many people believe he's the boss, and in a way he is. If he orders something to be done, we do it, no questions asked. We got to where we are because of the decisions and sacrifices he made for us. Not just Sean and me, but Jason too. If there is to be bloodshed, he does it when possible. He tried to protect us from that side of the business for as long as he could after being forced to take his first life at just fifteen years of age. It was to pay back some of our father's debts and ultimately the start of our now darker lives.

I watch the interaction between Christian and the two guys who were meant to keep our Jasmine safe and protected. They aren't going to see tomorrow. If he doesn't kill them, Terry will. There's no room for error in this life. People have your back, or they're against you. When people know as much as these guys know about us, the layout of our home, the security systems and whom we protect, they have to be handled properly.

"Please, Mr O'Reilly, sir, we swear we were just doing as we were told; it was just some girl." Christian shuts Wade up by grabbing him around the throat cutting off his air supply.

"Some girl? Would I pay you as much as I do to protect 'some girl'? No, I wouldn't. Jasmine Connors may not be an O'Reilly yet, but one day, she will stand at the top with the rest of us."

As quick as a flash, Christian retrieves his gun from the back of his trousers and pulls the trigger hitting Wade right between the eyes. Before Henry has even registered that his mate is dead, a bullet finds his head, too. Both slump in their chairs, blood dripping from their heads as Christian puts the gun back where he had it concealed.

"Let this be a warning to anyone who thinks Jasmine Connors shouldn't be protected at the same level as the four of us. You put her life in danger, or she gets hurt on your watch, your life is forfeited, understood?" Christian calls out as several of our guards stand around and look at the two dead men in the middle of the ring.

"Get these fuckers out of here and get this area cleaned!" Christian demands, looking at Terry and the guards, who all nod and step up to do their jobs. Christian looks at Jason and me.

"I think we have one more person to pay a visit to before we go home to our girl. Let's go and have a little *chat* with our father."

Chapter Twenty-Five

JASMINE

It's been a week since Jason and the guys saved me from the pathetic existence I was living. They've taken everything I hated about my life and started to make it right again. Honestly, they are the best thing to ever happen to me.

I thought things would be difficult with me being in a relationship with the four of them. That there would be an adjustment period where things would be complicated for a while, but in fact, it's been the complete opposite. Everything has fallen into place easily and feels so natural; like the rules we have set about sleeping arrangements. If my door is open, I'm happy for anyone to join me. But if the door is closed, I either want space or am already with someone, and we want time together. If I go to someone's room, whether sexual or just for a chat, the others give us space to enjoy our own company. So far, it's working out perfectly.

All four of the O'Reilly brothers have become my daddies. As Sean said I would, I found a way to distinguish between the four of them when they are together. Christian is just Daddy; I then have Daddy Jason, Daddy Sean and

Daddy Max. Maximus usually hates it when people shorten his name to Max. However, he agreed that Daddy Maximus is a mouth full, and because I'm his favourite person, he will allow me, and only me, to shorten it.

My Daddies have set a number of rules, the most important being that I have to greet them with a kiss every time I enter or leave a room. I also have to eat three meals a day and get to bed at a reasonable hour, and I am no longer allowed to work in the bar or clean at the school. They allow me to continue teaching the children classes as they know how much I enjoy them. I'm also no longer allowed to touch myself, which I didn't do a lot of anyway. I certainly don't need to now; I have four men who are more than happy to make me scream with pleasure whenever I want. I have never felt more cared for than I do now.

It's Saturday afternoon, and I'm enjoying some late summer warmth while sitting on a blanket in the garden. Maximus is training down in the gym, and the others are out and about doing God knows what. I popped down earlier to see him, and it was a sight I could have watched all day. The way the sweat ran down his back and chest was more of a turn-on than it should have been. I had to get out of there before I jumped into the ring myself and begged him to take me there and then against the ropes. Not that I think he would have refused me.

I stand up and stretch before picking up the blanket and my Kindle. The guys have promised to be home for dinner before they head off out to various locations. Saturday nights are always busy for them, apparently, and even though they offered to take me with them, I said no. I plan on having a bath and enjoying a couple of hours of rest before they come home. Tomorrow, we have planned a day out together followed by dinner, and I can't wait to just spend time with them.

I place my Kindle on the breakfast bar and fold up the blanket before putting it back in the cupboard where I found it. Hearing the door to the garage open, I spin around excitedly only to come face to face with my stepfather.

"Should have known you'd be here," he snarls, marching towards me.

"Hi Tommy," I reply nervously, taking a couple of steps back. "The guys are out at the moment, but Maximus is downstairs if you want me to get him for you," I offer, hoping he will let me leave quickly. Tommy may have never laid a finger on me before, but he has put me on edge, especially after threatening me once or twice about how much I tell the guys.

"So, it's true! You've gotten your nails into one of the lads, and that's why they cut me off!" he growls. He stops in front of me, and I realise I'm trapped.

"I had nothing to do with it," I protest, my voice shaking. Tommy glares at me, and I know there's going to be trouble.

"Don't give me that bullshit. You're just as much of a lying slut as your mother. What is it you see in them? The money? Power? I hope you enjoy it whilst it lasts because, from what I hear, everyone can't wait to get away from you!"

He steps closer again, and I go to move further away from him, but I'm backed up against a door that opens inward. Tommy's eyes gleam when he realises he has me cornered. He reaches up and grabs my face, gripping it hard, holding me in place. I want to push him away to get some distance between us, but I'm terrified of his reaction.

"This is what's going to happen. You're going to put everything right and get my lads to let me back in and for them to give me access to the money again. If you don't, I'm going to make it my mission to make your life a living hell. The guys won't want to know you by the time I'm done with you." I let out a whimper as he squeezes my face harder. I know I'm going to bruise.

"Get your fucking hands off her!"

Tommy lets go as Maximus grabs him and hauls him up against the wall before punching him as Layton and another security guard jump between me and the two O'Reillys.

"Jason isn't here to stop me from killing you this time!" Maximus growls at his father, who has his hands up defensively as his lip bleeds.

"It wasn't how it looked. Tell him, Jasmine," Tommy begs as he turns his head to look at me. "Tell him we were just talking."

"Shut the fuck up for once in your sorry-ass life, you piece of shit!" Maximus yells as he slams his father against the wall again.

"I just wanted to clear the air and -" Maximus cuts him off by slamming him back into the wall.

"And get back some of the money we are no longer paying you? Well, tough shit. Coming here and putting your hands on my girl was the biggest mistake you could ever make!" Maximus roars. Tommy looks between Maximus and me and smiles.

"You might think she cares, but trust me, son, she's just like her mother. Looking for a way to live a rich life without having to work for it. Trust your father; he knows how the Connors women work."

I feel sick. He really thinks I'm only here because of the

money. I have no doubt that's what drew my mum to Tommy, but that's not me.

"I don't want their money," I say quietly, unable to put any volume into my voice as I'm shaking so hard. Maximus looks over at me and sees me wiping a tear from my eye. I see the anger rising on his face as he turns back to his dad.

"You call yourself a father? Where the fuck have you been all our lives? If anyone is my father, it's Christian. He's the one who brought us up. Protected us when bastards you had ripped off came looking for payment. Everything we have is because of him, and you know it. You are just a worthless piece of shit."

As Maximus shouts at his father, I notice the security guard whisper something to Layton and rush out of the door that leads to the garage. Please let one of the others come back; they need to stop Maximus from killing his father. I go to step forward in the hope of getting him to calm down, but Layton stops me.

"Stay back," he orders as he holds an arm out in front of me.

"Maximus, I did everything for my boys; I'm trying to protect you now from her and the lies she's feeding you."

"Shut the fuck up!" Maximus roars as he punches Tommy again.

"Maximus, enough!"

We all turn to see Christian and Jason standing by the garage door.

"He fucking assaulted Jasmine!" Maximus yells.

"So, we hear. I will deal with him," Christian says in that calm but dangerous tone as Jason glares at his father, who's gone pale. "Get him in my car and stay there until I return," Christian orders Jason, who grabs their father and starts to haul him out of the kitchen. Tommy instantly starts to struggle against his son. Jason slams him face-first into a wall and holds his arms behind his back.

"Fucking keep fighting me, I dare you. I'm looking for a reason to end you," Jason growls. Tommy stares at me with pure hatred in his eyes, and I feel myself sinking back to get away from him.

"You fucking did this, you little bitch. You and your slut mother are nothing but trash," Tommy growls at me as Jason cuts him off by slamming him into the wall again.

"Maximus, get Jasmine out of here," Christian orders as Jason whispers something in Tommy's ear before pulling him away from the wall and towards the garage, where he starts fighting again.

Maximus walks up to me as Layton steps out of the way. He pulls me to his side and guides me out of the kitchen. As we get to the door, Christian is waiting for us.

"Did he hurt you?" he asks as he cups my cheek. I shake my head.

"Not really."

"The fact that he touched you is enough. I'm going to see to it he never touches you again." Christian promises before kissing me on the lips.

"Are you going to kill him?" I ask nervously. Christian shakes his head before looking up at Maximus.

"He is a low-life piece of shit, but he is still our father." Christian looks back at me and runs a hand over my head. "I won't have you scared in your own home; he will learn a lesson today," he whispers before standing tall. "Maximus, take her to the sitting room; Jason will be there in a minute."

Maximus guides me out of the kitchen as instructed.

"Come on, Shorty. Let's get you a strong drink."

Chapter Twenty-Six

JASMINE

Maximus guides me into the sitting room and sits me on a sofa before heading over to the mini bar. I'm shaking uncontrollably and blinking back the tears as my throat burns. I force myself to swallow whilst clenching my jaw, trying not to cry.

The way Tommy looked at me was like how my mother did the other day. Like I was the worst person in the world. Is that how the guys will come to see me in the end? Tommy's right; everyone does leave me; it's only a matter of time until the guys do too.

"Are you okay?" Jason demands as he rushes into the room and squats down in front of me, cupping my face. One look at his worried grey eyes and my last straw of strength snaps as I burst into tears.

"Oh, Jazzy," Jason coos, scooping me up and sitting on the sofa so I can curl up on his lap. I cling to his shirt as I cry into his chest. Jason runs a hand over my head and holds me tightly against him as he attempts to soothe me.

"I don't care if he is our father; I want the bastard to

pay," Maximus growls, passing a drink to Jason, who offers it to me.

"He's your blood," I whisper as I wipe my face before taking a sip. I shudder as the whiskey burns my throat and settles in my stomach helping me to relax a little in Jason's arms.

"He might be our blood, but he's never been a father," Jason replies as he hooks a finger under my chin and forces me to look at him. "Did he hurt you?"

I shake my head, but Jason gives me that look, and I know he doesn't believe me.

"A little, he only grabbed my face. I've had worse from my mother," I point out. Jason sighs, kissing my forehead.

"What did he say to you before I got there?" Maximus asks, sitting on the coffee table in front of me.

"Nothing."

"Shorty, tell us what he said!"

I sigh before repeating our short interaction. By the time I finish, both Jason and Maximus are furious.

"Don't let him get into your head," Jason warns. When I don't reply, he places a finger under my chin and forces me to look at him. "Do *not* let him get into your head. I don't care what others have done. We are never leaving you."

I nod as a single tear slides down my cheek. Jason leans down and kisses me. It starts as a light kiss on the lips, but as his grip on me tightens, I feel the kiss deepen. I realise how much I need him right now.

As always, he's putting me back together just when I think I'm about to break. He pulls away from me smiling with that twinkle in his eye I've noticed he gets right before things become heated.

"I think you need your daddies to show you how much they care," he whispers before looking up at Maximus. I turn my head to find him watching me with a grin on his face.

"I think she does." Maximus stands up as Jason removes me from his lap and places me on the sofa. Maximus sits so I'm between the two of them and kisses me as Jason's hand lands on my chest. As he pulls my top and bra down, exposing my breast, he takes my nipple between his teeth causing me to moan into Maximus's mouth, who pulls away from me, grinning.

"I could cum to that sound alone. Let me hear it again."

He reaches between my legs and slides his hands up my skirt and cups my aching pussy. I moan as his grip tightens, and my damp thong rubs against me in the right spot.

"So wet and ready for us, gorgeous," Maximus groans as his fingers slide under my underwear and through my swollen and waiting lips whilst Jason fondles one breast and has the other in his mouth. Jason lets go of one of my breasts and slides his hand down until his finger finds my clit at the same time as Maximus slides a finger into me.

"Yes," I moan as they start working me together towards an orgasm.

"Take her underwear off, Maximus. Our girl needs to cum," Jason growls before kissing me.

"Lift your hips, Shorty."

I do as I'm told, and Maximus makes short work of taking my thong off. Jason leans away, smiling.

"Turn around and hold on to the back of the sofa, Jazzy. Put that arse up in the air." I do as I'm told, and Jason moves, so he sits on the floor with his head between my legs. "I'm going to lick this delicious pussy whilst your daddy Max fucks it until you cum, and then we are going to swap places," Jason says as my pussy floods.

"Please, Daddy, I need to cum," I beg as I feel Jason's breath tickle over me.

"Let's give her what she wants, Maximus," Jason groans before I feel his tongue against my clit and a cock slide into me.

"Whatever daddy's girl wants, she'll get," Maximus growls as he moves within me. After a week of having sex at least once a day, it's no longer painful, just pure bliss. I groan as both start working me towards my orgasm and I know it isn't going to take long, not with Jason's tongue working my clit as Maximus fucks me from behind. He can get so much deeper in this position.

"Fuck, Shorty, you look so perfect bent over like this," Maximus growls as I feel him squeeze my ass cheeks. I feel a little pressure against my back passage and let out a loud, deep moan. Causing Maximus to chuckle.

"Shorty, I think we're going to find you are a kinky little minx," he growls before applying more pressure and letting his finger slide in a little.

"Daddy, don't stop!" I call as Maximus continues to move his finger in and out of my ass whilst fucking my pussy. Maximus continues to use both entrances as Jason licks me and my whole body comes alight.

"Shorty, you keep clamping my fucking cock like that, and I'm not going to last much longer!" Maximus growls through gritted teeth, but he doesn't stop stimulating me.

"Daddy, I can't hold off," I cry out as Jason sucks my swollen clit into his mouth, and I fall apart. "Yes!" I scream as I orgasm so hard my whole body starts to shake.

"Fuck," Maximus curses thrusting into me a few more times before filling me with his cum. His grip on my hips is so tight I know he will leave bruises, and I don't care.

Neither of us can move for a moment as we catch our breath.

"What did you do? I could feel her whole body vibrating," Jason asks as he comes out from between my legs, and Maximus slides out of me before leaning around to kiss me.

"Your sweet and innocent Jazzy likes anal play," Maximus chuckles kissing me again as Jason growls.

"Fuck, you just get better and better, angel," Jason curses as I feel his finger rubbing against my clit from behind. "Think you can take more?"

I look back behind me and smile. "Please, Daddy, I need you in me."

"Fuck, you are so hot," Jason groans, freeing his solid cock from his trousers and making short work of slamming into me.

Jason wraps my ponytail around his hand and pulls me so I'm on my knees leaning my back against his chest. Letting go of my hair he wraps his hand around my neck before squeezing, but not enough to cut off my air supply. I moan as he starts moving within me and keeps hold of my throat.

"Fuck, that looks so hot," Maximus moans in front of me as he reaches out and starts rubbing my clit.

"Whose are you, Jazzy?" Jason growls as he pounds into me hard.

"Yours, all of yours," I call as I take everything he and Maximus give me. I love it when they get rough. "Tighter, Daddy!" I call as I get lost in the moment. Jason's grip on my throat tightens, and I let out a deep moan, which causes Jason to pound into me harder. He's holding so tight I can only get a small amount of air into my lungs, but I don't panic as he restricts my breathing. Instead, I feel my pussy gushing from the excitement. I trust him implicitly, and he won't let any harm come to me.

"Fuck you are so perfect, so tight," he growls through gritted teeth. "One of these days, I'm going to tie you up and fuck you until you beg me to stop," Jason moans in my ear. "I'm going to find out every kink you have and give you everything you need," he adds before releasing his hold on my neck and pushing me so I'm back leaning forward.

Maximus is sitting in front of me, so I place my hands on his shoulders as he kisses me and reaches up to play with my breasts. I feel pressure against my back entrance again before Jason spits on it and pushes a finger into me. I groan with pleasure as he picks up speed with his cock and his finger.

"Now I know you like this; I'm going to claim it first. Christian might have taken your virginity, but I'm claiming your ass cherry," he growls as I feel him stretching me with a second finger.

"Take it, Daddy! Please!" I cry as I rush towards a second orgasm. Before I cum Jason pulls out of my pussy, and I feel his cock pressing against my puckered entrance.

"Stay still; let Daddy take care of you," Jason whispers as Maximus starts playing with my clit again whilst kissing me. Jason adds more pressure to my back passage, and I feel the head of his hard cock pop inside of me slowly, followed by more and more of it. Stretching me, making me his.

"Daddy," I call out as the pleasure becomes a discomfort.

"Shush, angel. Daddy's got you," he whispers as he works in and out of me, going a little deeper each time.

"Daddy, please," I beg as I close my eyes and realise the pain is adding to the pleasure.

"Fuck I thought your pussy was tight, but this is something else." Jason curses.

"I'm coming," I yell as my whole body tenses, and I shake violently as the orgasm crashes through me. Jason keeps pumping into me as I ride out the orgasm and quickly head towards another. Maximus pushes his fingers into my gushing pussy, and I hear Jason and Maximus both moan at the same time as me. I can tell Jason is getting close as his breathing picks up along with his thrusts, he's getting rougher which is pushing me closer to yet another orgasm.

"Fuck angel!" Jason curses as I cry out and feel him filling me with his warm release. I lean my head against Maximus's shoulder to keep me up as my whole body relaxes to the point I become floppy. As soon as Jason pulls out of me Maximus helps me onto his lap and holds me tight.

"That was fucking hot," he chuckles into my hair, as my eyes start to close, suddenly feeling exhausted but content.

"Come on, angel. Let's get you showered and into bed where you can sleep for a bit," Jason whispers as he presses a kiss to my lips. All I can manage to do is nod before Maximus stands with me in his arms and heads to my bathroom.

Chapter Twenty-Seven

JASMINE

"See you later, stompy!"

I rush past Danielle and her bitches and head to where I know Layton's parked, clinging to my bag for some sort of comfort. I keep my head down and pretend I don't hear them laughing at me.

I rush Around the corner and head straight to the car, throwing the back door open before Layton has time to open his own.

"Hey, everything okay?"

I fasten my seatbelt and look out of the passenger window so he can't see I'm holding back tears.

"I'm ready to go home," I reply quietly, refusing to look at him. I hear him shuffling in his seat before a hand lands on my arm.

"What's happened?" he demands. I shake my head and continue to look out of the window. "Either you tell me what happened, or I go in there and start asking questions. It's up to you."

The last thing I need is for him to make a scene.

Because Layton's window is down, I can hear Danielle's voice getting louder, and the last thing I want is to see her again.

"Can we just go? Please?" I ask quietly as I slide down in my seat, hoping to hide from her. Layton looks from me to where Danielle and her little gang are walking around the corner. I see the realisation on his face as he reaches down to unfasten his belt, but I grab his hand to stop him.

"Please, I just want to go home."

Layton looks at me and nods before pulling away from the school, and I finally relax a little.

As soon as we get home, I jump out of the car and head into the house before Layton can stop me. I know he'll be straight on the phone with Christian or Jason to let them know something's wrong, but I'm not ready for them to demand that I speak to them. I turn my phone off on the way to my dance room and push it into the bottom of my bag as I pull out my pointe shoes. I sit down and put them on, instantly feeling how damaged and worn they are, but if I can just get them to last a little longer, just until I can get some new ones, whenever that will be.

I get up, walk over to the music player, and select the music for the dance that I need to rehearse. I get into position as the music begins, and I start to dance.

I can feel every movement on my painful toes; everything hurts. I try to ignore it, but the more I move the more painful my toes become. I go into a toe lift and stumble as I curse in pain.

"I wouldn't let Christian hear you using language like that."

I turn around and find Sean leaning against the back wall. I slump down to the floor and pull off my shoes before massaging my toes as I blink back the tears that have been threatening to fall all day.

"Layton says something, or someone has upset you. What's up, princess?" I hear Sean ask as I start pulling off my other shoe.

"Nothing," I reply quietly, as I feel him getting closer. He squats down in front of me and takes my chin in his fingers before forcing me to look at him.

"Don't lie to me. Either you tell me what's wrong, or I call in the big guns, and I don't think you are in the mood to deal with Christian right now."

I shake my head as I feel the tears fill my eyes.

"Has it got anything to do with the fact your feet are obviously hurting you?" he asks.

"My shoes are dead, and I can't afford new ones." I blurt out as I throw my shoe onto the floor. "The bitch Danielle spent the whole morning taking the piss because I have nothing," I sob as Sean pulls me into his arms.

"When are you going to learn? You have money now and can buy anything you need," he sighs, running a hand over my head.

"You guys have money, not me. I can't just spend it," I protest as I pull away from him, wiping at my face feeling frustrated with myself for crying.

"Get some shoes on and meet me by the car. If you are not there in five minutes, I will find you and drag you out of the house." He doesn't wait for me to answer before standing up and walking out of the room, shouting, "Move it, princess!" as he goes.

I climb to my feet and walk over to my bag to grab my slip-on shoes. I slide them onto my sore feet and quickly turn everything off before leaving, knowing that Sean *will* drag me out of here if I try to hide from him.

I reach the car in time to see him ending a call on his phone. He turns around and looks at me, smiling.

"Do I need to tell Layton I'm leaving?" I ask, looking around.

"Already done. Now come on, I want ice cream, but we have to make a stop first." He holds the passenger door of his Jag for me. I quickly climb in and put my seatbelt on as Sean climbs in behind the wheel.

"Why aren't you working?" I ask as he presses the button to open the garage door.

"Because I couldn't be arsed today. I trained all morning and fancied skiving the afternoon," he explains before looking at me, grinning. "Bonus of being a rich bastard: I get to take time off and spend it with my favourite person whenever I feel like it," he throws in a wink for good measure as I roll my eyes. Sean pulls out of the garage and heads to the gates; they open automatically, and he drives through.

Sean puts his stereo on, and Nickelback fills the silence. Maximus and Sean always put on my favourite band whenever I'm in the car with them, even though they say they can't stand them. Sean doesn't say anything when I turn it up a little louder. He reaches over and takes my hand, giving me time to clear my head and letting me know that he's there if I need him. I'm so glad it was Sean who found me first today.

"Did Layton call you before?" I ask, turning to look at him.

"He knew I was home and came to find me," he answers as he stops at a traffic light. He turns to look at me.

"He was worried. Apparently, you looked ready to cry when you came out of the school."

I turn and look back out the window, as I blink back tears again. Sean squeezes my hand and carries on driving, not saying anything, just letting me process.

We come to a stop outside of the shop where I buy my dance clothes and shoes. I don't know why I didn't see this coming. I should have known he would bring me here. I turn and frown at him only to receive one raised eyebrow in return.

"Don't look like that. I'm not buying your shoes; you are."

"With what money?" I sigh, shaking my head.

"With *your* money."

"I don't have any," I point out.

"Yes, you do. You have twelve thousand pounds and an unlimited overdraft," Sean answers as he holds out my bank card. When I don't make a move to take it, he sighs and forces it into my hand.

"For the eighteen months you were living in the house, you paid six hundred pounds each month to Tommy. That money has been returned to you *by him*."

"You mean you guys made him pay it back." I point out.

"Of course we did! He stole that from you, princess! He had no right to take any money from you. We gave him plenty to live off. He is a selfish prick, and you didn't deserve to be treated like that!" Sean explodes. I lean back in my chair a little while I watch him run his hand over his face and take a deep breath.

"You are one of the sweetest people I have ever met. I hate that others see the kindness in you and use it to their advantage."

I look down at the card in my hand and blink back against the tears. I know Sean's right. If this is the money I paid Tommy then by rights, it's mine. I know, in reality, it's just his way of getting me to spend their money and to stop distinguishing between theirs and mine. I look back up at him and manage to force a small smile.

"Thank you, Daddy," I whisper.

"Anything for you, princess, you know that!" Sean replies before climbing out of the car and walking around to my side as I open the door. I'm just about to stand when he holds his hand out for me.

As soon as my hand's in his, he tugs me to my feet and into his arms. He slams the door closed before trapping me between the car and his broad, muscular body.

"Just so you know, unlike Jason and Christian, I won't force you to call me Daddy in public. You can introduce me as whatever you want, but I will not hide that you are mine, and no man, other than my brothers, can touch or look at you," he warns before moving so his lips are by my ear. "I will always be your daddy, and your needs are all I care about," he whispers before wrapping an arm around my waist and pulling me against him, causing me to gasp as I feel how hard he is. "Right now, I think you have needs you would rather I didn't take care of in public, so let's get you some new dance bits then Daddy is taking you home to see to them," he whispers grinding against me, making me moan aloud. Sean stands tall, grinning at me before giving me a wink and pulling me away from the car.

"You need to stop saying things like that to me in public," I chuckle as I fan my flushed cheeks. Sean glances at me, smiling.

"Why? You are so cute when you are flushed and aroused," he grins, before letting go of my hand and

Four Stepbrothers & I

throwing his arm around my shoulders, bringing me closer to him. "If it's any consolation, I'm now sporting a semi which is getting harder every time I think of you on your hands and knees in front of me as I fuck that tight pussy of yours."

"Stop!" I laugh, pushing him away as we both laugh aloud. I can't stop myself from glancing down and seeing a definite bulge in his tight jeans, which he is making no sign of hiding.

Sean holds the door of the shop open whilst waving me in. "Let's get these shoes, and then I'm taking you home," he growls in my ear, making me giggle as we walk hand in hand. I buy myself new shoes.

Chapter Twenty-Eight

SEAN

"I'm so sorry about this, princess. I promise I'll be as quick as possible." I open the passenger door and take Jasmine's hand, helping her out of the car.

"It's fine; I'm looking forward to having a look around one of your gyms."

I pull her into my arms and press a kiss to her lips. The last thing I want to do right now is work, but I received a call that someone has been tampering with the machines in one of our gyms, and I need to come and assess the damage.

"Do you want me to call Layton to pick you up?" I offer for the umpteenth time since I received the call. Jasmine shakes her head as she places a hand on my chest. Her smile lights up her whole face.

When she looks at me like I'm the only man in the world, it makes me want to drop to my knees and worship her like the goddess that she is. My brothers and I never back down from anyone, but one look from this woman in front of me is enough to bring us to our knees.

Not that we would ever admit that to her. Our little brat would be trying to get away with all kinds.

"No, for the last time, I'm happy to be here."

I press my lips to hers again before leading her with me into the building.

Inside, I'm instantly greeted by the manager, Keith, who looks flustered.

"Mr O'Reilly, I'm so sorry to call you out. But we've had to close half the gym down due to the damage and..."

I hold up my free hand to stop him before he gives himself a heart attack.

"Please, don't apologise; you did the right thing by calling. Why don't you show me where the damaged equipment is, and I'll see if I can fix it or if I need to order replacements."

The manager nods and quickly guides us to where we need to be. I glance at Jasmine and see her looking around. Her face lit up as she takes in all that's before her.

"I hope it's the gym itself you are gawking at and not the guys using it."

Jasmine looks at me with those big blue eyes, attempting to look as innocent as possible.

"What guys?" she asks, fluttering her eyelashes. I can't stop the grin that spreads across my face.

"Right answer, princess," I chuckle, pulling her closer to me whilst glaring at the guys who have the nerve to look her way. They all turn their heads and look in the opposite direction.

We come to a stop in front of the three machines that have been vandalised. I also spot a large, cracked mirror. I let go of Jasmine's hand and walk over to inspect the damage. Even though all three look broken beyond repair, I think I can fix them.

"How do you know so much about fixing this stuff?" I hear Jasmine ask whilst I am on my back inspecting the damage on one of the machines.

"What's the make, princess?" I ask, waiting for her to read SOR. I hear a small "Oh" and look up at her. "All designed by yours truly. Don't tell me you thought I was just a pretty face?" I add with a smirk.

"No, I thought you were just the knucklehead that liked getting knocked about," she replies with a wink. I stare at her for a moment before bursting out laughing.

"You have much to learn. Like when that smart mouth of yours will get you into trouble," I remark with an arched brow before sliding back under the machine to take another look, not missing the way she starts chewing on her bottom lip. If it wasn't for the fact her cheeks were bright red and her eyes glisten with arousal, I would think she was nervous.

We have yet to discipline Jasmine, but I have a funny feeling she's going to quickly become a brat when we do, especially as we are learning she has a lot of kinks. Choking and anal play are just two of them. I think she'll enjoy being disciplined, and I, for one, can't wait to see the way her ass cheeks redden under my hand.

Fuck, this is not the place to be having these thoughts. Especially when I'm trapped under one of my machines and unable to bury myself deep into her wet pussy.

I reach down and reposition myself. Hearing Jasmine chuckle as I do only heightens my arousal. I slide out from under the machine again and stand, smirking at her. She's still chewing on her bottom lip as if she's trying to stop herself from laughing. I want to take that lip between my own teeth before devouring that naughty little mouth of hers.

"Princess, you are very distracting. Why don't you go

and have a look around or wait in our office or the café ? I will come and get you as soon as I'm done here."

Jasmine looks around and smiles at me again.

"I'll have a look around if that's okay?"

I pull Jasmine to me and press a kiss to her lips before nodding and looking to Keith, who is trying to appear as if he hasn't noticed the huge flirt fest that's been going on between my girl and me.

"Can you show Miss Connors around, please, then to the café? I'll find her when I'm done," I ask, placing the car key into Jasmine's hand. She looks down at it, frowning. "Just in case you need to get in there," I add before looking back to Keith, who nods and starts leading Jasmine away.

"Behave," I warn, watching her firm ass swaying as she goes. She looks over her shoulder and blows me a kiss and a wink, flashing her devious smile as she turns back to Keith and starts talking to him.

Fuck, the things that woman does to me and makes me want to do to her. I shake my head and spot a member of staff tidying up the free weights.

"Hey, can you grab me the big toolbox, please? As well as a bottle of water?"

"Absolutely, sir," she replies before rushing off. I see Jasmine and the manager talking to a female customer and smile. Everyone she meets can't help but love her. It's no wonder my brothers and I fell for her so fast. She brought a bit of light into our dark lives just when we needed it.

I look back at the three machines and sigh. I need to get these fixed quickly so I can get my girl back home and lose myself in her.

I throw the screwdriver into the toolbox and wipe my forearm across my face. Luckily, I was able to fix all three machines with no problems. I've already sent off the measurements to our guy for a replacement mirror, and the manager has found out who was responsible and filed a police report.

Our gyms are our legit businesses, and we keep them that way. They are the front to the dodgy shit we do. Other than the occasional underground fight, Christian has always tried to keep me out of the darker side of our family's life. That doesn't mean I haven't dealt with my fair share of the shit, or that my hands are clean, but they are cleaner than his and Jason's. Christian says I'm too smart to be wasted on the uglier side of our world. With my passion for engineering and fitness, he was happy for me to focus on going to university and then on to the sports centres and the equipment we offer.

I take a sip of my water and look around at the gym in full swing. Every machine is in use, and everyone seems happy to be here. The staff are all busy with customers, either helping them through a fitness regime or spotting for them, some just offering a warm smile and encouraging comments when someone's struggling. I take great pride in knowing that our gyms are filled with the best equipment as well as professional and understanding staff.

"Mr O'Reilly?"

I turn and find Keith looking at me nervously.

"What's up?" I ask, squatting down to close the toolbox.

"Umm, I'm not sure where Miss Connors has gone. She isn't in the café where I left her, and she wouldn't have been able to get into your office."

I laugh as I hand him the tools.

"I'll find her; she won't be far," I reply, walking off.

"Knowing Jasmine, she would have seen a room where she could practice dancing and taken herself in there. Are any of the studios free?" I ask. The manager nods.

"Studio three should be empty. Do you want me to see if she's in there?" he asks. I shake my head.

"No, I'll go. All the machines are working again, and the mirror will be replaced tomorrow afternoon," I explain. I hear him thanking me as I head to the upstairs studios.

As soon as I get to the top of the stairs, I notice four guys standing around looking into the studios, all whispering to each other. It's not until I'm closer that I can hear their conversation.

"Fucking look at her, I bet we could have some fun with that pussy!"

My temper starts to rise when I realise it's studio three they are looking into, which means it's Jasmine they could be watching.

"I'm pretty sure you aren't meant to be looking into the occupied studios," I call out as I approach. All four guys turn around and see me walking towards them. I recognise one as a guy called Simon, with whom I have sparred once or twice.

"All right, Sean, it might be against the rules, but it's a sight worth breaking them for. Have a look and tell me you wouldn't do her," he laughs as I look through the window to see Jasmine practising inside. Her shoe bag to the side with her sewing kit and tape on the floor beside it having broken in her new shoes. I should have known it wouldn't take her long to get them on her feet.

"Oh, I would because that's my girl, which means she's off fucking limits!" I warn as I step back and cross my arms over my chest.

"You're one lucky son of a bitch," Simon laughs as he

turns back to the window, watching Jasmine as she dances. I can't miss the lust in his eyes. "I bet she's fun to fuck." My face must shift as his mates all start very quickly back away, muttering apologies as they go. "When you've finished with her, send her my way. I could do some fucking damage to that pussy."

All self-control snaps as I grab his t-shirt and pin him against the door, hearing the feral growl in my throat.

"What the fuck did you just say?" I get right in his face so he can see how furious I am.

"I was joking, dude! She's all yours," Simon splutters, holding his hands up defensively.

"Too fucking right she's mine, you piece of shit."

Just as Simon goes to push me away from him, the door opens, and we both fall into the studio, landing at Jasmine's feet as she jumps back.

"What the hell?" Jasmine gasps as Simon tries to climb to his feet. I jump to my own and push Jasmine behind me so she won't get hurt if he jumps at me.

"Fucking hell, Sean! Overprotective much?" Simon grumbles as he dusts himself off.

"Of my woman? Always!"

Simon nods as he looks at Jasmine behind me.

"Fair enough, mate, I didn't mean any disrespect," Simon says as he walks towards us. I manoeuvre us away from the door and watch as he leaves, knowing better than to argue with me.

As soon as he's closed the door behind him, I spin around and look at Jasmine. I expect to find her looking scared, but instead, she's staring at me with pure lust in her eyes. I grab the back of her head and pull her closer to me.

"No fucker touches you but me and my brothers."

"I don't want anyone but you four," she whispers, her

voice hoarse with desire. I reach her bag in seconds and throw her bits into it before grabbing her hand and dragging her from the studio. "Where are we going?" she asks, struggling to keep up with me. I can hear the excitement in her voice which causes the blood to rush straight to my cock, and I glance at her grinning.

"The one room where no one can disturb us."

Chapter Twenty-Nine

JASMINE

Sean pulls me into the office and quickly locks it behind us.

"Stay there," he growls before stalking over to the computer and clicking a few buttons.

"What are you doing?" I ask nervously. Sean looks from the computer to me with a look that makes my knees weak, and my pussy gush.

"I'm making sure all cameras in here are off because I don't want people to watch what I'm about to do to you."

An involuntary groan slips past my lips, earning me a raised brow from Sean.

"Come here," he beckons, and I head straight to him, my legs feeling like jelly underneath me.

There are two sides to Sean, he can be sweet and loving or will dominate me and use my body as he pleases. I can't tell you which turns me on more, as he always leaves me breathless and satisfied.

I stop by the desk as he leans back in the chair, his legs open and his arousal obvious. "Come here," he growls as he takes my hand and pulls me down so I am straddling his lap. He holds the back of my head and forces me to look at him.

"No one will come in here. You can scream, and no one would hear," he growls as his eyes darken. I can feel his arousal underneath me, and I can't help but squirm, which earns me a grin.

"Do you feel what you do to me? You and only you make me so hard I can't think of anything but being inside of your sweet fucking pussy," he growls before kissing my neck. My eyes roll, and I can feel every muscle below my waist tightening.

"That fucker and his mates were watching you, fantasising about sleeping with you. But you belong to us," Sean groans as his hand slides up the inside of my thigh and cups me hard. "I can feel how hot and wet you are through your clothes," he adds as he rubs me. "Did it turn you on seeing me declare you as mine?"

"Yes!" I gasp as he continues to rub me through my leggings.

"Yes, what, princess?" he asks as I feel a sharp bite on my collarbone.

"Yes, Daddy," I moan as he nips me with his teeth again. "I love it when you tell people I'm yours!" I wiggle on his lap and feel him getting even harder as he continues to stimulate me through my clothes. "I need you, Daddy!"

"Where do you need me? Here?" he squeezes my pussy again and I grind against his hand. But I want to play.

"No," I moan, causing him to look up at me with wide eyes.

"No?"

I shake my head and see a devious grin on Sean's face.

"Where do you want me, princess? If not in your greedy pussy."

"Here," I admit as I point to my mouth. "I want to taste you and feel you against my tongue," I gasp as Sean rubs me again. I watch his devious grin widen and know he's going to give me exactly what I asked for.

"Get on your knees."

I drop down in front of him as he leans back in his seat.

"Undo my belt and jeans."

I smile up at him through my lashes, not breaking eye contact once as I loosen his belt and free his restricted cock from his black jeans. I take him in my hand and slowly slide it from the base up to the tip and back down again. I hear Sean moan and look up to see him staring at me with a look that would bring me to my knees if I wasn't already on them.

I lift and keep eye contact as I slide my tongue from the base up and swirl it around the tip before taking it into my mouth.

"Fuck, your mouth is like a portal to heaven. I want to fuck it until tears stream down your cheeks as you gag on my cock."

I let him slide from my mouth and grin.

"Do it. I want to feel you down my throat to the point I can't breathe."

Sean stares at me for a moment in amazement before that devious grin appears on his face, and I know I've got him.

"Put your hair up in a ponytail," he demands. I quickly do as I'm told. "If it gets too much, slap my leg three times," he orders as I place my hand on his thighs and nod. He cups my cheek and smiles. "You are so fucking gorgeous there on your knees," he whispers before taking my hair and wrapping it around his hand.

Slowly, I ease my mouth around him and let it slide in.

Sean takes it slow to start with and lets me get used to him using my hair to control the speed and depth that I take him. I quickly learn how to open my throat so I can take him further into it. Before long, Sean is thrusting into my mouth so hard and fast I'm gagging, and tears stream down my cheek, and I love it.

"No fucker will ever get to touch you or fuck you. You belong to us," he growls as he picks up speed. He's like a madman desperate to claim what's his.

"We will give you everything you need. We will fuck you until you beg for a break. We will worship every inch of your body and treat you like the goddess you are," he growls as he thrusts into me repeatedly.

"Fuck!" he growls, suddenly pulling out of my mouth, taking a string of saliva with his rock-hard cock.

He grabs me and pulls me to my feet before turning me around and forcing me to lean over the desk. I feel him pulling at my leggings and underwear whilst one hand pushes between my shoulder blades, keeping my front firmly against the desk.

"Fuck, as dirty as your mouth is, I need to be inside you," he growls, positioning himself at my entrance and, in one hard thrust, filling my soaking wet pussy. I cry out as he stretches me and gives me everything I need in one move.

"No matter how loud you scream, no one will hear you. It's just Daddy and his princess," he growls through his teeth as he puts more of his weight on my back, as his other hand moves around and starts rubbing my clit.

"Daddy, I need more," I beg as I feel like I'm going to explode if I don't cum soon. Sean's growl deepens again as his hand moves from my shoulders and tightens around my throat. I instantly moan as he tightens his hold further.

"Fuck you are so wet, so fucking tight. I will never get sick of the feel of you around my cock."

Black starts clouding my vision as he restricts my breathing. Just as I'm about to tap his leg, he roars in my ear.

"Cum for me, princess!" and lets go of my throat. As the air rushes into my lungs, I fall apart. I cum with such force that I swear I'm going to pass out, and I'm grateful for Sean holding me against the desk.

As I fall apart at the seams, Sean follows me, and we both crash together screaming each others' names.

Chapter Thirty

JASMINE

Sean helps me out of the car before trapping me against the closed door with his firm body.

"Thank you for a fun afternoon," I whisper, with a broad grin on my face.

"You certainly made a work trip worthwhile," he replies, playfully kissing my neck before stepping back from me. I take his hand and follow him through the door leading to the kitchen.

As soon as we enter the building, the smell of roasted lamb and veg fills my senses, and I moan with pleasure. I turn to see Mrs Brown standing over the stove.

"Mrs Brown, something smells amazing," Sean declares. She turns and smiles at the two of us.

"I heard Miss Connors loves lamb, so I wanted to experiment with a new recipe."

"I can't wait to try it, and please call me, Jasmine," I reply. Mrs Brown nods as she does every time I tell her and turns back to the food. I know she'll still be calling me Miss Connors tomorrow.

"Let's go and find the others," Sean says, pulling me away from the kitchen and into the entrance hall.

"Everyone is in the sitting room," Jason calls as he walks down the stairs. He walks straight to me and wraps an arm around my waist as Sean lets go of my hand so Jason can kiss me. I place my arms around his neck and kiss him back.

"Hi, angel," he whispers, grinning at me.

"Hi, Daddy," I smile, just as happy to see him as he is to see me.

Jason takes my hand and pulls me down the corridor Sean has just gone down, where I know the other two are waiting for us.

As we walk into the study, I see Maximus and Christian going over some paperwork on one of the sofas. I let go of Jason's hand and quickly kiss them both before sitting down next to Sean on the other sofa. He places an arm around my shoulder as I lean into him.

"Why aren't you in school? You said you'd be there until late," Christian asks, frowning at his watch.

"I needed new pointe shoes. So, Daddy Sean took me to get some. Plus, the computer lab's closed, so I can't type up my essay," I answer quickly. Christian looks at me with an arched brow.

"Why do you need the computer lab for that? Why can't you do it here?"

"Because I don't have a laptop anymore, I sold it, remember," I remind them sheepishly. Christian shakes his head and looks over at Jason.

"When are you going to learn to just ask for something?" Jason sighs, walking over to me and placing a kiss on my head before leaving the room, announcing he's going shopping.

"When's your essay due?" Christian asks, looking back

down at the papers on the table. I chew on my lip and look down at my hands as I fidget with the cuff of my jumper. Christian notices the silence and looks back up at me.

"Baby girl, I asked you a question," he growls as I look at him.

"Tomorrow," I admit, as his eyes widen.

"And how exactly did you plan on getting your essay done in one evening?" he demands.

"It's done; I just need to type it up. I was going to do it on my phone once I got home and had internet access," I reply defensively.

"Give me your phone." Christian holds out his hand, but I quickly shake my head. He gives me his daddy look, and I realise I'm pushing my luck. "Now, Jasmine."

Fuck.

When any of the guys use my real name, I know I'm in serious shit. I pull my phone out of my pocket and hand it to him nervously. He looks at it and then up at me.

"How long has it been broken?"

"It's only the screen; the phone works fine," I reply quickly.

"How long?"

"A few months," I sigh, knowing he will get the truth out of me anyway.

"Why didn't you tell one of us? We could have gotten it fixed or replaced," Sean asks from his seat.

"Because it works!" I protest. But as I look around at the three guys, I know the answer is wrong.

"When is your upgrade due?" Maximus asks as he takes the phone from Christian and looks at it. "Is this even a contract phone? It's at least four years old," he adds, frowning at it.

"Some of us can't have top-of-the-line everything like

you guys," I snap as I go to snatch it out of his hand, but Christian stops me.

"But you can! All you have to do is tell us you need something," Christian growls. "This is a prime example of why you need us as your daddies. You can't be trusted to do what is best for you."

"It's just a broken phone," I sulk, noting the whine in my voice.

"No, it's not. First, you have let yourself get behind in your coursework to the point you have to type up an essay the night before it's due. Then you rely on the college's computers to do your work when you could use ours here or have your own. Plus, the fact that if that phone decided to stop working, you would have no way of getting in touch with us or your security team if there was an emergency."

"How did you do your essays before moving in here?" Sean asks as I slump back onto the sofa.

"On my laptop until I sold it. Then I used the school computer lab," I sulk as I cross my arms over my chest.

"Do you always leave them until the night before?"

I look at him and shrug. "Depends how busy I've been or how hard they are."

"Is this one hard?"

I shake my head. "No, it can be typed and uploaded in a few hours."

I hear Christian sigh and look up as he holds his phone to his ear.

"Add a phone and tablet to the list. Get whatever you think she needs: folders, notepads, pens, the works."

I stare at him open-mouthed and realise I can hear Jason's voice on the other end of the phone. "I'll set her up with a study area in my office. She can work there with one of us supervising as we work."

"I don't need babysitting!" I protest.

"Obviously, you do!" Christian snaps as he goes back to speaking to Jason on the phone. I feel Sean put his arm around me and pull me against his side.

I want to shrug it off and put some distance between us, but he just tightens his hold on me when I try.

"We are only doing this because we care and know how important your studies are to you."

"I know what I'm doing and how to study," I sigh as I turn to look at him. "Can't you tell him he's being unfair?" I ask as I look up through my lashes, but Sean shakes his head, smiling.

"That look won't work on me, princess. I agree with him. Now, how about we sit down and write up what work you have to do and when it has to be done? Then, we can work out a study schedule together. That way, you can show him that you are going to do as you are told and keep on top of everything."

"What's he going to do if I don't? Send me to my room like a naughty child?" I snap. Sean looks at me and shakes his head.

"No, but I will be withholding sex until you get back on top of everything, and I have a feeling your other daddies will be doing the same," he warns.

"You wouldn't do that!" I protest, but when Sean nods, he looks just as serious as Christian does when he hangs up the phone. "Fine, I'll get my bag," I sulk as I stand up and storm out of the room. Silently cursing each of them as I go.

As soon as I walk back into the study, the three guys stop talking and turn to look at me.

"What have I done now?" I demand, dropping my bag on the floor.

"Want to tell me the other reason you left school early?" Christian asks; for the second time I consider lying.

"Not really," I sigh, looking down at the coffee table.

"What happened, Shorty?" Maximus asks as he hands me a bottle of water. I look at the whiskey in his hand, and he shakes his head. "After you eat something," he warns before sitting down on the other sofa.

"I'm waiting, Jasmine."

I look up at Christian and let out a deep, annoyed breath.

"Because my shoes were dead, they were louder than usual, giving Danielle ammunition."

"I thought you said she wasn't giving you any more grief?" Christian asks. I shrug as I sit back down next to Sean, who puts his arm back around me and rubs my shoulder gently.

"She never really stopped; just gave me a break for a little while," I admit, chewing on my bottom lip.

"What's her problem?" Maximus asks. I shrug, as I've never understood what Danielle has against me. We were never friends that fell out or even had a reason to dislike each other.

"She's Peter King's daughter," Christian answers, not taking his eyes off me. "He spoils her, and she thinks everyone else is below her." Christian rubs the bridge of his nose as he leans back in his chair. "I'm not having you upset to the point you miss half a day of school just because of her. I'm going to call the school tomorrow and then her father."

"Please don't. I don't want them to think I'm a snitch who's gone running to her boyfriend for help!"

"Boyfriend?" Christian asks as his eyebrows disappear into his hairline.

"Obviously, you're more than that, but that's how they will see it," I reply quickly. Christian looks at me for a moment before beckoning me over with his finger. As soon as I reach him, he pulls me onto his lap and wraps an arm around my waist.

"I know you don't like the idea of me fighting your battles for you, but you need to learn that we are all here to protect you. We don't like knowing that someone is giving you a hard time, and if there is something we can do to prevent that, then we will," he explains.

"But if you go in there with guns blazing, it will make things worse. If you go to her father, you might as well paint a target on my back!" I argue. Christian seems to consider it for a moment.

"How about this? I will take you to school tomorrow for coffee. If she sees you and doesn't say anything, then I will leave it. If she does, I will tell the school that you haven't complained, I am, as I've seen first-hand the way she treats you."

"It makes sense, Shorty. That way, she can't put any blame on you," Maximus says next to us. I look at Sean, who gives me a reassuring nod.

"Okay," I sigh. "But you promise not to go over my head and complain anyway?" I ask, looking at Christian, who shakes his head.

"I wouldn't do that to you, sweetheart, but I will protect you. I wouldn't be doing my job as your daddy if I didn't."

I nod as I know he's right; he has always done whatever he can to protect me.

"Thank you," I whisper, kissing him. Christian tightens his hold and kisses me back.

"You're welcome, sweetheart," he whispers before I

notice a new look appear on his face. "Now, back to the 'boyfriend' comment."

I quickly put my arms around his neck and pull out the best puppy dog eyes I can manage.

"I'm sorry. You are more than just my boyfriend, Daddy. But I just meant that's how the school will understand it. What else could I have said?" I ask, throwing as much innocence into my voice as possible.

"How about Daddy? Love of my life? Significant other? Lover? Fiancé? Husband? Fucking Dom would be better than *boyfriend*!" He takes my chin between his thumb and forefinger as I hear Maximus and Sean both chuckle from their seats. "Never refer to any of us as your boyfriends again. Is that understood, baby girl?" Christian warns as his eyes bore into mine and I feel a fire erupt between my legs from the intensity of his glare.

"Yes, Daddy. Sorry."

Christian continues to look at me for a moment before a smile softens his face. He leans forward and lightly presses his lips to mine.

"Good girl. Now come on, it's six, meaning dinner will be on the table."

I jump off his lap and follow Christian and Maximus out of the room. Sean steps up beside me and places his arm around my shoulder, tugging me against him.

"Feeling better, princess?" he whispers into my ear. I turn to look at him and nod. "I'm glad to hear it," he adds with a smile before kissing my head and leading me into the huge dining room.

Chapter Thirty-One

JASMINE

"Morning, Daddy!"

I find Christian sitting in the kitchen reading something on his tablet, dressed in a designer all-black suit, drinking coffee. He turns and kisses me with a smile.

"Morning, baby girl. Did you sleep well?"

"I did," I reply, grinning, thinking of how well I slept after Sean, Maximus, and I made love for at least an hour. Mrs Brown places half a grapefruit and a cup of coffee in front of me.

"Thank you, Mrs Brown."

"You're welcome, Miss Connors," she replies with a smile.

"Please just call me Jasmine. I really hate being referred to as Miss Connors," I sigh as I look at the lady in front of me. She offers me a quick smile before turning back to the stove where I can smell bacon cooking.

"Why do you hate being called Miss Connors?"

I turn to find Christian frowning at me.

"I've never liked it. I wanted to change it to my grandparents' name when I was sixteen, but Mum wouldn't let me," I sigh, stabbing a piece of grapefruit with my fork and putting it in my mouth.

"And now?" Christian asks; I look at him and frown.

"Now what?"

"And now, what do you want to change it to?" he asks. I shrug and chew my food.

"Guess it doesn't matter now; my grandparents are dead, so what's the point in taking their name?"

"What about our name? Would you take that?"

I almost choke on the piece of grapefruit I'm chewing. "What?"

"It's a simple question: would you take our surname?"

"But I can't marry the four of you," I point out as my heart starts racing.

"You could marry one of us or just have a ceremony blessing our relationship. As far as I'm concerned, you're my wife."

"We've been in this relationship for a few months. You can't possibly know you'll never want anyone else," I point out, shaking my head, but Christian just watches me.

"I've known for a few years you were going to be my wife; we all have. That's not going to change now we finally have you."

I stare at him, rendered speechless. Christian rolls his eyes before leaning over and pressing a soft kiss to my lips.

"Don't worry about it, for now. Eat your breakfast and drink your coffee; we will leave in ten minutes," he says before turning to Mrs Brown. "Please feel free to call Jasmine by her first name if that's what she wishes."

"Thank you, Mr O'Reilly," she replies with a nod of her head before turning to me and giving me a wink.

Half an hour later, Christian parks his car in the school car park. My hands are sweating, and I feel sick with nerves.

"Sweetheart, you look pale. Are you OK? Did you get your essay submitted last night?" Christian asks, taking my hand. I nod, looking at him.

"I'm fine; everything is in," I reply, taking a deep breath. "I'm worried about how this will play out," I admit. Christian reaches over and cups my cheek.

"If she upsets you, I will take you home until the school deals with her. But I have a feeling all will be fine by the end of the day," he says with a wink before kissing me quickly on the lips. "Come on, I know you need more than one mug of coffee before class," he adds, climbing out of the car. I take one last deep breath and follow him.

I meet Christian at the back of the car, where he's standing with my bag. He takes my hand and leads me towards the entrance to the coffee shop.

"Have you been here before?" I ask, wondering how he seems to know the layout so well.

"No, but I've seen the blueprints," he explains.

"How?"

"Terry got them when we were discussing your security," he replies like it is a perfectly normal thing to get hold of.

"I don't think I will ever get used to how much you have access to." Christian looks at me, smiling.

"I think you are handling it just fine."

We get to the café, and Christian places my bag by a table and pulls the chair out for me.

"I'll get the coffee. Can you message Sean and see if he's up yet, please? I need him to do something for me."

I quickly agree, pulling my new phone out of my pocket as Christian heads to the counter.

I'm just typing out the message when I hear that laugh that makes my blood boil. I resist the urge to look in her direction and continue to type my message to Sean.

"Mr O'Reilly? I thought that was you. How are you?" I look up just in time to see Danielle standing next to Christian, who's frowning at her.

"Miss King, isn't it?"

"You remember me? I'm flattered, but please call me Danielle."

"I didn't realise you went to school here," Christian says as he hands over his card to the server.

"Oh yes, I'm studying for a degree in dance. You should come to watch a performance. I'm going to get the lead role this year."

"I wasn't aware the parts had been allocated yet," Christian answers, frowning at her.

"They haven't. But I'm the best dancer here," Danielle announces as she puts a hand on Christian's arm. I glare at her and want her to turn to face me. How dare she touch him; he's mine.

"I beg to differ, Miss King; I know for a fact there is a fantastic dancer in this school, one I've watched for many years and have a personal interest in."

"Oh, I see. Is it someone I know?" Danielle stutters.

"I'm not sure," Christian replies, not giving anything away. I realise he's playing a game with her, and she isn't enjoying it. He's waiting for her to say something negative about me or someone else so he can call her out on it. Clever, Daddy.

"Are you here for business or personal reasons?" Danielle asks as she slides her hand up Christian's arm. I swear if she flirts with him one more time, I'm going to rip her to shreds.

I never realised how possessive I am of my guys, but then I've never seen other women around them. They have always made a point of giving me their undivided attention wherever we are.

"Personal reasons. Someone very important to me is also a student here. Why don't you come and say hi?" Christian says as he picks up our drinks and walks towards me. He gives me a wink as Danielle follows him and starts looking around. When she sees me, she slides up a little closer to Christian as if it's her he's dating.

"There you are, sweetheart. Your favourite," Christian announces as he places the cup in front of me and leans in to kiss my cheek. Danielle stares at us as her face goes bright red. "Do you know, Miss King? It sounds like you must be on the same course," Christian says as he sits down next to me. He places an arm around the back of my seat and a hand on my shoulder.

"I do, yes," I reply as I smirk at Danielle, who, for possibly the first time in her life, has been rendered speechless.

"Miss King seems to think she'll get the lead role this time as she's the best dancer, but I beg to differ. There again, I'll admit it is only you, my brothers, and I see when you are on the stage, sweetheart," Christian says proudly.

"Stop it," I reply, blushing as he smiles at me. "I didn't realise you know Danielle," I add. Christian shrugs as he takes a sip of his coffee.

"I know her father," Christian answers, looking at his phone as it starts to ring.

"Excuse me, ladies," he says quickly before kissing me

on the lips, "I'll be right back," he stands up and walks away with his phone to his ear.

"What the hell? How long have you known the O'Reillys?" Danielle demands under her breath. "And how the hell did you get Christian? He's been dating the same person for years!" she hisses at me. I look at her with arched brows as I take a sip of my drink.

"Three years, to be exact," I reply. "I don't know how many times I've told you that some people don't like to flaunt what they have," I answer as she stares at me. "Word of advice, Danielle. Now you know the truth; I would be very careful how you continue to treat me. I may not have said anything yet, but all it would take is a comment to *any* of the O'Reilly brothers and your father's business with them would end," I point out as I lean in closer to the now pale Danielle.

"Also, a word of warning: if you ever place your hands on or flirt with any of them again, I will personally make sure you never dance here or anywhere for a very long time." I have no idea where this is coming from and what I would actually do, but the threat seems to be enough as she looks even paler.

"You can't possibly have all four to yourself," she growls. I just shrug and lean back in my chair.

"If you don't want to believe me, that's fine, but I dare you to test your little theory."

Danielle looks at me, and I see the colour returning to her face as she gets angry.

"Whatever, if they want to lower themselves to being with someone like you…"

"Now that's not very nice. Do you think you are better than me? Are you better than any of us in this school? Because you're not. Things are changing, Danielle, and it's time you realised the only thing going for you right now is your father's money, which is coming from *my men*," I point out. "Now move along and leave me alone. I want to finish my coffee in peace before I head to class."

Danielle flicks her hair over her shoulder before spinning around and storming out of the café as I sit back, smiling to myself whilst nursing my coffee.

"Looked like you were having fun, sweetheart."

I look up to see Christian sitting down in the chair next to me. He picks up his coffee and gives me a smile before taking a sip.

"You knew who she was the whole time," I say, shaking my head in disbelief.

"I may have made a point of turning up at her father's house one night unexpectedly to ensure I knew what she looked like and so she would recognise me," he answers as he continues to sip his drink.

"She said you have been seeing someone for years," I point out. Christian grins then and reaches up to run a knuckle down my cheek.

"It was always you; you just didn't know it," he whispers before leaning forward and pressing his lips to mine. "You were worth the wait," he adds as I feel my cheeks warm.

Christian sits back and glances at his watch quickly.

"I hate to leave you, but I need to be in a meeting in half an hour. Layton will be picking you up from rehearsal, and I'll see you at home later." He stands up and fastens the button back up on his jacket.

"Now she knows who you are; if she causes any more problems, let us know, and we will end our agreement with her father."

"I may have warned her if she so much as touches one of you again, I will end her dancing career," I reply with a smug shrug. Christian stares at me for a minute and starts laughing before leaning over and kissing me.

"See, spoken like a true O'Reilly," he whispers into my ear.

"No one touches my daddy," I reply as he stands up.

"And no one dares touch you, baby girl," he replies before turning around and walking away, leaving me looking forward to class and how much things are going to change around here.

Chapter Thirty-Two

JASMINE

I walk into the utility room and shake off my wet coat. All it has done all afternoon is rain. It's the first heavy rain of the season and it seems to be sitting on the pavement rather than running down the drains. Although Layton had parked as close to the school entrance as possible, I stupidly ran straight through a deep puddle, and now my feet are cold and wet.

I hang my coat up on a hook and pull off my trainers. Looking around, I spot some old newspapers piled on the side. Knowing they will help my trainers to dry quickly, I reach for the top one. As I grab the paper, I accidentally knock the pile over, and they all fall onto the floor in a mess. I sigh as I squat down to pick them all up. It's then an old headline jumps out at me.

Drug dealer found dead in flat

Sam Black, a well-known drug dealer, was found dead yesterday morning in his flat. It is thought that Black was killed due to a drug-related incident. Believed to have been dead for several days, he was only discovered after neighbours complained of the smell coming from his property. The police are asking for anyone with any information to come forward.

My hands start to shake as I read the article. I turn around, forgetting about my wet trainers and rush to Christian's office.

Throwing open the door, I see Christian sitting in his chair behind the desk.

"Hey, baby girl. How was school?" he asks as he looks up at me. I storm up to the desk and throw the paper in front of him.

"Did you have something to do with this?"

"I did," he answers, taking the paper and throwing it in the bin beside him.

"Why? Because of the flat?" I demand.

"As well as other things, yes."

"For fuck's sake, Christian, you can't go around killing people because they upset me!" I yell, throwing my hands up in the air.

"Watch your mouth, baby girl. He was a problem, so I dealt with it."

"He was just one fucking guy!" I yell again.

"He threatened you! I will not stand by and ignore that. Now, don't make me tell you again; watch your language!"

"He didn't deserve to die for one threat!" I yell, ignoring him. Christian points towards the bin, where the paper now sits.

"He had a diary in which he tracked your every move in that filthy flat he rented you. He had plans for you, which involved his friends. I will not apologise for removing that threat to you!" Christian answers, lifting his glass of whiskey and taking a sip.

"I'm here now. He couldn't have fucking touched me!"

Christian puts his glass down on the desk and stands. He walks around his desk and stops in front of me.

"I told you I would not allow him to live once he threatened you; you need to learn very quickly, I *always* follow through with a threat or promise. You also need to remember what I told you about punishments for not doing as you are told."

I stare at him as he unbuttons his jacket and shrugs it off.

"What are you going to do?" I ask as he starts undoing his cuff and rolling up his sleeve. "Spank me?" I ask as he starts to roll up his other sleeve.

"Exactly; glad to see you are finally catching on, sweetheart," he replies. I turn to storm out of the room, but Christian stands in my way. "I wouldn't try and fight this; you are only making matters worse for yourself," he warns before crossing his arms over his chest. A part of me is excited to see where this will go. Have I not been fantasising about him taking me over his knee? I want to know what it would be like. But I can also see I have made him mad, and that scares me.

Christian moves past me and sits on the sofa.

"Let's try this without you fighting me. Lie over my knee."

I stand there for a second, too scared to move.

"I won't tell you again," he warns as he arches one brow. I chew on my lips as I do as I'm told. As soon as I'm over his knee, he pulls my leggings down to reveal my bare ass. He starts rubbing it, and I have to stop myself from moaning. Why the hell am I as turned on as I am scared?

"You will receive fifteen. Five for each swear word that

passed through your lips. I want you to count each one, lose count, and I will start again."

"Daddy, please," I sob as the fear increases. "I'm sorry."

"I have told you numerous times to watch your language, but you continue to ignore me. From now on, every swear word out of your mouth earns you five smacks," he warns as he continues to massage my bare backside. Just as I open my mouth to apologise again, Christian's hand slaps against my skin; I cry out, not from pain, but from the shock. Christian goes back to massaging the cheek.

"I don't hear you counting,"

"One," I call out before he can say anything else. His hand quickly comes down again, and I cry out, "Two!" as my eyes start to burn. He forms a pattern: massage, slap, massage, slap, never landing two blows on the same cheek or in the same place. By the eighth, I'm no longer holding in tears; I'm crying as I count each assault on my now stinging backside.

"Fifteen!" I call aloud as he lands the last one.

Christian doesn't stop me as I climb off his lap and pull up my leggings.

"I hate you!" I scream, glaring at him through the tears.

"No, you don't," Christian says calmly as he stands in front of me. He reaches out to take my hand, but I snatch it away from him.

"Yes, I do! I hate you!" I yell at him again. I expect Christian to yell at me for screaming, but instead, he reaches up and cups my face lovingly.

"The fact that you are saying you hate me tells me a whole other story, baby girl," he says softly.

"That makes no sense," I sob, not even trying to get away from him.

"When was the last time you told anyone you hated them? Never," Christian explains as he looks into my eyes. He runs his thumb over my cheek, wiping away my tears. "You won't tell anyone how you truly feel because you are scared they will leave you. You hate your dad for leaving. You hate your mum for her abuse of you and the substances. You hate your grandparents for dying and leaving you, all of them leaving you alone and scared. So, you keep your true feelings bottled up and buried, scared that others will also leave you.

"But you don't hide your feelings from me and the guys. Why? Because you know we aren't going anywhere, you know we are here for you no matter how hard you try to push us away; that's why when you tell me you hate me, all I hear is how much you trust and love me."

I stare at Christian as my bottom lip quivers and my eyes and throat burn. "Whatever you need to throw at me and your other daddies, whether physical or verbal, throw it at us. We can take it and will never leave you alone."

I stare into his eyes as I realise he's right; I do know that they will never leave me. They have shown me again and again that they are going nowhere.

"I'm sorry," I sob as I start to cry. Christian pulls me into his arms and holds me tight as I cry into his chest. He runs a hand over my head and whispers words of encouragement, but now the floodgates are open, I can't stop crying.

In one swift move, Christian scoops me up into his arms and carries me out of the room. I continue to cry into his chest as he walks through the house and up the stairs.

At one point, I hear Maximus asking what's going on, but I don't hear Christian's reply as I cling to his shirt and cry even harder than I have in years.

Christian walks us past my room and takes us into his, where he places me on the bed and lies down with me, holding me tightly against him as I continue to cry into his chest.

"You have been through more than anyone I know, which has made you so unbelievably strong. But you have bottled up your pain and feelings for so long that you no longer know how to process them. You need to start letting us in and trusting us to know what you need," Christian whispers into my hair.

"I know," I reply as I wipe my face. Christian reaches into his pocket and pulls out his handkerchief. I take it from him and wipe my nose.

"I'm sorry for swearing, Daddy," I croak as I look at him. Christian nods and presses a kiss to my lips.

"I know, baby girl, and I know you are going to be more cautious of what you say from now on," he whispers as he runs a knuckle over my cheek. Christian presses a kiss to my nose before climbing off the bed and walking into his bathroom.

"Pull down your leggings and underwear, please, and lie on your stomach," he calls as I sit up and stare at the door.

"Please don't spank me again."

Christian walks out of the bathroom with a tube of something in his hand and a towel.

"I'm not going to spank you again."

I quickly do as I'm told, place my arms under my cheek, as I look to the side where Christian is unfolding the towel.

"Lift your hips, baby." As I do, he slides the towel underneath me and sits on the side of the bed. "Relax, I'm not going to spank you again, I promise."

I watch as he squeezes the tube over his hand and then reaches around and rubs the contents onto my butt cheek.

"Daddy, that stings!" I hiss as the lotion sinks in before it starts to cool, and I feel myself relax.

"It would sting more if I didn't put this on," Christian sighs as he starts rubbing the other side. He rubs the lotion into the skin and then places the tube back on his bedside cabinet; he sits back with his back against his headboard. I turn onto my side and rest my head on his chest as he strokes my head lovingly.

"I love that you feel confident enough to argue with me to get your point across. But just do it without cursing," he chuckles as he tightens his arms around me. I look up at him and into his blue eyes. I take in his soft smile, that he seems to save just for me. He has never once shown me the side of him I now know exists. I have never feared Christian; even as I lay over his knee waiting for him to spank me, I wasn't afraid of him, just the spanking itself. Christian, Jason, Maximus and Sean may have all done unspeakable things, and I don't want to know how many people they have killed or hurt, but I do know I am always safe with them; they will never hurt me as others have.

"I love you, Daddy," I whisper as I look into his eyes. Christian's smile lights up his whole face with those four words.

"I love you too, baby girl, so very much."

Chapter Thirty-Three

CHRISTIAN

I stay perfectly still as Jasmine sleeps against my chest.

We talked, and she cried again for nearly half an hour before she exhausted herself and fell asleep. It broke my heart to see her suffering, but I knew it was what she needed.

Jasmine has never allowed herself to show her true feelings before, and her fear of being rejected is always at the forefront of her mind. But I think we are finally getting through to her that we are here to stay, and no matter what she does, we are not leaving her. Do I wish I hadn't had to take her over my knee to get her to admit it to herself? Absolutely. But I will do it again and again if it means she will let the last of her walls down and let us in completely.

I hear a knock at the bedroom door and call out to whomever it is quietly. Jason pops his head into the room with a smile on his face.

"So, you finally did it then?"

I roll my eyes at my brother before looking down at the still-sleeping Jasmine.

"Yeah, she found out about the landlord and didn't take it well." I hear Jason hiss through his teeth before moving into the room.

"Yeah, I can imagine she was rather vocal with that one."

"Well, put it this way: I've told her we will spank her five times for each swear word and then issued fifteen."

"Nothing like easing her in gently," Jason jokes as I glare at him.

"Is there a reason you are here other than to annoy the shit out of me?" I ask as Jasmine moans slightly. We both watch her for a moment to check she stays asleep.

"Just to let you know, Sean and I are heading off to the club to sort out the latest issues with Taylor. You sure you still want us to cut all ties with him and withdraw all funds from his bars?"

I nod as I feel my phone vibrating in my pocket.

"Yeah, he owes us a lot of money, and until he starts making payments, he isn't getting another penny out of us. If he doesn't like it, then he shouldn't have pissed me off."

Jason nods as he turns his back on me and heads to the bedroom door.

"We only do business with him because of Tommy anyway. Tommy didn't want to lose the only friend he had ever had. Now we have cut ties with him; Taylor is of no benefit to us." Jason turns and looks at me as he gets to the door.

"I will ask Mrs Brown to plate up both your dinners. From the looks of it, Jazzy needs to sleep a little longer. I take it she finally cried?"

"A lot. We were right; it was what she needed," I admit as I pull my phone out of my pocket, as it vibrates again.

"Good. Hopefully, she'll start healing now. Tell her I will come and see her when I get back."

"Will do. Let me know how it goes."

Jason gives me a thumbs-up as he walks out of the door, closing it behind him.

For a moment, I close my eyes and just breathe. It should have been me going to this meeting with Taylor. It was me who called it in the first place, but right now I can't bring myself to leave Jasmine, and Jason saw that.

I sigh as I feel my phone vibrate again in my hand. Unlocking the screen, I see three messages, all from an unknown number.

The first message is a picture of Jasmine walking with another girl; I think it is Verity. From the looks of it, the picture was taken today at her dance school. I feel my jaw clench as I open the second message.

Unknown: I wonder what your Jasmine would think if she found out some of the evil things you have done. Do you need a reminder?

I may not have told Jasmine everything I have done over the years, especially during the early days when I had no choice thanks to my father's dealings, but she knows enough for nothing to come as a shock. The text doesn't annoy me, but the photo of her does, as they have been watching her. I will find out who it is and make sure they never go anywhere near her again.

I open the last message and freeze as bile fills my throat, and I look at the one face I will never forget. That still haunts my dreams.

The face of the first person I ever killed.

Unknown: Your time is coming to an end. It's time for you and your brothers to pay for all that you've done.

Bonus Scene

"Fine, I'm on my way. You better have a goddamn explanation when I get there!"

I look up from my new laptop in time to see Christian walking over to me while shoving his phone in his pocket.

"How are you getting on?" he asks, standing behind me as he runs his hand over my head.

"Almost finished, just tidying up the references." I don't miss the way he checks his watch before nodding to himself and kissing the top of my head.

"You have two hours until the deadline, so you've made good time on it."

"I told you there was nothing to worry about," I answer, rolling my eyes. Christian takes hold of my chair and turns it so I'm facing him. I instantly realise I may have pushed my luck.

"That's because Jason went out and got you everything you needed, including the laptop you are working on. If you hadn't had that, you would still be trying to write it up on a broken phone, wouldn't you."

I go to argue, but as soon as Christian arches that one brow at me, I know I will never win this one.

"Yes, Daddy," I answer, looking down at my hands on my lap. Christian places a finger under my chin and forces me to look back at him.

"I know you think we are being strict, but we know how important this degree is to you and how hard you have worked to get to where you are. We only push you because we care."

I stand and wrap my arms around his waist as he sighs and hugs me back.

"Thank you," I whisper, not being able to express how much it means to me to have someone caring about what matters to me. Before the guys, I've not had that for a long time, but now, not one but four men are willing to help me achieve all my goals.

"You are more than welcome, sweetheart," Christian sighs into my hair before stepping back. "I leave for a bit. Jason is already out, and Maximus is down in the gym. Sean will keep an eye on you to ensure you get everything done and uploaded."

I give Christian my best puppy dog eyes whilst smiling sweetly.

"It will be," I promise him. "When will you be back?"

"Not until late, but I'll still take you to school in the morning and see if we can get Miss King off your back." He leans down and kisses me quickly before turning away and walking towards the door. "Make sure she finishes that essay," he calls to Sean as he heads to his car, where no doubt Terry will be waiting for him. Turning back to the laptop, I make short work of typing up the last five references and let out a sigh of relief when I see that everything is completed.

"How much more do you have to do?" Sean asks from behind, startling me.

"Don't scare me like that!" I snap, turning in the desk chair to face him. Sean grins down at me playfully. I roll my eyes as I turn back to the laptop.

"It's not my fault you didn't hear me." He places a hand on my shoulder. "Uhh, Harvard referencing, I do not miss that!" I sometimes forget that Sean was the only one of his brothers to go to university. The rest left school to focus on the family business.

"Yeah, it sucks, but ..." I click a few buttons and sit back, smiling. "The essay is completed and uploaded for marking. I am done!" I look over my shoulder to find Sean smiling back at me. "Do I remember you saying something at dinner about a reward if I got everything in on time?"

Sean turns the chair before leaning on the arms so he hovers over me.

"Does Daddy's princess think she deserves a reward?" His voice deepens as he stares deep into my eyes, causing my whole body to come alive and my toes to curl whilst I nod in agreement.

In one smooth move, Sean pulls me to my feet as he leans forward and throws me over his shoulder, startling a scream out of me before I start laughing. He turns around and carries me out of the sitting room where we've been since after dinner.

"What is it with you and your twin having to carry me like this?" I laugh. Maximus is always throwing me over his shoulder when he wants to take me off somewhere, usually to rock my world.

"Makes it easier to do this..." a hard slap sounds as he spanks me. I moan in response before slamming my hand over my mouth, but it's too late; Sean hears and chuckles whilst spanking me again.

"I thought I was getting rewarded, not punished!" I cry out, still grinning from ear to ear. "Hang on, where are we going?" I ask as we pass the stairs.

"So impatient, princess." Sean spanks me again, and this time, my eyes roll to the back of my head. There's something about the way he does that, which heightens all my senses.

Sean continues to carry me into the kitchen and places me on the large counter in the middle of the room.

"Stay right there," he orders, giving me his best Daddy look before walking out of view. I turn on the counter and sit with my legs crossed as he pulls a plate out of the cupboard.

"What are you doing?"

Sean looks over his shoulder as he opens another cupboard and pulls out the tub where Mrs Brown keeps her homemade cookies. My eyes widen, and I grin excitedly. I love Mrs Brown's cookies; they are always perfect.

"Gimme gimme!" I giggle, holding out my hands, but Sean shakes his head, causing my excitement to disappear as I pout at him.

"You never eat Mrs Brown's cookies cold, princess. I thought you knew better than that," he grins, placing four on the plate. He walks over to the microwave with the plate in his hand, and I realise what he's about to do.

Everything Sean does, from placing the plate in the microwave to waiting for it to finish the thirty-second, he does with a devious grin on his face. Every time he looks over his shoulder at me, I can't help but squirm where I'm now sitting cross-legged.

When the microwave pings to signal the timers up, Sean

carries the now warm cookies over to me. Placing the plate on the counter, he picks up one and slowly breaks it in half so I can't miss the way the chocolate melts inside. Replacing half on the plate, he breaks the other half further before lifting it to my lips.

"Open that beautiful mouth, princess," he whispers seductively. I do as he asks, and he places the warmed cookie in my mouth. My eyes close as the sweetness of the cookie and the bitterness of the chocolate explode on my tongue. "Ready for more?" he asks as I swallow down the melted goodness. I open my eyes and nod before Sean feeds me a little more of the cookie.

Gradually Sean feeds me the cookies whilst his other hand rubs against my thigh seductively, causing my whole body to come alive. As he feeds me, he keeps eye contact the whole time, adding to my arousal.

"This is the last piece, princess. Open wide."

As he pops the last piece in my mouth, I notice he has some chocolate on his finger tips. With a smile on my face, I take his hand and suck on his fingertip before moving on to the next one and sucking them clean. I don't miss the way his jaw clenches, and his eyes darken as he devours me with one look.

"Only you could make chocolate so sexy," he declares as his voice deepens. "I have an idea." He walks away from me and heads back to the cupboards. As I turn to see what he's doing, he gives me a firm look. "Face forward and no peaking." I quickly do as I'm told, knowing that when Sean wants to play, he makes everything so fun and sexy.

Listening to him rummaging in cupboards and placing things on the side, I hear him approaching again. It takes every ounce of self-control to keep facing forward and not looking to see what he's up to.

"Do you think you deserve more of an award for submitting your essay?"

"Yes, Daddy," I answer as sweetly as possible whilst giving him my puppy dog eyes, knowing all the brothers struggle to ignore them.

"Then get down off the counter, princess and do everything you are told." Sean holds out his hand, which I take. He smiles as he leads me to our small kitchen table and makes me stand in front of it. "Take off your clothes," he orders, causing my eyes to widen from shock.

"Here?" I ask, sure I must have misunderstood. I start looking around

"Yes, here. Don't make me repeat myself." Looking around nervously, I start pulling off my clothes. Sean smiles at me as I do as I'm told. "Good girl, princess," he grins, knowing full well what his praise does to me.

Once I am naked in front of him, he closes the gap between us, places his hands on my hips and lifts me to sit on the edge of the table. Threading his fingers into the hair at the back of my head, his lips brush against mine tenderly.

"I want you to lie back and close your eyes, keeping them closed whilst I give my good girl what she deserves." He kisses me once more before releasing me and stepping back. "Lie down and close your eyes."

"Yes, Daddy." I slowly ease myself back until I am lying on the table as instructed. Lifting my foot onto the table to push myself back further, I hear Sean clearing his throat.

"Stay just where you are, but open your legs a little so I can get between them," he orders, and I instantly do as I'm told. I take a calming breath before closing my eyes and waiting to see what Sean is going to do to me.

Anticipation floods through me, heading straight to the apex of my thighs as I wait for some kind of indication of what is happening around me. I listen to Sean's footsteps, leaving and quickly returning before something is placed on the table beside me.

"What did you learn today, princess?" he asks as his hand slides up the centre of my body before massaging my left breast.

"To ask for help when I need it," I answer, my body coming alive from his touch.

"And?"

"To not leave my coursework until the night it's due in," I gasp as something drizzled onto my right breast.

"And?" he asks again. I try to think of something else to answer but get distracted when his tongue licks up whatever he poured on my breast. I realise I can smell chocolate and not just from the cookies he warmed up for me a few minutes ago. "And?" he asks firmer this time. Forcing me to try and focus on his words, not his amazing tongue.

"That I'm not to let people bully me and stand up for myself." How I managed to get all of that out, I don't know, as Sean is now dripping something onto my left breast and quickly starts to suck it off, to the point I know he will leave a mark.

"And when you feel you can't stand up for yourself?" he asks, drizzling what I now believe is chocolate sauce down my stomach.

"If I can't stand up for myself, you guys will help me," I gasp as Sean slowly and purposely licks from between my breasts down my stomach, stopping just above my clit.

"We will always have your back, princess. No one will ever hurt you while we are around."

"I know, Daddy."

"Good." Before I get the chance to say anything else,

the tip of Sean's tongue flicks across my clit and all coherent thoughts vanish as he devours me as if he is starved.

Sean slides one and then two fingers into me as he continues to flick my clit while his fingers rub all my buttons on the inside.

"Oh my god!" I cry out as my back arches off the table. I no longer need to remind myself to keep my eyes closed. I don't think I could open them if I tried. The pleasure rushing through my body is making every nerve stand on end. My whole being feels alive as Sean guides me closer and closer to that sweet release.

"Daddy." The name flows from my lips before I can stop it. Sean doesn't reply; he continues his assault on my clit. Between his fingers and tongue, it doesn't take long before I'm screaming his name as I cum hard.

Sean removes himself from between my legs as I gasp for breath, still unable to open my eyes.

"I hope you don't think I'm finished with you, princess. Because I'm far from it." I hear the zip on his jeans being pulled down before the sound of the denim sliding down his legs. Opening my eyes, I look down at my body to where he is positioning himself at my entrance.

We look at each other for a moment, and I can't miss the fierce look in his eyes as he stares at me.

"You are fucking perfection." Not giving me a chance to reply, he grabs my hips and slams into me hard and fast. I cry out, not from pain but from the overwhelming sense of completion I get whenever one of the guys takes me. I never feel whole until I am with at least one of them. The O'Reilly's complete me in a sense no one else ever could.

Everything is fast and hard for a few minutes, as it always is with Sean. He slides a hand up between my breasts before gripping me around the throat and applying a little pressure, knowing how much I love it when he chokes me.

"You are ours to take care of and love, princess," he declares between gritted teeth. "No one but us will ever touch and fill you ever again."

"I'm yours!" I cry out as I start heading towards another orgasm. "I'm all of yours!"

"To fucking right you are! You belong to us!" he roars as he pushes himself so deep I cum, crying out incoherent words as he fills me with his release for the second time today.

Seans leans over and kisses me whilst we both try desperately to catch our breath.

"You are so fucking perfect, it hurts. You turn me feral," he gasps as he pulls me up so I'm sitting on the edge of the table and can lean against his chest.

"You do the same to me," I grin, pressing my cheek to his chest.

"Mrs Brown isn't going to be happy."

Sean and I both look to the kitchen door to find Maximus grinning at us whilst leaning against the door frame. Sean laughs, stepping back enough to pull his trousers up.

"Do I even want to ask what started that?" Maximus asks before frowning at my body. "Is that chocolate sauce?"

I look down and smile when I see remnants of the sauce Sean must have licked off me.

"We were celebrating her submitting her essay and got a little carried away," Sean laughs. "Plus, it tastes even better when licked off her sweet skin," he winks at me as Maximus stalks forward. He leans in and licks my breast, coaxing another moan out of me. Maximus lifts me before I get a chance to comment, so I'm thrown over his shoulder.

"What is it with you two and acting like cavemen?" I cry out as Sean laughs.

"Sean, grab the clothes and the sauce. I have an idea, but we will need to do this somewhere Mrs Brown won't kill us for making a mess," Maximus declares as he carries me out of the kitchen and heads straight for the stairs. "We will be in her room!" he adds before slapping my ass, causing me to cry out. "I think it's only fair I get to reward you as well," he adds as I make a mental note to ensure all essays are completed early if it means I get these kinds of rewards.

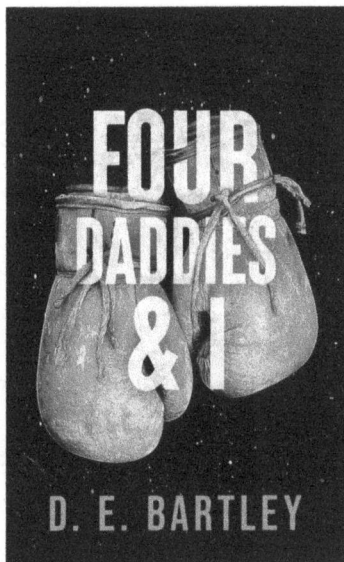

vinci-books.com/Fourdaddies

She's the light in their darkness—and now she's in danger.

Jasmine finally feels safe in their arms, but the O'Reilly brothers' past is closing in fast.

They'll protect her or burn everything trying.

Turn the page for a free preview…

Four Daddies & I: Chapter One

"Jazzy, there is a perfectly good desk over there," Jason sighs stepping over me as he heads to the bar.

"I know, but I prefer it here," I reply, sticking my tongue out for good measure.

"How the fuck can you sit like that?"

I look up from the floor where I'm working on my laptop and see Maximus looking over the back of the sofa he is sitting on.

"What? It's how I always sit when I work," I protest looking at my legs on either side of me in a perfect box split.

"I guess it explains how you're so flexible," Sean adds with a wink, from beside his twin. I smile before going back to my essay.

Being a ballerina certainly helps with my flexibility, and having four hot daddies who love to bend me to their will helps too.

Three months ago, my life was a mess. I'd escaped my abusive drug addict of a mother by living in a run-down shithole of an apartment and working in a dive of a pub. I couldn't even afford to eat properly because I needed any cash I made to pay rent and tuition fees for my dance school. I'm training to be a ballerina and studying for a degree in dance. I hid the extent of my issues from everyone, including my four hot and very rich stepbrothers.

Christian, Jason, Sean and Maximus O'Reilly were the best stepbrothers a girl could ask for; there was nothing they wouldn't do for me. But because people abandoned me throughout my life, the thought of losing the O'Reilly brothers was too much, so I hid everything from them. Until Jason found out, and I finally confessed to how bad things had become.

Instead of running off and leaving me to deal with my life on my own, he bundled me into his car and brought me to the house he shares with his brothers. That was the night my whole life changed for the better. The O'Reillys are no longer my stepbrothers; they've become so much more.

You see, I'm in a relationship with not one, but all four of the O'Reilly brothers. With our parents now divorced, they have lost the title of stepbrothers; they are now my daddies. I no longer need to worry about where my next meal is coming from or if I can make payments for my dance school. They pay for everything and look after me in a way no one has since I lost my grandparents.

I know how that sounds, and no, I'm not with them for their money, although they have a lot of it and make thousands of pounds an hour. I'm with them because they make me happier than I have ever been; they show me nothing but love, and I love them all just as much. But having been alone for so long, it's been hard for me to accept they aren't going anywhere. However, every single day, they go out of their way to show me they are here to stay.

"You never said how the meeting went this morning. Is

the fight on for a week Saturday?" I hear Sean ask. I look up to watch his interaction with his twin, Maximus.

"Yeah, all set. We finalised everything with the other fighters and their managers. Word got out, so it should be a good turnout."

I look at Maximus as he sips his whiskey.

"You have a fight coming up?"

He looks down at me and nods.

"Can I come and watch?"

"No."

I look to Christian, who's sitting opposite the twins. His eyes not leaving the tablet in his hand as he sits back relaxed.

"Why not?" I demand moving so I can see him better, making it easier for me to argue with him.

"Because it's an underground fight. You can go to the next competitive one," he replies, not looking up from the screen. "Plus, you have an essay due three days after."

Out of all my daddies, Christian is the strictest and least likely to back down. He is also the most likely to dish out punishments, too.

"But what if the essay is done early? Can I go then? I want to watch Daddy Max fight," I argue. Christian looks at me then and gives me the 'Daddy' look I've learnt there's no point arguing with.

"I said no. These fights are not like competitive ones. They're loud, full of drugs, with highly dangerous men and women present who aren't always on their best behaviour. The fights are dirty with no rules; it's no place for someone like you."

If I missed the warning to stop arguing in his tone, I certainly don't miss it in his cocked brow. When he gives me that look, I know it's his way of warning me to behave, or there will be consequences.

"I can't see it being a problem, Christian."

I turn and look at Jason, who's filling up his glass. "If it was both the twins fighting, then yeah, there's no way she could go. But Sean and I can stay with her the whole time, and there's already going to be plenty of security. It's on our turf as well, so we can get her to safety quickly if there's a problem," Jason continues as he turns around and looks at Christian whilst leaning against the table behind him.

"Jason's right. If we stay with her, no one will try anything. They know we are always armed at these things. You can concentrate on Maximus and the business side, and we'll watch Jasmine," Sean adds. I watch Christian looking at his two brothers before turning his attention to Maximus.

"You've met the other guys; what do you think?"

Maximus shrugs as he looks at me. "I get where you're coming from. My first instinct is to keep her as far away as possible. But if Shorty's going to be in our lives, she needs to see what we do. She never needs to go again if she doesn't like what happens. At least this way, she's protected by Jason and Sean. You could also ask Terry to have Layton guard her. I don't think anyone is stupid enough to try something on our turf anyway," Maximus says as he looks between me and his big brother.

"Plus, it will help get the word out that she is ours and what will happen if anyone hurts her." I chance a look at Jason, who gives me a little wink, obviously realising that he's winning this argument. I look back at Christian and chew on my bottom lip nervously. Christian lets out a sigh.

"Fine, you can go."

I jump up and rush to him, squealing excitedly. "However!" he announces as I jump onto his lap. "There are rules."

I put my arms around his neck.

"I will stick to them!" I promise quickly. Christian rolls his eyes before looking at his brothers.

"You two don't let her out of your sight. If she needs to pee, you go with her. If she wants to leave, you go with her."

"You aren't the only one who gives a shit, Christian," Jason warns as he walks away from the bar to sit on the third sofa.

"No, but I know she can wrap you around her little finger when she wants to," Christian says as he looks at me. I give him my best puppy dog eyes.

"I'll be good, I promise," I declare, making a cross over my heart.

"Jason, you'll need to sort her outfit, and I'll speak to Terry about having extra eyes on her."

"Christian, she'll be fine; stop worrying," Sean says from his spot on the other sofa. I watch as Christian's blue eyes frown at his younger brother. "I dare anyone to try anything; I will kill them myself," Sean adds. Christian nods, and I hug him tightly.

"You are going to see a side of us that might scare you, but I promise we will *never* be like that with you," Christian says firmly as he looks into my eyes and tucks a section of hair behind my ear. "Why do I feel like I'm going to regret letting you come?"

"It'll be fine, I promise, Daddy."

"It better be because I will kill anyone who hurts you."

Four Daddies & I: Chapter Two

JASMINE

I open the messaging app on my phone and stare at it for a moment before closing it. I stare at the locked screen and unlock it again before growling and shoving the phone into my pocket.

Get a grip, for fuck's sake, Jasmine.

It's been three months since I last had any contact with my mother, and I know I should reach out.

The last time I saw her, she was dirty, skinny and addicted to all kinds of drugs as well as alcohol. She stood in front of Christian, Jason and me, shouting all kinds of vile shit. Although I like to think it was mainly the substances talking, I know it wasn't.

My mother and I haven't been close since my father left us when I was eight. Mum always blamed me for him leaving, even though it was mainly due to her substance abuse and shopping addiction. I missed him for the first few years and would often dream about him coming back for me and saving me from the abuse Mum would dish out when high or drunk. But he never came. By the time I was a teenager, I had given up on those dreams and threw myself into my dancing as a way of escaping the shitshow that was my life.

That all changed three years ago when Mum got sober and met Tommy O'Reilly. She fell head over heels in love with him, and they married shortly after. Even though her marriage didn't last, and they divorced less than three years later, their marriage led me to my four guys, and I will always be eternally grateful for that.

The problem is that although I'm the happiest I've ever been, I know Mum is struggling with her addiction again, and I want to help her. Yes, she said some horrible things to me the last time we spoke, but she is still my mum and the only blood family I have left. I want to reach out and message her to check that she's okay and at least alive, but I can't seem to do it.

I look down at the phone in my hand and come up with an idea. I might not have the guts to message her, but I can at least check that she has everything she needs and see for myself that she is still breathing. I throw my phone into my bag and head out with a plan of action.

"I don't care what you say; I'm coming into that house with you, Jasmine. The O'Reillys would kill me if anything happened in there."

I turn to face my personal bodyguard, Layton and smile.

"They wouldn't *actually* kill you."

Layton looks at me with arched brows, and I hiss through my teeth.

"Okay, yeah, they might," I admit before smiling.

The O'Reillys are successful businessmen who own hundreds of fight clubs, gyms, and other sporting venues, but they are also very powerful and dangerous men. Their father, Tommy, dragged them into the darker world from a young age, and they built up quite an empire. I don't know much about what they do, but I know they have all killed people to get to where they are. But I also know I am safer with them than I have ever been with anyone else.

"Fine, you can come in, but keep your mouth shut. My mother doesn't do well with new people."

We climb out of his car and head around to the trunk. Layton collects the bags of food I brought for Mum, knowing there won't be much in the house. When I go to grab a bag, Layton gives me a look, which promises an argument if I even attempt to take one.

"You are worse than my daddies at times," I sigh as I reach up and close the trunk for him.

"That's because I have seen what your daddies are capable of. I don't plan on being the receiving end of one of their moods," Layton says as he walks next to me.

"Are they that scary?" I ask. Layton nods and turns to look at me.

"I've seen them at their scariest, and I have seen the way they are with you. They really would burn the world to ashes to protect you."

"Do you ever regret working for them?"

They employed Layton after seeing the way he looked after me one night about nine months ago when I was so drunk I couldn't stand. He had been a bouncer in the club I'd been in. Maximus and Sean found me and took me home after giving Layton their business card; the rest is history. He now works for them full-time, watching my back. It's a role he takes seriously, but sometimes, it's easy to forget he is paid to be with me. We have developed a good friendship during all the time we spend together.

"No, not only is the money good, but I enjoy my job, even when you are being difficult," he adds with a smirk. I slap his arm as we reach the front door. Coming to a stop, I feel my chest tighten. Now I'm here, but I'm not sure this is a good idea.

"You don't have to do this, you know. You could just leave the food on the doorstep and go."

I shake my head and take a deep breath before opening the door.

"Be careful. It was a mess last time I was here," I warn him before stepping through the door.

Inside the house is quiet. I can't hear or see anything. I head straight to the lounge and look around.

The place seems a little tidier than it did the last time I was here. It's still far from how it was when I lived here alone, but there are no obvious signs of drugs and empty cans and bottles. It smells a damn sight better too.

"Mum? Are you here?" I call out, only to be greeted by silence. "I guess not," I sigh as I continue to walk through the house and into the kitchen. I find the kitchen much better than it was three months ago. The bin is no longer overflowing, and the sides are cleaner than they were.

"Let's just leave this stuff on the table, and she can put it where she wants it," I sigh as Layton places the bags down. We quickly arrange the bags, and I put the milk and cheese in the fridge before leaving a note.

Mum,
I popped by to see you and see if you needed anything. I hope you are okay.
Happy birthday.
Jasmine x

I place the note on top of the cake box, which contains a rich chocolate cake, her favourite, and look at Layton.

"Let's get out of here."

He offers me a sad smile, and we head out of the door and back to the car.

I take one last look at the house before we drive off. I hope she is happy and safe, whatever she's doing.

Grab your copy...
http://vinci-books.com/Fourdaddies

About the Author

D.E. Bartley lives in Wales, UK, with her husband, three feral boys, four cats, and a budgie.

To say her home is a madhouse would be an understatement, but she wouldn't have it any other way.

When she isn't running around after her tribe or driving her husband up the wall, she can be found reading and hoarding books like a dragon.

Nothing is as important to her as time with her family, and she loves her trips home to Cornwall with them more than anything in the world. What could possibly compare to sitting on a Cornish beach, with a glass of Cornish gin in one hand and an authentic Cornish pasty in the other, while the monsters, I mean children, play and bodyboard in the sea?

Absolutely nothing.